Further Praise for *The Turk and My Mother*

"Comic, touching, erotic, sad, violent, innocent, harsh and crafty, just like the world it describes. . . . The characters are seized by music, food, the old and new languages and each other. They believe in the evil eye, the wages of sin and prayers that God hears. They may be without power or position, but they have much to lose—their families and their sense of belonging on this earth. The power struggles of the 20th century seemed hell-bent on taking both from them. Stefaniak's book tells their stories in a poetic and gently humorous voice."   —Jim Hazard, *Milwaukee Magazine*

"Compulsively readable, brilliantly constructed, and filled with funny, flawed, unforgettable characters, *The Turk and My Mother* reinvents the family saga and the art of storytelling as we know it."   —Lan Samantha Chang, author of *Inheritance*

"*The Turk and My Mother* is a wild ride through a symphonic family history that carries you breathless with laughter and curiosity to a most satisfying conclusion. This innovative and wholly engaging novel, tossing its cast across history and oceans, immerses you in a culture of the absurd and bittersweet."
          —Sandra Scofield, author of *Occasions of Sin*

"The beautiful voices in *The Turk and My Mother* speak to us across the generations with overwhelming intimacy. Written with humor and affection, Mary Helen Stefaniak's first novel breathes life into the hardships, secrets, and enduring love that bind an American family to its immigrant past."

—John Smolens, author of *Cold* and *The Invisible World*

"With wonderful insights into the immigrant experience—and with a sense of humor that encourages the reader to laugh out loud—Mary Helen Stefaniak tells an unforgettable story."

—Eleanor Edmondson, president, *Bas Bleu*

"*The Turk and My Mother* sparkles with originality, humor, and insight. Mary Helen Stefaniak has a true gift for making the ordinary feel magical and the exotic feel hauntingly familiar. I love this novel!" —Elizabeth Stuckey-French, author of *Mermaids on the Moon*

"Stefaniak brings the immigrant experience to life and weaves together a intricately tangled plot. She exactly captures the difficulty of trying to get family stories unraveled. I think that *The Turk and My Mother* will connect with readers interested in a cleverly told, multigenerational story."

—Daniel Goldin, Harry W. Schwartz Bookshops

THE TURK AND MY MOTHER

ALSO BY MARY HELEN STEFANIAK

Self Storage and Other Stories

THE TURK AND MY MOTHER

A Novel

MARY HELEN STEFANIAK

W. W. Norton & Company New York • London

For information about permission to reproduce selections from this book, write to
Permissions, W. W. Norton & Company, Inc., 500 Fifth Avenue, New York, NY 10110

Manufacturing by The Haddon Craftsmen, Inc.
Book design by Chris Welch
Production manager: Anna Oler

Library of Congress Cataloging-in-Publication Data
Stefaniak, Mary Helen.
The Turk and my mother : a novel / Mary Helen Stefaniak.
        p. cm.
ISBN 0-393-05924-3 (hardcover)
  1. Russian Americans—Fiction. 2. Children of immigrants—Fiction. 3. Siberia
(Russia)—Fiction. 4. Milwaukee (Wis.)—Fiction. 5. Immigrants—Fiction. I. Title.
PS3569.T3389T87 2004
813'.54—dc22

                                                                    2004001102

ISBN 0-393-32699-3 pbk.

W. W. Norton & Company, Inc., 500 Fifth Avenue, New York, N.Y. 10110
www.wwnorton.com

W. W. Norton & Company Ltd., Castle House, 75/76 Wells Street, London W1T 3QT

1 2 3 4 5 6 7 8 9 0

For the real George and Madeline,
in memoriam,

and for Marie

THE TURK AND MY MOTHER

"Whatever evil I had suffered, I forgot."

—CZESLAW MILOSZ, "GIFT"

AUTHOR'S NOTE

Staramajka is the Croatian word for *Grandmother*.

I

The Turk and My Mother

*T*oward *the end of his life, and even afterward, my father became quite the storyteller. He said*:

IT'S HARD FOR me to picture my mother in love. I can't help thinking that she seemed too old for it, even when she must have been young. People aged faster in those days, I suppose, especially people who lived hard lives in tiny villages like hers, in a part of Europe that was so used to being cut up and handed around like cake at the end of every big and little war that my mother could tell you who was king when she was a girl but not what he was king of. I remember her the same way you do: she was a stern, stout woman with a babushka on her head and a mole on the side of her nose worth mentioning as a distinguishing mark on her naturalization papers. What she disliked most about America was the way women walked around half-naked whenever it was warm outside. "No wonder God don't give us nice weather in Milwaukee," Ma used to say. When I visited the village myself—this was many years after she died—I met an old, old woman there, somebody's cousin, and she told me that even as a girl my mother had always worn her skirts longer than everybody else. You can see why forbidden passion is not the first thing that comes to my mind at the mention of my mother's name, which was Agnes.

But I do know this. When Ma was in her seventies, we took her to see *Doctor Zhivago* at the Riverside Theater downtown. Four of us went: me, Ma, my sister Madeline—she must have been in her early fifties then—and you. You were what, ten? Eleven? This would be in 1965 or '66. Do you remember?

"How could I forget? Grandma *genuflected* before she went into the row of seats."

That's right! She did. You have to remember that my mother spent a lot more time in church than at the movies. This one she had asked to see, though. She had a picture from the newspaper ad. Omar Sharif and Julie—what was her name?

"Christie."

Right. A picture of Omar Sharif and Julie Christie with far-off looks on their faces and furry hats on their heads. Ma cut it out of the paper and said she wanted to go. At first, she seemed to be loving the movie. Everything was fine until the scene where Omar Sharif says good-bye to Julie Christie at the military hospital—remember that? He was a doctor and she was a nurse, but they hadn't laid a hand on each other yet. That part came later, after the intermission. I'll tell you, Mary Helen, if your mother had known how steamy those scenes were, she never would have let you—

"But what about Grandma?"

I'm trying to tell you. There he was, Omar Sharif, standing on the veranda in his military uniform, watching this horse-drawn wagon take what's-her-name away, when all of a sudden, my mother stands up and starts stumbling over everybody's feet to get to the end of the row.

"I don't remember that."

You were busy watching the movie. I thought she was just in a hurry to find the restroom, having sat through almost half of the three hours already, but no. Your aunt Madeline, who followed her, learned the truth. It was Omar Sharif's brown eyes full of tears that caused my mother to flee, weeping, to the Ladies Lounge.

That's how I know there must be *something* to the story of my mother and the Turk.

It started, at least from my point of view, with my sister Madeline's troubles in the summer of 1932, when she got fired by the Beymors. She had already lost most of her customers to the Depression by then. In fact, it wasn't too long after the Beymors fired Madeline that Mr. Beymor went downtown and took a flying leap off the seventh-floor balcony in City Hall. Ma's friend Mrs. Tomasic happened to be there waiting in line at the Relief Office when Mr. Beymor landed on the top of his head on the marble floor in the lobby, seven stories below. She said he stood on his head for a second or two before his legs came crumpling down. You'd have thought he was doing a parlor trick, she said.

On the day my sister got fired, she had just finished ironing Mr. Beymor's special white shirt, the extra expensive one about which he was, as Madeline used to say, "overdue particular." This shirt couldn't be hung on a hanger. It had to be buttoned and folded and laid in the box from the shop in Paris where

Mr. Beymor had bought it. Madeline was leaning over this box, smoothing the handwoven cotton, buttoning the mother-of-pearl buttons, folding the sleeves and shaping the collar just so, when her nose betrayed her. Without warning, a burst of bright blood poured out all over the snowy white shirt.

"Mother of Jesus, help me!" poor Madeline cried, bringing Mrs. Beymor, a maid, and the other laundress, the one who was not permitted to meddle with Mr. Beymor's white shirts, running to see what had happened. They found Madeline still on her feet but swaying beside the ironing table, her head thrown back and her face as white as the special shirt had been. They caught her in their arms before she fell, removed her blood-stained apron, brought a cold wet cloth for her nose, and laid her gently on the bed in the guest room where she did her ironing. In hushed tones, Mrs. Beymor told my sister to rest until she felt better, while the other laundress carried the shirt away to see if anything could be done. After a time, when Madeline found that she could stand up without sending the rest of the room careening around her, she was given her hat, her bag, and her last day's wages. On her way out to the alley, she passed the clothesline. The shirt and the apron—still wet but looking white again—waved good-bye.

On the streetcar, my sister nearly gave in to despair. She was only seventeen, and she knew that she was caught. My mother had often described the monumental nosebleeds she suffered when Madeline herself was on the way, gory messengers that announced to the whole village what kind of parting gift her husband had given her before he left for America. Bending over in the fields brought them on, my mother said. So did the surge in her blood pressure caused by thinking about the thousands of miles that lay between her husband in Milwaukee and herself. She never really forgave him for leaving, not even later, after the war took every able-bodied man from the village and left pieces of them strewn along the Russian front. My father set off for America in March of 1914, the archduke was murdered in June, the war began in August, and Madeline was born in December—my mother's little contribution to the bloody events of the year.

Madeline's next nosebleed was almost as ill-timed as the cloudburst over the shirt. It happened in church the next Sunday, when she was sitting between me and my mother, singing "Tantum Ergo," the offertory hymn. All of a sudden, gush. All over her prayer book and down the front of her dress. The people in the pews around us were sympathetic. The nearest ones sent the usher for wet cloths and stretched Madeline out on the wooden bench, lifting her feet gently. The ones a little farther away but close enough to see what was happening went on singing bravely, so that my sister would not suffer the additional embarrassment of having brought the hymn to a fluttering halt. (Faintings in church were extremely common in those days, nosebleeds less so.) The only person whose stony face betrayed no sign of sympathy was my mother. She gripped the back of the bench in front of her and didn't turn around to help or even acknowledge the people ministering to her daughter. Being not quite twelve, I failed to make a connection at that point between Madeline's distress and the gory messengers in my mother's past, if I knew about them at all. I was embarrassed by Ma's hardness of heart.

When we got home, Madeline went straight to the room she shared at that time with Staramajka, my father's mother, whose face—when she opened the front door and saw Madeline's pallor and her stained dress—collapsed into the very picture of woe. As soon as the bedroom door closed, Staramajka turned to my mother. Knowing the signs—Staramajka's lips pressed together, the rigid set of my mother's jaw—I was prepared to back away from a sudden flood of angry words. But there was no flood. They merely stood, eye to eye, my grandmother's sadness holding its own against my mother's hard gaze. When I finally asked, "So what's the matter with Madeline?" they both looked at me. Then they sent me outside.

⚜

I HAD PROBLEMS of my own on the street. According to Chuey Garcia, who had grabbed my sleeve on the way out of church and asked me what the hell was wrong with my sister— earning himself a rap on the back of the head from Mrs. Garcia—Pete the Cop had been strolling around the neighborhood already this morning with a section of the Sunday *Journal* under his hat. In it was a picture of four boys in the canal, three of them swimming in the shadowy canyon between a moored freighter and the wooden pilings that served as the shore, and one standing on the pilings, mugging for the camera as he prepared to dive in. "One Way to Beat August Heat," the caption under the picture said. Pete the Cop was showing it to people, asking if they recognized the boys.

"Can you tell it's us?" I whispered.

"You can tell it's Frankie, that's for sure," said Chuey. He was safe now, his mother having moved ahead to shake hands with the priest in the doorway.

"Sonovabitch," I said through my teeth. An usher in the last pew frowned as I passed.

Officer Pete Moldenowski, who walked the beat from Lincoln Avenue north to National and from Kinnickinnic east to the lake, claimed to be concerned only for our health and safety, but there was no predicting what cruel and unusual forms a cop's concern for your safety might take. When Pete the Cop caught us in the canal back in June, he had grabbed Frankie's little brother Tony Tomasic by the back of his wet undershirt and held him out over the water. He had pointed with his nightstick at the oil slick flecked with floating garbage—tin cans, cardboard, pieces of wood, dead fish, blackened leaves—that coated the surface of the canal. (We always threw a big rock or chunk of wood into the water to clear a space before we dove in.) "How can you swim in this cesspool?" he'd asked, while Tony's skinny legs bicycled in midair. "Why don't you go to the natatorium?"

We said nothing. He knew why. It cost a dime plus carfare, as well as a between-the-toe inspection—an indignity to which none of us would submit.

"Or the lake?" Miles of beach stretched north and south from the Port of Milwaukee. When none of us answered, he nudged me with the nightstick.

"Lake's too cold," I said.

Pete the Cop had swung Tony back in over dry land and dropped him in a heap. "I'll let you off this time," he said, "but if I catch you diving in the canal again, I'm hauling you in. Then you can explain to your folks why you like this soup so much that you're willing to pay a fine for the privilege of poisoning yourselves in it."

Sweating in the sun on our front porch steps, I pondered the best way to get a look at the picture in the *Journal* without having to pay for a paper. The only people I knew personally who subscribed were the Tomasics, but I didn't want to incriminate myself by going over there. I figured Mrs. Tomasic was giving Frankie and Tony hell already. (As a matter of fact, she had clipped the picture and tacked it up in her kitchen, for all her boarders to see. Mrs. Tomasic would have forgiven her boys for robbing a bank as long as they made the papers.) My best bet seemed like Solapek's tavern on the corner, where I knew I'd find the Sunday paper strewn across a long table by the windows. I went in the back way, through the kitchen, stopping long enough to promise Mrs. Solapek a couple of snapping turtles for soup. By the time my eyes adjusted to the dimness in the tavern, I'd found something I wasn't looking for. Veiled in old cigar smoke, Pete the Cop was standing at the bar.

I tried to duck back into the kitchen but old man Solapek spotted me in the doorway. "Speak of the devil," he said. "Georgie! Come and look at this."

They had the local news section spread on the bar between them. In the middle of a page full of stories about the heat wave, Frankie Tomasic stuck his big ears and skinny shoulders out of a grainy picture of the canal, three dark heads bobbing in the water behind him. Pete the Cop asked me if I recognized any of the boys.

"No, sir," I said.

"Really? I was thinking this one here"—he pointed to one of the heads in the water—"looks a lot like you."

Instead of hauling me in, he marched me two doors down the block and up the stairs to the little landing outside our front door. My grandmother opened it, looking very cross. This was her normal door-answering demeanor—useful with bill collectors and salesmen—but I think Staramajka's deep-set eyes and almost toothless scowl may have startled Officer Moldenowski a little. At any rate, he kept it brief, showing her the picture, at which she scowled even harder in her efforts to focus, and issuing the usual warnings about what would happen the next time I was caught up to my neck in the canal. When she made no response (Staramajka did not speak English), he thanked her for her time, replaced his cap, and retreated down the stairs. I was congratulating myself on my lucky escape when Staramajka opened the door wider and I saw that my mother had been standing within earshot the whole time, her face as stony as it had been in church.

"So," my mother said to me. "Are you going to stand out there all day?"

With dread, I stepped over the threshold. Staramajka closed the door behind me. My mother said, "Georgie, don't swim in that filthy water no more. It makes you stink."

That was it. She went back to the kitchen and sat down at the table, looking at nothing but her hands around the cup in front of her. My grandmother raised an eyebrow at me, then headed the opposite way, into the front room. Hinges creaked as she went out on the porch. There was no sign of my sister, except for the closed bedroom door. Try as I might, I could think of only one kind of trouble she could be in that was big enough to overshadow my bringing Pete the Cop to our door. Though days would pass before people uttered any of the tactful expressions we used to avoid the word, I finally guessed the truth. My sister Madeline was pregnant.

⁂

THE FATHER OF my sister's child was named John and he married my sister eventually, but he doesn't play much part in this story—not counting his role at the very beginning of it. Neither does my own father, although I did run to the railroad yard looking for him on the morning my sister's hands were burned. I didn't find him. My father worked two jobs: he was a coal sorter at Milwaukee Solvay Coke Company and a gandy dancer for the railroad (one of a few non-Italians in that whole sledge-hammering crew at the time). He was seldom home during waking hours. Over the years, I collected a mental list of questions I wanted to ask him if I ever got the chance. One of these was whether he knew how my mother had punished Madeline with the lye. By the time I got a chance to ask him that one, I had been to the Philippines and back with the U.S. Army Air Corps, and my father, whose lungs were destroyed by his years in the sorting room, was on his deathbed. I tried to put the question vaguely, in case he *didn't* know, and ended up making hardly any sense at all. "Pa," I said to him. "Did you know about the lye Ma put in the water—when Johnny was on the way?" He wheezed, "Of course I knew. Am I blind?" and then he closed his eyes, fooling me for one panicked moment into thinking that he had uttered his last words. He had only fallen asleep, though. He died later, in the early hours of the following morning, not long after calling me to his side and whispering to me, while my mother knelt at the foot of the bed and my sister wept by the window, "She never meant to cause so much pain."

❧

I SUPPOSE MADELINE should have been able to smell something funny about the bucket of soapy water my mother left for her in the kitchen on Monday. They hadn't spoken to each other since the nosebleed in church. Madeline had spent the rest of the day in bed, avoiding Sunday dinner, a tense occasion at which my mother shocked me by telling my father only that Madeline was suffering from a particularly bad case of the cramps that always assailed her on what they called special days. Staramajka, who still ate her meals out on the porch to protest the Sears bathroom recently installed where our pantry used to be, was not party to this deception, although I noticed that she didn't set him straight when he mentioned it later.

Madeline rose very early that Monday, slipping out of bed without waking my grandmother, and, though she urgently needed to use the bathroom, she waited to hear my father's workboots clomp across the front room, out the door, and down the steps in the hall outside, before she opened the bedroom door and scuttled to the back of the house. She expected to find my mother in the kitchen cleaning up after Pa's breakfast. When she found the kitchen cool and empty instead, she took it upon herself to warm a pan of water, dissolve a cake of yeast, and mix it up with flour and salt. As Madeline kneaded and punched the dough, watching long strings of it stretch between her knuckles and the mottled white ball in the bowl, she planned all the chores she was going to do in reparation— not to wipe away her guilt, for she knew there was no task big or difficult enough to do that, but just to show Ma that she was still Madeline, still here, very scared, and hoping to be forgiven. She covered the dough and left it to rise while she went downstairs to start the wash.

When the clothesline in the yard was full, Madeline emptied the washer, came back upstairs, and found the bucket of sudsy water and a scrub brush waiting on the kitchen floor. She smiled to herself at the practical bent of Ma's silent treatment, and taking the hint, she went down on her knees and pushed her sleeves up further, remembering to keep her back straight and nose held high to guard against bloody surprises while she washed the floor. Reaching for the brush, she considered ways to get a message to her young man, who worked with Pa at the coke plant. Should she enlist the little Serbs downstairs as messengers, she wondered, or get her brother Georgie to take the streetcar to the young man's rooming house on Canal Street? And what, she also wondered as she prepared to plunge the scrub brush into the water, should her message be? Preoccupied with these questions, she had both arms in the water halfway to her elbows before she noticed that her skin was on fire.

SNAPPING TURTLES ARE heavy. The ones we caught in the Kinnickinnic River at dawn and dusk, using lengths of twine baited with bread dough, weighed twelve to fifteen pounds apiece. I was laboring up the street with two big ones clamped by the jaws on the ends of two sticks, one over each shoulder like hard-shelled hobo bundles, when I heard the first scream. It stopped me in my tracks, my turtles bouncing. The second scream was long and muffled, with as much disbelief as pain in it. The third brought people out onto their porches to see what was wrong. Standing on the sidewalk, I could see in the spaces between buildings that Mrs. Tomasic was on the next block, running up Hilbert Street from her boardinghouse. By the time she disappeared behind Solapek's tavern on the corner and reappeared in front of it, I didn't need her or anyone else to tell me where the screams were coming from. I dropped the turtles and raced to the house, taking the porch steps in one leap, tearing open the door, and pounding up the stairs to the landing, with Mrs. Tomasic behind me calling, "Georgie! Georgie, wait!"

They were in the kitchen, Madeline and Staramajka at the sink and my mother mopping up foamy water from an overturned bucket on the floor. My sister was hunched over with her elbows on the edge of the sink, one ankle curled around the other, her knees buckling, her whole body writhing and twisting against my grandmother. Her screams had subsided to shuddering sobs. Staramajka was holding her by the forearms, keeping her hands under the running faucet. Nobody looked at me when I appeared in the kitchen doorway, but when I bent down to pick up the scrub brush that lay in a puddle on the floor in front of me, my mother said sharply, "Don't touch that!"

The next day my sister's hands looked like red claws. When Staramajka applied a salve to the blisters, the pain of contact lifted Madeline off her chair, it made drops of sweat bead up on her forehead. "Offer it up," my grandmother whispered, meaning the pain, offer it up to Jesus or maybe to the Blessed Virgin. "For your sins," she whispered. "For all our sins." Beads of sweat rolled down my sister's temples and slid to the tip of her nose.

For days afterward, my mother avoided everyone. She worked two shifts cleaning cars at the railroad yard on Monday, came home late, and left the next morning before the rest of us were up. After work on Tuesday, she hid out at Mrs. Tomasic's. (Staramajka told everyone that it was an accident, that too much lye got into the bucket by mistake. Mrs. Tomasic knew the truth.) From our second-story back porch, in the late afternoon, I saw my mother and her friend sitting on the rear steps of the boardinghouse across the alley: two thick-waisted women with flowered aprons over their housedresses and babushkas tied at the back of their necks. My mother sat facing the alley, her arms folded across her knees. Mrs. Tomasic leaned toward her, waving her hands as she spoke, sometimes touching my mother's arm or her shoulder. Every now and then, while Mrs. Tomasic was talking, my mother would curl slowly forward until her head rested on her arms.

The days after the incident were lonely for me, too. My friends were lying low because of Pete the Cop. My sister emerged from Staramajka's nest of featherbeds only to visit the bathroom. Most of the time Staramajka was holed up with her, the two of them sending a tantalizing murmur through the wall into the front room. I remember standing outside their door at the end of the second or third day, trying in vain to make out a word or two. Eavesdropping seemed my only prospect for another long summer evening, when Staramajka suddenly opened the door, almost catching the toes of my left foot under it, and invited me in to hear the story of my mother and the Turk.

STARAMAJKA HAD HER own style of storytelling, a style that did not accommodate her listeners in any way. She never started right in with what happened, which was, of course, what you wanted to hear. First, she had to make you see where the story took place, especially if it took place in her village, which was where most of the stories she considered worth telling took place. You had to hear about the fence cleverly woven of branches, the dirt yard full of chickens, the four fat pigs that her son sold off when our mother was pregnant with Madeline and couldn't stand the smell of them. "What's the matter with *her* nose, huh?" Staramajka asked us. "Everybody else can stand to smell a pig, no matter what special condition they are in, but my Marko, to make his brother's wife happy, he sells all the pigs. 'I can buy them back later,' Marko said, but then the army came and took him, so we ended up with no men and no pigs either. That's why the mayor asked us to take the Turk in the first place—no pigs on the premises."

My ears perked up at this early mention of the Turk, but it was a false alarm. We had yet to hear (not for the first time) about the crucifix that guarded the end of the single street flanked with yellow houses, about the thick clay walls of the houses and their thatched roofs, about storks who liked to nest in summer on the chimneys—big birds with long pink legs. "Pretty to look at but they make a big mess. Not at our house, though, because of my rooster. He didn't like those storks. If one came, he would crow like crazy and make it fly off. He was better than a guard dog, my rooster. When soldiers came to the village and stole our chickens and pigs, they never laid a finger on that rooster of mine. Your grandpa called him—" and for the rooster's name, she always switched from Croatian to Hungarian, which my sister and I had never learned to speak, adding, as if she were sorry to inconvenience us, "His name means something I can't say to children."

"We're not children," I protested, but my sister Madeline, who was sitting in a cloud of featherbeds with her greased and gauze-wrapped hands in her lap, looked satisfied, under the circumstances, to be a child for a while. I think she liked Staramajka's long preambles anyway, probably because she remembered the village herself—she was five or six when they left it—and she liked to have the lines and shapes of the place redrawn for her now and again to keep them sharp and clear.

"Speak for yourself," she said to me. "And don't interrupt."

Staramajka made a great show of ignoring both of us, sitting back in her wooden rocking chair. This was the same chair she hauled out to the porch every fine morning and dragged back inside every night, the same one in which she spent most of her evenings beside the radio in the front room, listening to the Voice of Firestone, the same one in which we would find her dead one day, looking very much the way she did right now: her eyes closed and her face toward the ceiling, the cheekbones high and round like apples, the rest scooped hollow by her lack of teeth. When she was ready to resume her story, she opened her eyes and peered at us from deep caverns under the bony shelf of her forehead, making us feel that we were in the presence of one both ancient and timeless. In years, she must have been about sixty-five.

"Inside our house," she went on when she was satisfied that we were listening again, "was one big room with the stove and two nice beds and our table and benches to sit by the window and smell grapes or roses, it depended on the time of year. By the other window was the loom. We only had one. Your mother was never very good on it, but Rosa, she could weave like the dickens. If it was nice Egyptian cotton that we bought in Szigetvar or that stiff hemp we pounded and soaked in the river, it didn't matter to Rosa. Her fingers flew."

I had forgotten who Rosa was, if I ever knew. Staramajka was from a tiny village, but her stories had casts of thousands. You needed an index to keep track.

"It was all very nice—can you see? White walls, and by the loom our extra special piece of wooden floor your grandpa put in, just as nice as Begovacz's, which he also put in. Begovacz had the only other wooden floor in the village and she hated that we had one, too. It was made of split logs from trees—that was before the soldiers cut down all the trees—sanded so smooth, it was better than packed dirt under the feet." She paused and looked around her narrow bedroom as if she were surveying a different scene, checking to be sure there were no properties missing before she continued, no details forgotten, except for the kind my unromantic father would have added to her picture of the village: no heat, no lights, no running water, mud in the street to your knees every spring. I took advantage of the pause, curiosity overwhelming my better judgment, to ask, "Who's Rosa?"

Staramajka looked at me, shocked. "Who's Rosa?" she said. "Rosa Zarac is your aunt. Your mother's sister. She looked just like Madeline—tall, dark hair—only Rosa's eyes were brown like chestnuts. You don't remember Rosa?"

"Did I ever meet her?"

Staramajka shook her head and pressed her lips together. Living in America meant not only that your grandson had never met his aunt, but that he didn't know he had one. "No," she said. "Of course you didn't meet her. And your mother hardly mentions her name, so why should you remember?"

Madeline squinted down at us from her white mountain. "I remember her," she said. "A little. She doesn't seem like Ma's sister, though, not how I remember."

"That's because Rosa was much younger than Agnes," Staramajka said. "Ten years at least. There were two girls and a boy born between them, but every one of them died right away. Eva Zarac—your ma's mother—she had trouble keeping her babies alive. Only the two survived. When Rosa was about four years old, Eva died herself. And that same year, Wendell, the father, he died, too." Staramajka leaned back in her rocker. "It's true that your mother didn't have it easy. She was only fourteen when she had to become mother to her sister. Couple years later, she married my son Josef, and both girls came to live at our house."

"What did they die of?" Madeline asked.

"Who?" said Staramajka.

"Everybody," said Madeline, looking pale. "The babies and Ma's mother and father—all of them."

Staramajka thought for a minute. "Different reasons," she said. "The babies were weak, probably made wrong on the inside somehow. Eva was worn out, and Wendell? He got run over by a wagon. Who knows all the reasons? People die." She rocked three or four times, creaking pensively. "Come to think, Monda," she said to my sister, "I wouldn't be so surprised if you didn't remember Rosa either. She was hardly ever home, always over at Mrs. Begovacz's, starching that woman's aprons, shining her boots, weaving fancy stuff for her on the loom. That was your mother's idea, that Rosa should get in so good with Widow Begovacz and her twenty acres and her flat-headed son."

I already regretted my question about Rosa and I could see that my sister was wondering about this Mrs. Begovacz, so I jumped in and tried to steer my grandmother in another direction. "What about the Turk?" I said.

"Hold on. I didn't get there yet," Staramajka said, but she straightened up in her chair. "Okay, here's how it was. When your uncle Marko came home from Barcs—did I ever tell you how he went to Barcs to learn the shoemaker's trade?"

"Yes!" Madeline and I cried together.

"Okay," said Staramajka. "He came home, and since we

didn't have pigs no more, he said he could build a room on the front of the barn and sleep back there, at least in summer, so Josef would have more room for the family when he came home from America. Now that was before your pa's letter came from Milwaukee, bragging about where he was living, what a fancy house, with running water!" (Plumbing was an especially sore point with Staramajka, since running water had led to the toilet in the pantry.)

The letter she spoke of was the last one they received before the war put a stop to the mail, and reading between the lines, both Staramajka and my mother could tell that my father's plans—to make his fortune and return to the village with it—were already changing. When the letter arrived, Marko was gone to the fort at Kaposvar, having been drafted, along with most of the men and boys in Novo Selo, into the army of the Hapsburgs. "How could Marko know," Staramajka asked the ceiling tragically, "that his only brother was never coming back from America?" My sister and I already knew, from previous sad stories, that Marko had gone from Kaposvar to Bohemia (a move specifically aimed at taking him away from his mother, Staramajka said, since Kaposvar was close enough for weekend furloughs in the village, whether authorized or not), and from Bohemia to Galicia, where Marko disappeared in action almost as soon as he arrived at the front. "Later," Staramajka said, wiping her eyes with her apron, "after he was gone almost two years already"—it was unclear here whether "he" was Marko or my father, but we knew better than to ask—"the mayor came, like I said before, to ask if he could use the little room in our barn to house the Turk."

By the spring of 1918, three years after Marko disappeared at the front, the war in Central Europe had almost run out of men. Even in the wildest, southernmost Slavic regions of the Austro-Hungarian Empire—from my grandmother's Podravka district, where people learned Hungarian in school if they learned it at all, south to Croatia and Bosnia and Herzegovina— the villages had been all but emptied to keep the trenches full. Sixty men went to war from ninety-three households in Novo Selo alone, my grandmother told us. Twenty-five were lost. By 1918, as the weather grew warmer, strange men came walking through the village almost every day, wearing raggedy clothes that used to be uniforms, their paper-soled boots—if they had them—on strings around their necks, coming from who knows where, going home if they could find it, trying to avoid troops who might seize them as either enemies or deserters, depending on the language they spoke or the sound of their accent or the spelling of their names. So it was nothing too unusual when the mayor of Novo Selo called the people together in front of the church that April and presented to them a man he called the Turk. Staramajka recalled the scene clearly for us: a small crowd of villagers, mostly women, jostling one another to get a better look at a man with dark hair to his shoulders and a serious mustache. Towering over the old mayor, the Turk looked strong, even handsome, in ragged pants of indeterminate color, a dirty white blouse and black vest, and a blood-colored fez like a little flowerpot overturned on his head. (He looked, of course, like Omar Sharif, but Staramajka couldn't know that.) She remembered how still he stood, like a stone carving of a man, she said, staring over a sea of black babushkas in the churchyard as the women sized him up. The mayor called him Tas Akbulut, said he was a prisoner of war, and offered his services to anyone who needed help with heavy work.

"Wait a minute, wait a minute," I objected. "If the village was in Hungary, how could a *Turk* be a prisoner of war? They were on the same side." This I had learned from one of the priests at St. Augustine's, a veteran of the Great War who taught military history—complete with body parts left in trenches and corpses bloating in no-man's-land—during catechism class. When the nuns complained, Father Wojcek said grimly, "These boys need to know what happened over there."

The question of the Turk's allegiance made no sense to my grandmother. Anyone who wore a fez and prayed to Allah was obviously the enemy—or at least the opposite—of Catholics like herself and the other villagers. Instead of answering my question, she told us that chopping wood became the specialty of this particular Turk, who also repaired wagons and roofs. He did very little in the fields, she said, since women were not inclined to waste him on things they could handle themselves, and there was little to plant and less to harvest anyway by that time. Early efforts to post a guard at the door of the barn where he slept soon came to seem unnecessary, even embarrassing, and for half a year, the Turk went freely about the village, unguarded, sought after, feared—if at all—only for the strangeness of his religion. For at daybreak, noon, and dusk, when the church bells rang the Angelus and the more devout among the villagers pulled out their rosaries or mumbled the "Magnificat," the Turk stopped wherever he was, faced the east, and dropped to his knees in prayer.

"He could have been an enemy soldier, pretending to be a Turk," I said. My grandmother looked at me.

"Oh, hush," said my sister. She settled back into the featherbeds and added with satisfaction, as if it were all that mattered, "He was an infidel."

For my sister did remember the Turk. A man as dark and spare as a tree in the winter, with very sad eyes and white teeth that surprised her when a rare laugh suddenly parted the curtain of his enormous mustache. Madeline was barely four years old when he left the village, but she had two distinct memories of him. In one, he was kneeling in the hard-packed dirt of the yard, touching his forehead to the ground. ("Why does he smell the dirt?" Madeline asked her mother, who told her to hush and said that he was praying.) In Madeline's other memory of the Turk, he was sitting at the table while her mother—her blonde, round, pink and white mother—glided around him, from stove to storeroom to table, setting out bowls and whisking them away without seeming to pause in her gliding. Little Madeline had thought of him as an important visitor, an official of some kind, even a prince. (He was very tall and somber.) She didn't know that he was merely the Turk, a prisoner (or something) quartered in the barn behind the house. And when, on occasion, the Turk took her solemnly on his knee, she didn't know she had a father in America who would not approve.

"WHAT I AM thinking, Agnes, is this. It don't look good, that man under the same roof as three women. A Turk. An infidel." So saying, the Widow Begovacz set the spindle down in her lap for the third time and slipped her fingers under her black scarf for a good scratch. By the time Agnes stopped the spinning wheel, big loops of thread were already tangled on the bench between them. Agnes did not want to offend Mrs. Begovacz, the way her sister Rosa often managed to do, so she chose her words with care, slowly turning the wheel to gather up slack in the thread before she spoke.

"Of course, he is not living under the same *roof* with us," Agnes began, but Mrs. Begovacz interrupted, plucking the spindle from her lap with such energy that the little spinning wheel teetered between Agnes's feet.

"He eats from your table, he sleeps—"

"In the barn!" Agnes said, dismayed to feel her cheeks getting warm.

"I only mean to say, Agnes, that people talk. They imagine things. It's evil of them, we know that, but still they talk." Mrs. Begovacz stood up. She scratched her chin and looked across her well-swept yard past the barn to the empty field beyond it, which would have been dotted with the backs of workers wielding scythes against Mrs. Begovacz's wheat if soldiers hadn't marched through the village last winter and stolen every sack of grain they could find. "I'll be lucky to get ten loaves of bread from twenty acres," the Widow Begovacz complained to neighbors who would have much less. Now she stopped and turned in her doorway to frown at Agnes, her eyebrows bristling across the bridge of her nose. "It's not good to keep an infidel in the house. *Or* the barn. That's all I'm saying to you. It's a dangerous thing."

Agnes was silent.

The Widow persisted. "Why does he not return to his home, or his army, or something?"

"He is a prisoner," Agnes answered.

"Is he?" said Mrs. Begovacz.

"Isn't he?" said Agnes. The mayor said he was.

"If he is a prisoner, where are his guards?"

"He doesn't need guards," Agnes said.

"Is that so?" said Mrs. Begovacz. She leaned out of the doorway. Something was tugging at the corner of her mouth—a scowl or a smirk or a smile. On Mrs. Begovacz it was hard to tell the difference. "Then you must ask yourself what keeps him here," she said before she stepped backward out of the sunlight, into the house.

It was on her way home from Begovacz then, stung by the Widow's insinuations, that Agnes first examined her conscience in regard to the Turk. Although there was not much to examine—her encounters with him were so few—she took the long way around the village, avoiding the street and its interruptions by walking along the edges of the fields to the bottom of the hill behind the church. While she walked, Agnes reviewed the months that had passed since the Turk appeared. During most of that time, she had hardly spoken to him, and when she had, they had not so much conversed as delivered lines to one another. Agnes said things like:

"Come and eat."

"The mayor has sent for you."

"You will need this blanket."

"I have sewn the sleeve of your shirt."

"Madeline gathered these two eggs. She says they are for you."

For his part, the Turk replied in kind, speaking surprisingly good Croatian for an infidel:

"Thank you, madam."

"I go at once."

"You are kind."

"You are very kind."

"The child is generous, like her mother."

As for eating under their roof, it was Staramajka's idea to invite the Turk inside to their table, instead of carrying his food out to him "like oats to a horse," she had said. Certainly there was no harm in treating him like a human being, she said. He sat alone at the table—except for those occasions when little Madeline climbed into his lap—there being no other men in the house to sit with him. And when the weather turned suddenly cold last week, human decency had required Agnes— had it not?—to wrap a steaming pot of hot water in a cloth and carry it out to the barn, where she set it down in the straw in front of the door to the Turk's little room. After knocking twice, she had turned to flee, but the door opened so quickly that she slipped instead and fell to one knee in the straw.

"Madam, I am sorry!" Tas Akbulut had exclaimed, reaching down with an arm (hard and veined like marble) to help her to her feet. "Please forgive a clumsy fool!" After a moment's hesitation, she had taken the offered hand (which felt warm, unlike marble), regained her balance, and fled. Looking back at the barn from her doorway, Agnes saw the Turk stoop to lift the pot of water. He stood for a moment inside the barn door, half-hidden by shadows, his place marked by the sun shining on his trousers and the rising wisps of steam.

There was also the one conversation they had by the Drava—but that was really Rosa's doing. When Tas Akbulut came down to the river to help the women rake a week's worth of mud and snakes and frogs off the bundles of hemp they had left soaking in the water, Rosa had dared Agnes to speak to him. "Instead of looking at your feet whenever he comes near!" Rosa had said, laughing. The work was almost finished—most of the hemp rinsed and tossed on the bank, most of the leeches plucked from the legs and feet of squealing girls, most of the women sitting on the grass to spread the damp hems of their skirts and aprons in the sun—before Agnes found the nerve to take up her sister's challenge. She and the Turk had stopped to rest for a moment on the bank, having pulled the last big bundle out of the river. They stood side by side under the canopy of trees. His pants were rolled up almost to his thighs. Beneath her calf-length skirt, her legs were bare. They avoided looking at each other by gazing south across the slow green current to an identical leafy bank on the other side. Thinking that Rosa and her friends would be watching, Agnes had gathered her courage and asked an easy question. "So," she said, "your homeland is south from here, across the river, is it not?"

"Yes," said the Turk.

They were silent again, but Agnes felt pleased with herself. A breeze blew her wet skirt against her knees. Shivering a little, she asked, "Do you miss it?"

"Yes," said the Turk.

"And your family, too, I suppose," she added.

"My mother is always in my prayers," said the Turk.

"Only your mother?" Agnes said. Immediately, she regretted this. She glanced at him long enough to see something fluttering across his face, perhaps the hint of a smile, but when their eyes accidentally met, they both turned back to the river at once.

"My father died when I was a child," the Turk explained.

"I'm sorry to hear it," said Agnes. She wrung out the hem of her skirt until threads snapped. "My parents, too, are gone."

"I have not yet been blessed with a wife," the Turk admitted further.

Agnes released the twisted hem of her skirt. It trailed again in the water. She looked over her shoulder to see if her sister was watching, but Rosa was at the center of a group of girls sprawled on the grass, examining each other's legs for leeches. Agnes turned back to the river. "I'm surprised to learn this," she said. "A man like yourself, strong and healthy and—strong. Willing to work hard."

The Turk gave his mustache a tug. A long pause followed. Finally, he said, "I am sorry that your husband is missing."

This startled Agnes almost enough to make her forget to avoid eye contact with the Turk. She had never thought of Josef as *missing*, and yet, in a way—in many ways, in fact, in nearly every way that mattered—he was. "I used to think he would return," she said, surprising herself with her frankness.

"You must not give up hope!" said the Turk. He turned to her earnestly. "The war plays odd tricks on us, it keeps many secrets. I myself am thought to be dead." At that moment a cloud of laughter rose from the girls sitting on the grass behind them.

Agnes looked at him now. "Josef is not dead," she said.

"I am *certain* he is not," said the Turk. "Many, many of the missing will return."

"He is in America."

These words produced so profound a change in the Turk's expression—the brown eyes widened for an instant and then narrowed, hiding under a black ridge of lowered brows—that Agnes wished at once to take them back. Suddenly, she understood. For months, Tas Akbulut had been hearing Staramajka talk about her son who was missing in the war, and he had assumed, naturally, that Marko and Agnes's absent husband were one and the same. In a rush of words aimed solely at removing the bewilderment from his face, Agnes explained the mistake. By the time she finished explaining—how Josef had planned to return in a year with money to buy land on the other side of the river, but then the war had broken out and put a stop to travel and mail, and now she was no longer certain of her husband's situation—the Turk's calm had returned. He said, "I am surprised that a man would leave his wife and child behind."

Agnes considered telling Tas Akbulut that she couldn't be sure, given the timing, that her husband even knew he had a child, but before she could find the words, the Turk had excused himself with a polite, *"Izvinite, gospođa,"* and moved off down the bank. She watched him carry two armloads of hemp up to the wagon waiting on the road. Later, at home, she went back to the field behind the barn where she and Rosa had spread their hemp stalks to dry and found her little daughter strutting back and forth between the rows. Madeline was wearing a wig of long white fibers tied together at the top of her head and reaching to her elbows.

"Monda!" Agnes said. "What are you doing? Where did you get that on your head?"

Little Madeline pointed to the haystack, where Tas Akbulut sat on a stool in the shade, his foot holding down the hinged end of a wooden *stupa* while one hand drew a bundle of stalks through it. His other hand lifted and dropped the top rail onto the stalks, chopping away the casing and softening the fibers into long white hair of the kind draped over Madeline's head.

"I am the queen of heaven," Madeline announced as she marched past her mother, keeping time to the Turk's *chop-chop-chop*. Agnes stroked the wig and found it slightly damp.

"The hemp is still too wet," she told him.

For a long time—five seconds, then five more—he didn't answer but only went on chopping as if Agnes hadn't spoken at all. Then he stopped and looked up at her—not over or past her but at her, his brown eyes brimful of something. What he said was, "I could not have left her behind."

Agnes stopped short at this point in the examination of her conscience. She had reached the steepest part of the grassy hill behind St. Anna's. It was mid-October, and the air should have been buzzing with cicadas, but they had fallen silent in the noonday heat. All that she could hear when she stopped was grass rustling in the dry wind and the beating of her heart. After a breathless moment, she resumed her ascent. But of course he couldn't have left her behind, Agnes told herself sternly. Everyone knew how the Turk loved children! She swatted absently at the heads of tall grass that clung to her skirt. How many times had she seen him carrying a load of firewood in his arms and a child—Madeline, or little Paul next door, or Eva's girl Marica—on his shoulders, the child's fingers clutching the Turk's black hair like the mane of a pony? Once, she had even heard him singing, while the child on his shoulders used his fez for a drum. It was an old and silly song about a rooster. Agnes had been amazed at the happy voice coming out of him.

She reached the churchyard and hurried through it to the street, anxious to be home now, before the Angelus rang.

And what about Vincent Zarac? she thought. Tas Akbulut had saved that boy's life! Not that Vincent was a child, exactly, but he was certainly *like* a child—a sweet, slightly slow-witted young man, distant cousin to Agnes, with blond curls and blue eyes like hers, and a clubfoot that had kept him out of the army. Last month, the mayor had sent Vincent to Szigetvar with a cart full of hemp sacks to trade for wheat, flour, onions, lard, potatoes, whatever he could find. Vincent had memorized a whole list of things he was to try to obtain. It was a task he had performed admirably in the past—counting and bartering being two of his strengths—but this time the marketplace had little to offer. When he returned with the only food he could find—which turned out to be a cart full of flower bulbs disguised by a layer of onions—the Christian women of Novo Selo had grabbed handfuls of bulbs from the cart and waved them by their hairy roots in Vincent's face. "Do these look like onions to you?" they had sneered at him. "Are onions this small and hard?" The women were so disgusted—as well as frightened to think there was so little that resembled food to be had in the market town of Szigetvar—that they pelted Vincent Zarac, whose foot deprived him of the chance to flee, with bulbs. Then they backed him against the wagon and pressed the bulbs to his mouth, crying, "Do they *taste* like onions, fool?" They were threatening to burn the wagon—bulbs and driver and all—when the Turk stepped in.

Agnes had been watching him all along. From the edge of the crowd she had seen him take the mayor off to one side, the Turk so tall that, leaning toward the mayor's ear, he could almost rest his elbow on the shoulder of the dusty black suit of clothes that old Bunyevach felt obliged to wear on the street as a badge of his office. At first, the mayor had looked alarmed and helpless, hunching his shoulders and turning his palms toward the sky. The Turk leaned closer. The mayor frowned and tugged on his ear. Then Agnes saw Tas Akbulut plunge into the crowd, pulling the mayor after him. When they reached the wagon, the Turk half-hoisted the mayor onto the seat, boosted Vincent up beside him, and stood guard silently, his arms folded across his chest. From the wagon seat, the mayor held forth about God's mysterious ways and the punishment that surely awaited those who would destroy what the Lord had made, leaving it up to his audience to decide if he referred to the bulbs, or the boy, or both. Hesitant at first, the mayor had warmed to his speech, bouncing a little on the balls of his feet as he decreed that Vincent Zarac, with the help of the Turk, would plant these flower bulbs along the road, from the crucifix at one end of the village to the blacksmith's shop at the other. "In the spring," the mayor had concluded grandly, putting his arm around a bewildered but grateful Vincent Zarac, "we shall see what kind of gifts God has given us."

"If we live that long!" Mrs. Begovacz had cried from the middle of the crowd. Later she complained, "That old *patrici* sounds more like a priest every day," but like all the other women in the village she let them plant the bulbs along the road in front of her house, reserving a few from the pile for her hired girl to cook and taste to see if they were good for something after all. They were so bitter that the poor girl vomited them up on the spot.

Agnes reached her own gate as the church bell began to ring the Angelus. For many years afterward, the round and heavy sound of iron bells would summon Tas Akbulut to her mind as she saw him now from the gate: sitting on his heels in the grassy part of the yard between their long yellow house and the neighbor's, his body curled forward and his face to the earth. Even from a distance of several yards, she could see his black hair mingle with the grass, baring the back of his neck like an offering. The Turk at prayer had fascinated Agnes from the beginning. She knew many women who were devoted to their rosaries and novenas, but never, aside from the priest, had she seen a man so devout. She was surprised, too, at how small he could make himself, folding his long legs under his chest, humbling himself before God, not in the shadows of the sanctuary but openly, outside on the grass in the noonday sun. She saw him lift his shoulders slightly now, as if with a deep breath or a sigh, and then drop them again to the earth. His bare feet curled more tightly together with the intensity of his prayer, which reached her ears like a bee humming. His chest bounced lightly against his knees.

It was at this point that she meant to open the gate, but found to her surprise that her hand refused to lift the braided loop of rope that held it shut. She was still puzzling over the rebellion of her hand when the fluttering began in her stomach. Her knees felt odd, too, as if suddenly uncertain of their function. Unable to do anything else, she held onto the gate while Tas Akbulut prayed. She watched him straighten up and square his shoulders, then get to his feet, moving slowly. When he saw her, his eyebrows rose.

"Madam," said the Turk. And then, seeing her face, her hands on the gate, he added, "Agnes?" It was the first time she heard him say her Christian name.

"Tas Akbulut," she said. She tried to sound distant and official but succeeded only in giving the syllables of his name, like all the words she had ever addressed to him, more weight than other, ordinary syllables. She couldn't help but see that his skin had paled under its leathery tan, and that his hands, too, were trembling. She remembered the knowing smile of Mrs. Begovacz and her throat grew dry, while other places dampened. *Mother of Jesus, help me*, Agnes thought, but when he took an uncertain step toward her, she hastened to open the gate.

❧

FROM TIME TO time, whenever she felt that she had said enough rosaries to earn a piece of good news about her missing son Marko, Staramajka sent Rosa and little Madeline—

together, for the mutual safety of their souls—to Gospođa
Dragovich, the wax lady, who lived behind the store. For the
price of one *krunar* (or a chicken or two extra large loaves of
bread), Gospođa Dragovich would take the wax you brought
to her—wax, say, from a candle burned down to the tin holder
beside a sick person's bed, or, in Marko's case, from the candle
Staramajka lighted while she prayed for his return—and she
would melt it in a metal spoon, pour it into a cup of water, and
read in the shapes that formed in the cup the answer to your
question. If the doctor over in Lukovišće was stumped by your
symptoms, the wax lady could read a diagnosis for you in the
clumps and threads and ribbons of wax. She could tell you
what was wrong, who did this to you (whether God, the devil,
or a spiteful neighbor), even what might happen next. That no
soldier or vagabond had ever stolen any scrawny chickens
from the yard of Gospođa Dragovich was testimony to the
breadth of her fame. So far, every *krunar* that Staramajka had
put into the wax lady's pocket had brought the same news: *He
is alive*. Nothing more, nothing less. When, on occasion, she
asked abut Josef in America instead, the answer was the same.
He is alive.

"You are wasting your money," Agnes always said to Staramajka when Rosa came back with the drippings from the candle, rolled up now into a ball the size of an apricot and
impressed with the fingerprints of the wax lady. If Staramajka
didn't grab it first, Agnes would take the ball of wax from her
sister and flatten it, first squeezing it between her thumb and
forefinger, then finishing the job with the palms of her hands,
holding it there for a moment between them. "Of course, she

says they're alive. If she tells you something else"—here Agnes would slap the flattened coin of wax back into her sister's hand or drop it on the table—"you won't be coming back with another *krunar*, will you?" Staramajka always threw such wax away at once, fearful that Gospođa Dragovich would somehow get hold of it again and read therein the handprint of her daughter-in-law's scorn.

It so happened that Staramajka was waiting for Rosa and little Madeline to return from a visit to the wax lady—she had come to the window, in fact, thinking that she heard them at the gate—when she looked out and saw the Turk and Agnes standing there instead. Agnes was gripping the wooden sticks of the gate with a look on her face like a person poised at the edge of a cliff. The Turk, facing Agnes, was swaying like a sapling, but he had his back to the house and without a look at his face, Staramajka could not be sure what his swaying might mean. Her daughter-in-law's expression had certainly provided a clue, but Agnes had unfortunately chosen to bow her head at this crucial moment, hiding her face from Tas Akbulut as well as Staramajka, who moved from the window to the door and hoped that Rosa and Madeline would show up soon, so she wouldn't have to resort to throwing a stone at her rooster. (Once he started crowing, they would have to throw more stones to make him stop.) From the doorway, Staramajka saw Tas Akbulut lift his hand to the side of his head. She saw him take a step toward Agnes, who looked up as she opened the gate, her round face full of disbelief, like a person who had already leapt off the cliff. Rosa and Madeline still did not appear. Staramajka drew in a long breath. The Turk took another step, tentatively, as if he were testing to see if the ground would bear his weight, and then, in slow motion, like a tent folding, he collapsed at Agnes's feet.

By the time Rosa and Madeline finally came running down the street to the gate, Agnes and Staramajka had pulled the groggy and feverish Tas Akbulut up off the ground. They staggered, bearing most of his weight between them, to the house. "Keep the little one outside," Staramajka puffed at Rosa. Inside, Staramajka helped Agnes stretch the Turk out on the bed, both of them grunting with the effort of lifting his legs, of tugging at his boots. When she saw over her shoulder that Rosa was in the doorway, watching, with Madeline behind her trying to see, Staramajka asked, "So what did the *gospođa* say?"

Rosa hesitated. She looked down at the soft, warm ball of wax in her hand. All the way home she had tried in vain to imagine some harmless meaning for the words the wax lady had uttered.

Staramajka turned around. "Rosa, I'm waiting," she said. "What did the woman say?"

Rosa held out her hand as if to say it was the wax, not she, that spoke. "Gospođa Dragovich said, *'He falls a stranger.'*"

Staramajka scowled briefly and turned back to the bed. "Of course," she said, loosening Tas Akbulut's shirt, "Dragovich speaks of the Turk."

※

INFLUENZA HAD WAGED a deadly campaign through the neighboring district of Baranya the previous winter, and although it had so far spared Novo Selo, no one was taking any chances early in the fall of 1918. Once the Turk fell ill, an invisible wall went up around the house where he slept fitfully under the same roof with no one at all, for Rosa and little Madeline had gone to cousins in Lukovišće, and Staramajka, after burning the Turk's straw mattress and sweeping all the hay out of the room in the barn, had taken her bed out there.

Agnes had made a bargain with God and did not sleep at all. It was not lost on her that the Lord had seen fit to strike down the Turk in the very moment of their temptation. (If only He had struck her down instead!) In exchange for his return to health, Agnes vowed to relinquish the sight and even the thought of him: if only God spared him, she would give him up completely, like coffee during Lent. She would send him away as soon as he could walk. If he couldn't go back to his homeland, then he would have to live with the mayor until the war ended. She would think of no man but her husband, and she would join him in America if that's what he wanted, unless, of course, Rosa married the rich Begovacz, or anyone prosperous enough to support them all, in which case Agnes would live like a nun in her village forever. She laid out these terms to the Heavenly Father while Tas Akbulut lay delirious, and she refused to leave his side until she knew if God was planning to keep His end of the bargain or not.

In the meantime, tossing feverishly in the same bed where Agnes had slept with her husband and suffered through the begetting and birth of her child, Tas Akbulut clung to her hand and moaned. She touched his face. He sighed. She wiped the sweat from his forehead, his cheeks, his chin, his throat, and his long arms. She covered him with sheets she had embroidered for her marriage bed. Once, when she was sure that he was so ill he couldn't know what she was doing, she laid her head on his chest and bathed him with tears. At dawn, noon, and dusk, when the church bells rang, she prayed the Angelus for him first, then faced the east and begged *his* God to spare him, addressing Allah shyly and asking Him to look with mercy upon the Turk's unfailing devotion. "You know he saved the life of Vincent Zarac," Agnes reminded both Gods, "and he planted all those bulbs."

Whether it was due to her tears, or Staramajka's herbs, or the combined power of two great religions, three days after Tas Akbulut fainted in the yard, his fever broke, and even before his eyelids started to flutter, Agnes had run away to Lukovišće, the better to keep her vows. For several days, until she was sure that she wasn't going to be ill herself, she stayed in the dryest corner of a half-burned house abandoned at the edge of the village. Rosa and Madeline, who were staying with the mother of Vincent Zarac, brought her meals every day. Agnes would stand by the window and watch them set a basket and a pitcher on the boards that covered the well in the yard. Perched on Rosa's or cousin Vincent's shoulders, the better to see her mother in the window, little Madeline threw kisses and shouted out how many days remained, cleverly counting backward—"*Sedam! Šest! Pet! Četiri!*"—until Agnes would be free. When she went outside her hermitage, Agnes skulked in the shadows, staying out of sight for fear that Tas Akbulut might show up looking for her, at the same time dreading that he would not. At night, when she was alone inside the cold clay walls, listening to scurryings in dark corners and rustlings in what remained of the straw roof over her head, she suffered from shortness of breath, dryness of throat, and a racing heart, pressed by the full weight of knowing she would never see him again.

Left in the care of Staramajka, who fed him sparingly and continued to dose him with herbs and teas, Tas Akbulut was soon on his feet again in Novo Selo, where, miraculously, no one else fell ill that fall. Restoring him to health was easier, Staramajka found, than getting him to leave. When she told him how Agnes had vowed to go to her husband in America as soon as the war was over, the color left his face again, but this time, instead of fainting, he asked Staramajka where in America Agnes would be going, how she would get there, how he could be sure that she was safe.

"How will she find her husband?" Tas Akbulut demanded to know as he helped Staramajka drag the mattress off the bed and out into the yard for emptying. He followed her in and out of the house while she cleaned and swept. "Will he meet her at the boat? How will she know where to go? Is it far from the sea to the place where he lives?"

Staramajka, who had made it her business to know as little as possible about America, had no answers to these terrifying questions. She could only tell him that her son Josef was a good man and would see to it that his wife and daughter found their way safely to him when the time came. When he saw that he could get nothing else out of her, and that Agnes would not return while he remained, Tas Akbulut finally accepted the cloth-wrapped bundle of bread and dried peppers that she kept offering him and left the village one night after the first good rain of autumn. The next day, a search party that the mayor felt obliged to assemble followed the Turk's footprints on the muddy road along the Drava for a mile or so until the prints turned left and slid down the bank into the water. The search party came back. A few weeks later, past the middle of November, the people of Novo Selo were roused from their naps after dinner not only by the growling of their empty stomachs, but by the sound of the little mayor's drum and the shouted news that the war was over. No one had to tell them they were on the side that lost.

IN THE BEDROOM on East Bay Street, we thought that sounded like the end of the story, but I could tell by the way her eyes were glowing that Staramajka was not finished yet. She leaned toward Madeline and me like a conspirator. "Two secrets," she said. "First, the Turk—he ain't a Turk."

"What do you mean?" said my sister.

"I mean he ain't a Turk. His mother was from Barcs, where Marko went to learn his trade. That's about fifteen miles from Novo Selo, right on the Drava, just like our village. You could ride a bicycle up that nice road by the side of the river all the way there. In Barcs, that's where they got the big bridge for wagons to go across."

"Into Yugoslavia?"

"Yeah, only it's not Yugoslavia. Everything on the other side of the river—*preko*, like we say, across—*preko*, everything used to be Austria and Hungary, but it belongs to the Serbs now."

"Do you mean it belongs to the Serbs *now* or *then*?" I asked her.

"When?"

"When the Turk—or whatever he was—came from there. Did it belong to the Serbs then?"

"Came from where?"

"From Barcs! You said the Turk was from Barcs."

"I never said anything like that."

"Yes, you did!" I began, but my sister gave me a look to shut me up.

"I said his mother was from Barcs. Her folks moved there from Lukovišće—next village from ours. We used to go to market all the way to Barcs sometimes and I saw her there. From Barcs she's going all the time across the bridge to Virovitica. Pretty soon she meets a guy there—a clerk who works for the government, collecting something for the Hungarians—and they get married. They move way over into Serbia someplace, by Vojvodina, which is where her boy is born."

"Her boy?" I said.

"The Turk! Only he ain't a Turk, you can see now, he's a Serb—at least by birth. About the father, I don't know. He was dead already before the war."

"Well," I said, "now that makes more sense—to have a Serb prisoner, because they were on the other side."

My grandmother looked crabby. "The other side, the other side of what?" she said. "Too bad I'm not on that other side. Then maybe my boy could have come home to me."

Staramajka was still so jealous of the Turk's mother, who had had a chance to rescue *her* son, that she could hardly tell us the next part of the story. Unlike Marko, by the time the Turk was reported "missing" from his army, he was already on his way home to his mother. The way Staramajka heard it, he had scuffled with a superior officer in a village near the Danube after the officer had threatened to cut off the nose of a Gypsy girl who spurned him. Somehow the superior officer, who had been drinking heavily, ended up dead. To save the Turk's life, three of his comrades in arms had invented a midnight ambush that left the officer slain and the Turk captured by enemy soldiers in a daring foray across the river. The Turk, meanwhile, made his way by night through the countryside to the town where *his* widowed mother had been praying night and day, no doubt, for his safe return, just as Staramajka prayed in vain for Marko's. The Turk's mother hid him in a wagon and drove him north to the banks of the Drava River, somewhere between Novo Selo and her family's home in Barcs. There he was to make honest men of his comrades by swimming across and getting captured by none other than his uncle Janos, his mother's younger brother, the smart one who studied in Pécs and was now a captain in the Hungarian army division stationed in the Podravka. Knowing that the true story of what happened to the superior officer was likely to come out sooner or later, Uncle Janos had advised his nephew to be Tas Akbulut, a Turk, accused of unspecified crimes by a military tribunal and sentenced to hard labor in the countryside. Then he turned him over to the mayor of Novo Selo—a not-so-distant cousin of both of theirs—for safe keeping. "If only I had such a chance to save my Marko," Staramajka said. She lifted the hem of her apron up to her nose.

"So the Turk was a deserter?" To me, this was disappointing news.

"That's right." Staramajka frowned at me. "I suppose you think it's better for him to be a corpse. They would shoot him for killing that officer, no matter what."

"But I don't get it. Which army did he desert from?"

Staramajka thought for a minute. "That I couldn't tell you."

"How do you know all of this, *Baka*?" my sister asked her.

"I told you. I knew the mother."

"But about him deserting and swimming across the Drava and everything. How did you learn all that?"

"What do you think? The mayor told me who he was."

"You mean you knew who he was all along?"

"Of course I knew. You don't think I would let him into my house if I didn't know who he was? So close to my little grand-daughter and my son's wife? The mayor figured he had to tell me and he was right. Although, to tell you the truth, I think everybody figured out who he was after a while. Everybody but Agnes."

Madeline looked as if she had just thought of something. "Then Tas Akbulut wasn't really an infidel?"

"Sure he was—why not? Some of those Serbs, they changed their religion long, long ago. That wasn't his real name, though, and you know it's a funny thing. I can't remember his real name. I know his mother was a Bunyevach, like the mayor."

"Wait," I said. "Do you mean to say that everybody else knew who he was, except for Ma?"

"That's what I said."

"Why couldn't she see it?"

"Why? Because your mother was in love with a Turk! That's why."

My sister and I were quiet for a moment. I, for one, was trying not to look stunned. Then Madeline asked Staramajka, "Did you tell my mother these things about him? After he left?"

"Not until what happened with her sister—your aunt Rosa. When she took up with that other Serb, the young soldier who guarded the river, and your ma made like the end of the world was coming. Then I told her the truth about her Turk."

"Wait a minute, Staramajka," I said. "I thought Rosa married the rich guy. Begovacz."

Staramajka snorted. "If she did, Agnes and me would still be in the village, and you wouldn't be sitting here to ask."

⚶

THE SAME WEEK that the Widow Begovacz announced the engagement of her son Andras, newly returned from the fort at Kaposvar where (thanks to well-placed bribes) he had safely spent the war, to Elanka Jankovich, daughter of the second richest man in the village (Andras being the first), Rosa Zarac, now sixteen years of age, revealed to her sister Agnes that she intended to marry Tomas Novakovic, a soldier in the victorious Serbian army occupying the area. Rosa had made the young soldier's acquaintance during a series of heated arguments she had with him in his capacity as guard at the ferry crossing that linked Novo Selo with the village on the other side of the river, which was now located in the Kingdom of the Serbs, Croats, and Slovenes, soon to become the federation of Yugoslavia. (Rosa didn't see why she needed some kind of stupid passport, with her picture on it yet, to go across. Did he know how much that would cost her in Barcs? *Eight krunar!* She wasn't going to spend that kind of money just to dress chickens and do laundry on the other side of the river.) When Agnes heard of Rosa's plan, she cried, "He is a soldier in the Serbian army!" and then added what was much worse, "He is the fifth of five sons! You told me yourself he has nothing! Not a pig, not an acre!" Rosa calmly said that pigs and acres mattered nothing to her.

"I love him, Agnes."

"You *love* him," Agnes said. "Three months ago you were playing games with your friends in the street. Now all of a sudden you're a grown-up woman? How do you know it's not just another game you are playing with this Serb boy?"

Rosa hesitated, then squared her shoulders and said, "I am carrying his child."

Instead of flying into pieces at this bit of news, as Rosa expected her to, Agnes stopped pacing back and forth like a caged animal, turned, and focused a sharp gaze on her sister. "You are carrying whose child?"

"Tomas Novakovic's!" Rosa said defiantly.

"How do you know it is his?" Agnes said.

"What?"

"It could be anyone's," Agnes said, feeling almost as astonished to have said such a thing as Rosa looked to hear it.

"What do you mean?" cried Rosa. "Do you think I've been

with every man in the village?" Not that there were so many after the war.

"Not *every* man," Agnes said as she resumed pacing, slowly now and thoughtfully. "But one man, perhaps. Or one boy. One snot-nosed, flat-headed boy who would *have* to marry you then." She stopped. "No matter what kind of big ideas his ma has about Elanka Jankovich!"

Rosa looked at her sister in pity and disbelief. "Andras?" she said. "Andras Begovacz? Ha! He couldn't plant a seed in a chicken!" She snorted. "Although, from what I hear, he has probably tried."

Rosa was quietly married (a sad little business compared to the three days and nights lavished on Elanka Jankovich) and moved to the village on the other side of the river. Vincent Zarac, who had hoped to take Rosa's place on the trip to America, was arrested by the Serbs for stealing pigs from wealthy landowners and selling them to the local people at lower prices than he charged the Serb soldiers. (It was widely believed that Mayor Bunyevach was the brains behind this scheme.) Vincent was still under guard in a barn in Lukovišće when Agnes got a letter from Josef with coupons for the steamship tickets they would buy at Boulogne-Sur-Mer and the fifty American dollars they would need at the other end of their journey to prove they were not indigent. Agnes had resigned herself to the will of God and her husband, although she did permit herself to pray until the day of their departure for a miracle to keep them home—Josef's sudden return to the village, perhaps, or news from America that he had taken another wife. (She was willing to grasp any straw.) There was a gathering of official papers from the parish records and a hasty trip to Pécs to seek Vincent's release from the barn in Lukovišće. Rosa's young soldier, who had advised them to go through Zagreb not Budapest, gave Agnes the name of a man and wife, formerly of the Podravka region, who ran a reputable hostel there. He wrote a letter to the couple, telling them when Agnes expected to arrive in Zagreb and mentioning that she knew their family back home.

Staramajka, meanwhile, was asking everyone, "Why does my son Josef send money for a ticket for me? Does he think I can let his brother come home to an empty house and all the family gone?"

Continuing to believe that Marko would return to save her from exile in America, she watched for him every day for more than a year, right up until a gray morning in the early spring of 1920, when they helped her into the loaded cart and put Madeline in her lap. The church bells did their part, tolling the Angelus as the wagon rolled over the muddy street covered with straw past the crucifix that guarded the last house in the village. While Agnes looked backward, keeping her eyes on the street and its border of daffodils until the road curved and the yellow stripes in the distance were lost to view, Staramajka looked ahead, craning her neck and straining to see down the road once lined with linden trees, hoping to spy a tiny figure that would grow larger and larger until it turned into her son Marko, with his fiddle on his back. Or even without it. All the way to the train station in Pécs, she strained her eyes in vain.

⚜

"SO THAT MUST be the other secret," I said when Staramajka finished this part of the story. She and my sister were
both sniffling and dabbing at their eyes.

"What do you mean?" said Staramajka from behind her
apron.

"You said there were two secrets—first, the Turk wasn't a
Turk, and then this one, about Aunt Rosa and the rich boy and
the Serb."

Staramajka made a blowing noise, dismissing this comment.
She dropped the hem of her apron and smoothed it over her
lap. "That was no secret. Everybody knew what your ma had in
mind for her sister, and everybody knew how it all turned out
instead."

"Well, *we* didn't know," I said.

"Because you don't know something, does that make it a
secret from the world?"

"Then what *is* the other secret?"

Staramajka pressed her lips together into what was for her a
grin. You had to give her credit. She knew how to keep a person listening. "The other secret is also about the Turk."

"Who was really a Serb," I put in.

"Here," she said, "is what you still don't know about him."
She paused. We waited. She said, "He followed your mother to
America."

"He followed her?"

"All the way to our porch downstairs."

WALKING DOWN BECHER, having taken a streetcar from the train station to the street the Greek told him about that looked like the same word twice, the man that Agnes knew as Tas Akbulut held in his hand the page torn from her prayer book, a soft and crinkled piece of paper that had made the journey from Europe inside his shoe. The only blurry letters he could make sense of were the ones that spelled "Milwaukee"—he was already there—and the more challenging "146 East Bay." To start with, he'd had no notion of what "East Bay" might be—a street? a building? a village? A Greek selling stuffed grape leaves outside the train station had helped him out. He seemed to speak every language known to man, and tried several on the Turk before explaining in passable Croatian about street names and house numbers. The Greek told him which streetcar to get on, where to get off, and how to get from Kinnickinnic and Becher to East Bay. The Turk thanked the Greek and bought three stuffed grape leaves from him. They were delicious.

When he got off the streetcar, his heart was pounding, and when, after walking a block or two, he saw the sign that said E. BAY ST., his heart climbed into his throat. He knew that she was married. But it was possible, he also knew, that she had never found her husband. He had a cousin Sonja who for years wrote letters to her mother from America, telling about her husband, her lovely home, her children. She sent pictures. (Her mother never did find out who the children in the pictures were.) Not until Sonja died did her neighbors in the rooming house where she lived in Cleveland, Ohio, find her family's address in the old country among her things. They found someone to write to her mother there, and only then did the family learn that cousin Sonja had lived and died alone in Cleveland, after eleven years of supporting herself by questionable means. Tas Akbulut did not expect that Agnes had sunk so low as that, but he knew that husbands in America cannot always be found and he could not live with himself—he could not live at all—not knowing her fate. If she was in need, he would rescue her. If she was not, at least he would see for himself that she was well and happy.

She was seven months' pregnant and sitting on the front porch with her friends Ludmilla Tomasic and Mrs. Solapek from down on the corner when he found her. She had been talking to Mrs. Tomasic and at the same time watching a tall, dark, handsome man (who looked, remember, like Omar Sharif) as he walked slowly up the street. She saw him pause before Solapek's tavern to look down at a paper in his hand and back at the front of the tavern, before he moved on to do the same at the next house—searching the front of the building, then consulting the paper in his hand—and the next and the next. By the time he reached the grocery store alongside the house, Agnes's voice had faded away in the midst of a tale about the size her feet had swollen to by the end of her shift at work the day before. Her friends watched her face grow deathly pale and then flush bright pink like a sudden sunburn.

"What is it, Agnes?" Mrs. Tomasic said in alarm.

The tall, dark, handsome man was standing now on the sidewalk in front of the house, next to the postage-stamp yard, staring up at the three women on the porch. The piece of paper in his hand fluttered, as if threatening to fly away, and he closed his fist around it. Mrs. Tomasic asked him, first in Croatian, then in Polish (he had those Slavic cheekbones, the deep-set eyes, and broad brow), and then, when she got no response, in English, "Can we help you?" He only stared.

In the meantime, Agnes stood up slowly. They looked at one another for a long time, Tas Akbulut with his hand still raised in front of him, the paper closed in his fist. Finally, he cleared his throat.

"I see you found your husband," he said.

"HOW HE MUST have loved her," said my sister, and it was at that moment I saw the feet blocking the light under the door. I nudged Madeline out of her dreamlike state—"What?" she said—and I nodded my head in that direction. Her eyes got big. Staramajka looked where we were looking, and without a moment's hesitation, she said, with volume and gusto, "That was a terrible trip. You remember that?"

"What?" my sister said again, her eyes darting from the door to Staramajka and back to the door.

"First a guy drops dead at the train station so we don't get into Zagreb until so late we can't get into the nice place Rosa's young man told us about and we have to go stay somewhere else. Then all the lights go out in this other place—I think it was really a warehouse or something, not an inn—and your ma's beautiful wedding shawl gets stolen in the dark. You remember that?"

Madeline shook her head, looking at the bottom of the door, where feet that had to be my mother's still blocked the light. Staramajka rolled her eyes and sighed. "And in Bologna Surma, before we got on the boat? That was the worst of all." She looked at me. "They took all of our things, Georgie, even our clothes." She looked at my sister. "You remember that?"

"A little," said Madeline.

"They made us sit around naked wearing white coats," Staramajka said. She waved a hand at my sister as if to say, *Talk.*

"How could you be naked if you were wearing white coats?" I said. The feet were still there.

"*Underneath* we were naked, and they weren't our coats! And when we got our bags back again, all my plants were gone except the grapevine I had in the lining of that little valise Marko made for me out of cow leather."

"What plants?" I said.

Finally, Madeline spoke up. "Staramajka had a whole garden in her bags! She had poppy seeds and rose cuttings, grapevines —and bulbs." She looked at Staramajka. "You even had daffodils! Were those the same ones that he—?" She put a hand bandaged like a mitten to her mouth. Staramajka nodded sharply. Madeline swallowed and went on. "You showed me before we left. All the different kinds of bulbs, each kind in a different piece of cloth so you could tell them apart."

"Why did you bring plants along?" I said.

"To plant them in America, in Milwaukee!" said Staramajka, "but those bums took every one away in Bologna Surma. They probably went home and planted them in their own gardens. That's why all we got here from the old country is the grapevine.

That's it. That's the only thing from home. No roses, no poppies"—she sighed pointedly—"no daffodils."

We all felt rather than saw a movement that drew our eyes to the door. Together, we watched the feet move silently away, leaving an unbroken strip of sunlight behind. When we heard the muffled sound of a door closing in the back of the house, my sister and I exhaled loudly together. We looked at Staramajka, who raised an eyebrow at us and said, "You know? I think I got an idea about those plants. Where did you say that young fella of yours lives, Madeline? On Canal Street?"

Before I could ask her what she meant about the plants, my sister whispered, "But how on earth did he know where to find her?"

❧

I HAVE TO admit to you, Mary Helen, many years passed before I realized that Staramajka wasn't telling me and Madeline the story of the Turk and my mother for *our* benefit, that she had been waiting for my mother's feet to appear at the bottom of the door, and that even when they were gone, Staramajka knew that Ma was still following the story, still listening to every word.

"In her heart, you mean?"

No. By the furnace in the basement. The heating ducts in that house were a communications network. If you had a secret, you didn't tell it by a heat register, not unless you wanted everybody else in the house—upstairs and down—to know. I finally realized what my grandmother was up to at

Ma's funeral, in 1967. I was thinking about my mother and the Turk the way you think about things at a funeral, you know, wondering if she'd spent her whole life regretting what she had given up over there. I pictured Madeline sitting up on the bed with her bandaged arms, listening to the story, and Staramajka in her rocking chair with her stockinged feet pressed up against one of those fancy wrought-iron heating grates we all fought over to warm our feet in the winter, and that's when it hit me. It was *August* when she told that story. There was a heat wave, remember? She wasn't warming her feet by the heat register. She was using it as a telephone. She knew that my mother would go straight downstairs to the furnace, put her ear to the right flue, and get the whole story, better than through the door.

That's why Staramajka went on for so long about the flowers and this idea she had for Uncle John—Madeline's young man, that is—to plant daffodils around the yard out front, saying how that would melt my mother's heart. We did that eventually, we took a basket of bulbs over to his rooming house on Canal Street. He thought we were crazy. I remember he said they wouldn't grow, it was too early for planting, the timing was bad, and Staramajka told him, with me translating into English, that it was too late to worry about timing. She said he should have worried about timing before. He turned red as a beet, and so did I, but he took the bulbs.

Planting daffodils in the front yard turned out to be a good thing—a few were blooming already when Johnny was born in April—but Staramajka was only stalling when she came up with the idea. She was giving my mother time to get to her listening post in the basement before she answered Madeline's question, which is your question, too, I'll bet.

"How *did* he know where to find her?"

⁂

THE NIGHT BEFORE they left for Pécs, Agnes couldn't sleep. For a long time she watched a blue beam of moonlight from the window over her head fall on the wall opposite, inching its way down as the moon rose, turning Rosa's loom into a harp with silver strings. When the moon was so high that the beam reached the floor, she sat up and pushed the featherbed down to her feet, careful not to uncover Madeline, who slept beside her. Her mother-in-law was a gently snoring lump in her bed on the other side of the room. Rosa was long gone. Except for the beds, the loom, and a trunk piled with cloth bundles, the room was bare.

Outside, the ground felt cold under her feet. The sheds, the wash house, the privy, and the well all cast sharp shadows across the path. Next to the barn, the haystack spread a dark double of itself on the grass. Beyond the barn and the shadows, beyond the fence at the end of the garden, Agnes could see the long, narrow pasture with a tree in new leaf in the middle of it, and then more fields and the little rise that hid the river, all of it silver. She would never see these fields by moonlight again—a thought that made her stomach drop, her fingers ache.

After a stop at the privy, where she left the door open for light, she pulled her shawl up from her shoulders over her head and took careful steps toward the barn. Sleepy clucks bubbled from the doorway of the chicken coop as she passed it, followed by a short, sharp crow from the rooster whose name was a curse. Agnes had never uttered the name, *Jabotevrag*, not even the way Staramajka said it, running it together into one word that didn't really mean *Thedevilfuckyou*, Staramajka said, that didn't mean anything at all, she said, except to her and the rooster. Tonight, however, seemed like a night for first and last things, and so Agnes called softly, *"Jabotevrag!"* taking a peculiar satisfaction in the way her cheeks grew warm with the saying of it. "Shut up, Old Man," she added. "It isn't morning yet."

It was darkest beside the haystack, where all kinds of rustlings and squeaks ran ahead of her across the invisible path. Agnes didn't need the path—since last fall she had been walking around the yard and the village, often with Madeline by the hand, doing her best to memorize every tree, every stone, every plank in the barn—but she walked slowly anyway, looking down to where her feet were vague gray shapes beneath the hem of her nightgown. She wished that she had pulled on Staramajka's boots—the last pair Marko had made for her before he left for Kaposvar and oblivion. What if her bare foot found something that scratched or bit? What if she stepped on a toad or a snake? Agnes slowed to a stop and heard in the hay a rustle that was too long and deliberate to be a mouse or a fox. A few yards ahead, the mounded edge of the haystack seemed to grow a second, smaller mound that bulged from its side and then unfolded upward into an appendage as tall as a man, the moon behind it casting its features into deep shadow against the light. "Agnes?" it said.

Light-headed with terror, Agnes answered. "Josef?"

A long, rustling silence followed, during which the man of hay shook out his long legs and brushed off his arms, and Agnes realized the foolishness of her mistake, for her husband was thousands of miles away, marking days on a calendar. Still silent, the figure bent to pull hay from its legs.

"Tas Akbulut," Agnes whispered.

The figure straightened. Haloed by moonlight, he said, "They told me you are leaving."

"Tomorrow," said Agnes. She didn't ask him who had told him, or where he had been keeping himself through two winters and the year in between. They told her he had left the village, he had crossed the river and was gone. Agnes thought he had gone back to his own people. Had he been here instead—all the while that she had taken pains to imagine the next day and the day after that with the room in the barn empty, while she had learned not to look out the window when the Angelus rang to see if she could spot him curled close to the earth—all that time, was he waiting nearby? Was he in Barcs or Virovitica? Or in the village across the river? All winter long, when she went down to the Drava to wash clothes in the freezing water, was he watching her from a screen of tangled brush and black tree branches on the other side? Had he been waiting all this time to see what would happen, to see if she was really leaving? Whatever he thought, wherever he had been, Agnes could feel the air vibrating around him now.

"My cousin Vincent Zarac is dead," she said.

"I know," said the Turk.

"Vincent shot the guard—that nice boy—with his own gun. He was trying to escape in time to come with us to America."

"Agnes."

"What are you doing here, Tas Akbulut? Why haven't you gone home?" She saw that he was wearing some kind of uniform.

"I did go home," he said. "I came back."

"Why?"

"To see you."

"But we are leaving tomorrow."

"I would have you stay," he said.

That he would express his desire made the ground feel unsteady under Agnes's feet. She felt a cold breeze fluttering the fringes of her shawl, and although she pulled it closer to her face, a spot of cold slipped through and traveled down her spine.

"I can't stay," she whispered.

The Turk said nothing.

"You know that I can't."

"Then at least you must tell me where in the world you will be!" he cried, and in a flurry of words he begged her for the name of a town or a city, a street, a building, something, anything. He told her about his cousin in Cleveland and asked her, "How will I know that you have found your husband? Will he meet you at the boat? Will he show you where to go? Going to America is not like walking to the next village, or taking a wagon to Barcs!"

Having thus uttered more than Agnes had ever heard him

speak at one time, the Turk sat down hard in the hay, as if he were suddenly tired, and dropped his head into his hands. When he looked up at Agnes again, his eyes were dark circles, his face blanched by moonlight and despair. "I just want to know where you are," he said. "How can I eat or sleep if I don't know where you are?"

It was mostly to escape the anguish on his face that Agnes ran back into the house, pulled her prayer book from one of the bundles on top of the trunk, and tiptoed out again. As she approached, Tas Akbulut rose and stepped into the cascade of light the moon was pouring over the top of the haystack now. He watched her as she opened the little book and fingered the first page thoughtfully. She was asking herself, *What harm can it do?* She scored the inside margin with her thumbnail and tore the page carefully from the binding.

"Here," she said.

He took it from her delicately, a white scrap of moonlit paper, tissue thin, a tiny thread of gold leaf glinting on three sides. "What does it say?" he asked.

Without looking at the blue ink handwritten in the top margin of the page, Agnes said, "It says the name of the place where my husband lives in America. Where we will live," she added.

"What does it mean?" he said.

"It's a place in the city called Milwaukee." She said it "Mil-VOW-key."

"But the words? The numbers? Here. Do they name a street? A house? What do they mean?" He turned the paper sideways, so that the writing went down the side of the page.

"Not like that," said Agnes.

"Then how? Come," he said. "Show me."

Agnes stepped into the light, into the air trembling around him. She took his hand and turned it so that the blue writing was again at the top of the page. He caught her hand in his— careful of the scrap of paper—and put his arm around her waist, and the cold spot she could still feel at the base of her spine became an ache, it warmed and spread, it weakened her knees, it made her head feel light, her arms and breasts heavy. Over their heads, the moon had reached the zenith and seemed to wait there, unwilling to begin its descent.

Who knows what happened that night, or what would have happened, vow or no vow, before the brightness of the moon fooled that crazy rooster into thinking it was dawn? *Ah, Jabotevrag!* The rooster ignored the handfuls of dirt and stones that Agnes threw at him, keeping up his devil's racket until Tas Akbulut had no choice but to escape, a gold-trimmed piece of paper tucked into the pocket of his coat. As soon as the Turk was gone, the rooster retreated, strutting back toward the coop, where chickens calmed him with gentle pecks and clucks.

Agnes returned to the house. She paused in the doorway, leaving dusty handprints on its wooden frame as she listened to her daughter's even breathing and Staramajka's gentle snores. They had slept through it all, Agnes thought, deafened by dreams, sleeping the sound sleep of the blameless. As she crept into bed next to Madeline, Agnes felt as if she might never sleep again. It was as if she had dissolved into the air, as if a cloud of her filled the room. Everything that touched her—the rough sheet under her, the featherbed on top, the loose, warm limbs of her daughter—felt heavy and strange. *All this time he had dreamed of her. He had waited for her. And when hope was gone, he had come to say good-bye.* Agnes pulled up the covers—leaving dusty prints there, too—and pressed her face into Madeline's warm back.

Then Staramajka's voice rose in the milky darkness. "He asked me, too, where to find you," she said. There was no trace of sleep in her voice.

Agnes took so sharp a breath that Madeline squirmed away from her.

"Before he left, he asked me," Staramajka said. "When you were in Lukovišće."

Agnes was no more now than her own voice, whispering, "Did you tell him?"

"No," said Staramajka, and after a silence long enough for poor Agnes to die a thousand times of shame, she added, "I couldn't find that prayer book."

⚜

IN THE BASEMENT of the house on East Bay Street, Agnes sat on an upturned bucket next to the furnace, with the hem of her skirt dragging on the dirt floor and a crink in her neck from keeping her ear to the flue. She had held her breath during much of Staramajka's version of the night before they left for Pécs, and sighed in relief when the rooster began to crow. Now the room upstairs was quiet, and Agnes was left to think about a part of the story that Staramajka couldn't tell.

This was a secret Agnes had kept in her heart, wrapped in guilt and longing, for more than a dozen years, and one that she would keep for thirty more, until the day she begged forgiveness from her gray-haired daughter as they both sat weeping on a vinyl couch in the Ladies Lounge at the Riverside Theater downtown. In the meantime, it would cause her many sleepless nights and more than one bad confession. It would make her feel and do things that she did not understand—flying into a rage when her husband dozed on the sofa Sunday mornings, ashes spilling from his pipe, or punishing her daughter, God help them both, with a bucket full of lye.

It was a secret about hands.

IN THE ROOM where the Turk lay ill, the darkness before dawn covered even the table by the window, where Agnes poured water carefully from a pitcher to a bowl, watching bits of silver fall through the air, listening to the rising splash as the water deepened. When she judged by the sound that the bowl was half full, she set the pitcher down. She draped a fresh supply of linen cloths over the crook of her elbow and lifted the bowl from the table with both hands, careful not to let it slosh over the rim. Then she turned slowly on her heel, keeping her eyes on the water in the bowl, and took three careful steps toward the bed. She looked up. A moment before, Tas Akbulut had been lying with his back to the room, a white sheet draped over the sharp ridge of his hip, leaving the hot, dry skin of his back and arms bare for bathing. Now, Agnes saw, he lay flat on the bed, the sheet fallen down across his legs, and from the dark, gleaming place at the top of his thighs rose something white—a rod, a column of white. It pointed straight up at the ceiling.

Agnes dropped the bowl of water. It hit the floor with such force that a bowl-shaped tide rose from it, drenching her feet and legs, darkening her skirt, scattering shards of red and black pottery across the floor, and sprinkling the Turk from head to toe. He never moved, not at the noise, not at the water drops on his face and chest and everywhere else, although his penis changed direction, pointing now as if to draw her attention to his flat belly, his countable ribs, and above them, his gaunt but handsome face. Her first thought was that he must be dead if he didn't hear that crash, and her second was to shield him from view. The sheet was tangled around his knees—tugging at it was impossible—and the linen cloths had hit the floor with the bowl and water. All Agnes could think of was to cup her hands together side by side, thumb to thumb. With the shield they formed, she covered him.

Only now did she think to look over her shoulder to see if the noise had summoned Staramajka. The doorway behind her was empty but growing paler. She turned back to the Turk and searched his face for any sign that he felt her hands, her presence, but found none. His eyes were closed, his breath came and went raggedly through dry, half-parted lips. Agnes looked around for another sheet or blanket, but there was nothing within reach, not while she stood this way, with her hands over him. She half-twisted away from him to see if she could reach any of the linens she'd dropped, and it was while she looked about her that her hands drifted gently down until they touched him.

No one heard her little gasp.

Agnes's hands had never touched the penis of a man before. (She had soothed the bare-bottomed little boy next door when a gosling nipped at him in the yard, but that was the extent of her experience.) She was surprised by its softness. The skin felt to her quivering fingers like a newborn's cheek, or the petal of a rose. The truth is that Agnes had never even looked at her husband in such a state (although she had seen enough of cattle and horses to suspect before the fact that her wedding night would not be easy), and she was astonished, now that she had seen, to think that something so large could have gained entry to her. Now she understood the blood and the pain. What a strange way, she thought, for God to arrange things! Looking down at her hands, she saw that her fingers had parted a little. She closed them again. Like petals at dusk, she thought.

Agnes couldn't say how long she stood that way, not quite touching him. When her arms grew so heavy that she had to let them drop to her sides, she saw that the penis of Tas Akbulut had also retreated. She put her hands behind her back and held her breath, waiting for him to open his eyes, wondering what it would mean to him—this unsought intimacy between them—but his eyes didn't open, not even when the rooster crowed outside and Agnes ran to the chest for a blanket. By the time she returned, she could see by the pale square of light the window had become that Tas Akbulut's skin was damp, almost glossy. This was the sign Staramajka had told her to watch for, the sign that his fever had broken. Agnes spread the blanket over him and pulled it up to his chin. When the rooster crowed a second time, she went to the window, but instead of hissing its name like a curse, she called softly, *"Starac!* Hey, Old Man! Be quiet! A man is sleeping in here." Her voice danced away from her. "Do you hear me? A man is *sleeping* under my roof!" Then, heedless of broken pottery, she faced the east and knelt on the wooden floor so smooth it felt like cool earth under her knees. With her palms and fingers pressed together to keep them still, she thanked his God and hers for their mercy.

Years later, sitting in the coal dust beside the furnace on East Bay, Agnes looked down at her hands, palms up, palms down, spreading her short, broad fingers. They had always been clumsy hands compared to her sister Rosa's. They were hands without mercy, she thought, red and rough only from hard work and years, not like Madeline's hands, blistered red and bandaged, the wrong hands burned. A wave of grief washed over her. As if it were yesterday and not a dozen years ago, she remembered how, for many months after her son was born, she had touched his cheek or his arm or his soft baby's belly with her guilty hands and remembered—no, she had by an act of her own will *imagined*—how it felt to touch the Turk. Agnes bowed her head and put her hand against the cold furnace for support. The summer evening had turned into a moonless night, erasing the outlines of the basement windows and leaving Agnes in the inky dark. It was where she belonged: cast into darkness, her sins (most of them anyway) laid bare to her children. From the room upstairs came only silence now. The story was over.

Then the singing started, causing Agnes to stand up in surprise and bang her head hard on an overhead flue. There was a brief pause in the melody while the echoes thunderously died, and then Staramajka's thin voice flowed again through the heating ducts, tremulous and hollow, accompanied by the squeak of her rocking chair, right into Agnes's soot-covered ear. It was a tune Agnes hadn't heard since she left the village, a silly little song about a rooster. It opened a door in her heart.

PETE THE COP placed no value upon surprise as a law enforcement technique. It could be hazardous, after all, to startle a person in the middle of committing a burglary or picking a barroom fight, especially if he happened to be armed, and Pete knew that a lock-picking penknife or a broken bottle was as lethal as a pistol in certain circumstances. The way Officer Moldenowski looked at it, his job was to prevent bad things from happening, not to make matters worse by getting himself killed or injured in the line of duty. And one of the most effective ways to change a potential criminal's mind about the act he was about to perpetrate was to let him know you were coming. Many a would-be thief saw the error of his ways while making good his narrow escape.

So when Pete the Cop came around the corner in front of Solapek's tavern one fresh night in September and spotted the shadowy lump wielding shiny objects in one of the patches of grass they called a front yard in this part of town, the first thing he did in his capacity as an officer of the law was to start whistling "The Beer Barrel Polka." Lustily. With satisfaction,

Pete the Cop watched the shadowy lump straighten up and drop the shiny objects—a hand spade, Pete could see as he drew nearer, and a little rake. By the time Pete reached the yard in front of 146 East Bay Street, the young man inside the picket fence was on his feet, wiping his hands on a canvas work jacket. Looking down, Pete could see that the grass inside the enclosure was dotted with mounds of dirt, as if a gopher had run amok there. A basket at the young man's feet looked to be full of little onions. Pete waited for an explanation, but the young man only stood and stared, brushing and brushing his palms against his jacket while his eyes darted from Pete's badge to his gun to his nightstick. It was clear to Pete that he would have to open this conversation.

"Odd time for gardening," he said, twirling the nightstick on its leather thong.

The young man didn't argue.

"You speak English?" Pete asked, and then, remembering the people who lived at this address, he added, *"Hrvatski?"*

"English," the young man said.

"Good," said Pete. "Now do you mind telling me what you're doing here with all this"—he poked his nightstick at the basket and the tools—"at one o'clock in the morning?"

"I work second shift," the young man said.

"Looks like this is overtime for both of us," said Pete.

"I know the people who live here," the young man offered. He tugged at the visor of a shapeless cap and then, on second thought, he pulled it off and shoved it under his arm, leaving dark hair that stuck out over his ears.

"So do I," said Pete. He was about to tell the young man to

come out from behind the fence with his hands held out where Pete could see them, when the front door opened and the lady of the house upstairs—not the silent, toothless one, Pete was glad to see—came out onto the porch, wiping her hands on a towel. Her appearance seemed to turn the young man to stone.

"It's okay, officer." She said it "offeetser." "I know these fella."

The young man revived a little at that. He stepped off the grass onto the sidewalk. Pete said, "Do you know he's out here digging up your yard?"

"Sure, I know it," Agnes said. "I ask him to do it."

"In the middle of the night?" asked Pete the Cop.

"Sure!"

"Why?"

Agnes put her hands on the porch rail and looked at Madeline's young man, at his basket and his tools. Tas Akbulut had stood on the same sidewalk twelve—no, thirteen—years ago, almost in the same spot. He looked different in some ways from the last time she'd seen him—the baggy brown suit, the gleaming hair cut to the top of his stiff white collar, a tweed cap instead of the fez. In other ways—his brimming eyes, his mustache, the hand that held the gold-trimmed page from her prayer book—he looked the same. When he mentioned her husband, Agnes had blurted, "My husband is not at home!" (This was true: it was Sunday, and Josef had taken Madeline on the streetcar to South Shore Park.) After that, Agnes seemed unable to say anything at all. Speech, it turned out, was not required of her, for Staramajka had spied the Turk from an upstairs window, and before Agnes's heart had a chance to start beating steadily again, Staramajka was out on the porch, too, smacking the Turk's chest with the flat of her hand by way of welcome—welcome!—and telling Mrs. Tomasic and Mrs. Solapek that this—this!—was the son of an old neighbor from Lukovišće by way of Barcs—did they know Barcs? On the Drava? Only a few miles from her village up that nice road by the river? She pushed and pulled them all upstairs for coffee and *kolače*, the Turk protesting all the while that he didn't have much time before his train left for Chicago.

"So," said Mrs. Tomasic, settled down at the table across from the guest, "you are going to Chicago?"

The Turk looked at Agnes, who was following Staramajka's orders as best she could, bringing cups and saucers from the pantry. He said, "I am going home."

Agnes did not drop the cups.

"And where is home?" asked Mrs. Tomasic.

"Near Barcs."

The cups rattled again but made it safely to the table.

"You are going back to the old country?" Mrs. Tomasic said.

"*Now* you are going?" said Staramajka. She was standing stock-still at the stove. "You are going *home*?"

The Turk lifted his shoulders. Agnes was behind him now, leaning against the wall. "I have seen what I came here to see," he said.

"Well, God bless you then and safe journey," said Mrs. Tomasic. "I envy you! It would be good to see the old village, eh, Agnes?"

From the porch they all watched him walk down East Bay Street to Kinnickinnic to catch the streetcar. Agnes—with her big belly, her full heart, and her swollen feet—gripped the porch rail, leaning over it so far when the streetcar pulled up to the corner, sparks flying from the cables, that Staramajka told her to be careful she didn't topple over the railing into the yard.

"A handsome fellow," Mrs. Solapek said after the streetcar had come and gone. "Too bad Joe missed him."

"He don't sound like he's from Barcs," said Mrs. Tomasic. She stole a glance at Agnes.

"I said his *mother* is from Barcs," Staramajka snapped before she went back inside.

Now, leaning over the same porch rail toward Madeline's young man, Agnes felt like a passenger on a ship leaning toward the shore. He was a nice-looking fellow, too, even with dirt streaked across his face: tall, a little too thin perhaps, white teeth (he was biting his lip) under a black mustache. He held the basket of bulbs in both hands, as if to offer them to her. She remembered the policeman had asked her a question. Why *did* she want this young man to plant these bulbs in her yard at this hour? "You come around in spring," Agnes told Pete the Cop. "You gonna see why."

II

UNCLE MARKO
AND THE HOLLYWOOD PLATE

You know i met that fellow, the Turk, years and years later. Watch out for my umbilical cord, Mary Helen.

"What?—oh, the hose!"

You keep stepping on it like that and your dad will be turning a pretty shade of blue.

"Should I turn up the oxygen?"

Just watch your feet. He did look a little like Omar Sharif. Without teeth.

"Where did you meet him, Dad?"

In the village. When I went there with my cousin Marie Sinyakovich in 1982. He must have been in his nineties. Pushing a hundred maybe.

"So then he didn't go home to Serbia—or wherever. He went back to the village."

That's right. He lived by himself for a long time in Staramajka's house. It was vacant after they left for Milwaukee. Nobody seemed to care. And then, in a really funny twist of fate, when he was in his fifties, he married my uncle Marko's wife. His widow, I mean.

"Uncle Marko. You mean Staramajka's son, the one who disappeared in the war? He had a wife?"

That's why my cousin Marie was a little funny about the Turk. She didn't want to have anything to do with the old guy, maybe because he took her father's place. But it was years after Uncle Marko died before they got married. The wife was in her forties already. Her name was Natasha—no, not Natasha, but something like that. I guess everybody was pretty surprised when she got pregnant. She and the Turk had the one boy. I met him, too.

"So you're saying that Marie Sinyakovich—your cousin from St. Louis—is Uncle Marko's daughter?"

That's what makes her my cousin. Nadya! Uncle Marko's wife was named Nadya.

"But I thought Uncle Marko died in World War I."

Is that what you thought? Join the club. We didn't find out any different until 1934, when the priest in the village sent us a letter saying that Uncle Marko had come back from the dead. Staramajka didn't ask any questions. She didn't ask why it had taken her son sixteen years to make his way home after the war. She didn't express any surprise about the wife and four children and the wagon full of shoe-making equipment that he brought back to the village with him. By the time my father got to the end of the letter, she was on her way to the bedroom to pack her bags. And although my mother took a sharp breath as if to speak, perhaps to remind my grandmother of how many thousands of miles an old woman and her bags would have to travel to get from Milwaukee to the village of Novo Selo, not a person in the room—and we were all in the room—said a word to stop her from packing them.

At the beginning of the war, remember, Uncle Marko was

stationed at the fort in Kaposvar, only twenty miles from Novo Selo. The army was not a bad thing for him at first. His uniform was unlike any clothing he had owned in his life and there were frequent visits home to the village to show it off. Due to his small stature—he was five feet four in all but the most elevated boots—Marko was designated a courier, one of three in his company. The courier's job was to ferry messages back and forth between command posts in the field. Every time Marko came home, Staramajka's house would fill with visitors, and she would explain again why her son wore on his collar a beautiful brass pin that looked like a shoe with wings.

Soon, however, the commanding officer at Kaposvar got tired of retrieving his men from unauthorized furloughs made possible by the fort's proximity to their homes in the villages along the Drava. It wasn't long before Marko was transferred, along with sixty other men from Novo Selo and nearby Lukovišće, to some place in far-off Bohemia, and from there to a vast city of tents in Galicia, where he was attached to a company on its way to the front. Somewhere on that long march, Marko looked up and saw that he was one in a line of men walking two abreast that stretched as far as he could see, to the front and to the rear, from horizon to horizon. He hadn't known there were that many men in the world. Marko's company spent their first night at the front in muddy trenches at the edge of a forest bristling with Russian artillery. They might have marched into an ambush if they hadn't approached from downwind and smelled the Russian uniforms, which were woven of wool and cow hair and bathed in carbolic acid against the lice.

In the middle of the night, the Russians commenced firing. The new recruits, exhausted by the day's march, awoke from dreams of their villages to a nightmare of terrifying light and sound. Each bursting shell turned the muddy clearing beyond the trench into a bright room furnished with burned and broken trees, the black border of forest rising around it like a wall. Every boom dealt a sharp and personal blow to the chest and ears. An hour before dawn, the bombardment stopped as abruptly as it started, and the lieutenant sent the first courier out of the trench. In the cottony silence that filled their ears, the men could hear the *plop* and suck of his boots as he ran through the mud. Marko counted to twenty before a single shell exploded and the first courier flew up in the air. Immediately, the second courier scrambled out of the trench—encouraged by the lieutenant's bayonet at his back—and set off zig-zagging across the mud. Marko counted to fifteen before machine gunfire raked across courier number two.

Marko was courier number three. To keep himself upright, he had hooked his arm over a tree root that protruded like a crooked elbow from the dirt wall of the trench. He felt dizzy, not only with terror but also from holding his breath in suspense between the whistle and the boom of each shell. He waited until he felt the tip of the bayonet through his uniform and then he was out of the trench and running for his life in near darkness, able to see his feet only when shells flashed. He saw courier number one's head staring skyward in its helmet in plenty of time to avoid stepping on it before he, too, was hit.

Back in the trench, the lieutenant saw Marko go down and cursed. He was all out of couriers.

❧

STARAMAJKA HAD NEVER for a minute believed that her son Marko was dead. She hadn't believed it during the fourteen years she'd spent in Milwaukee, and she hadn't believed it back in the village in 1916, when she received a different sort of letter, one of many to arrive at the post office in Lukovišće in envelopes emblazoned with the seal of the monarchy. "Very fancy," the postmistress said bitterly as she handed it over (having received one herself), "but that doesn't change what's inside." Staramajka had taken the fancy envelope to the very same priest who would one day write to us about Marko's return, a young man who had gone to grammar school with her son Josef but who, unlike Josef, had the good sense to become a priest in Lukovišće instead of going to America. In 1916, he was only a deacon. He read the letter aloud to her, first in Hungarian, of which she understood only enough to deepen her dread, and then, translating loosely, in Croatian. When he fell silent, she asked him, "What does it mean, my son is missing?"

He said, "It means he is unaccounted for," and when she still looked blank, he added, wanting neither to crush her nor to raise false hopes, "God help him, *gospođa*, he is lost."

To Staramajka this meant only one thing: that her son had given the army the slip. Marko was such a clever boy, much quicker in his wits than Josef in America. She was certain that he had hidden himself behind the Russian front, which she pictured as a wall of gray cloud, like a long and compact fog, opaque but not impenetrable, and that he was even now find-

ing his way back to her. She had spent the rest of the war waiting for him to show up at the gate with his fiddle strapped to
his back. (She didn't know that he'd left the fiddle behind in
Kaposvar with a mixture of regret and relief.) When someone
reminded her gently that two, three, four years and more had
passed since the word that he was missing, she always pointed
out, "It's a long way to walk."

Now, almost twenty years after he disappeared, it seemed
that my grandmother had been right about Marko all along.
The letter announcing his return, in which the priest praised
God and his Blessed Mother for a miracle and then described
the wagon full of shoe-making equipment—the sewing
machine, forms and stretchers, cutters and awls—was followed
one week later by a package containing a pair of small black
boots. The boots, said a note painstakingly written by Marko
himself, were a present for me, his brother's son. Someone in
the village had apparently misinformed Marko as to my age (I
was almost fourteen), so the boots went to Johnny, my sister's
little boy, instead. They were too big for him, but he stuck his
fat legs in them anyway and clomped down the slight incline
between the kitchen and the front room of our upper flat like a
fisherman wading back downstream toward home.

Staramajka wanted to sell the house and buy steamship tickets for everyone—my mother and father, my sister Madeline
and her husband and their little boy Johnny, and me. When my
father vetoed that idea, she sent Frankie Tomasic down to the
depot to buy her a ticket for Chicago, which was all she could
afford. Mrs. Longinovich had warned her about Chicago,
where a woman she knew boarded the westbound train by mis-

take and missed the boat, but Staramajka had no intention of ending up in Omaha.

"Jesus, Maria," she kept saying. "I am going home."

⁂

BEFORE HER SON Marko came back from the dead, Staramajka's attitude toward the American dollar was similar to her feelings about the Catholic Church in America. She had no faith in either one. The cause of the Depression was obvious to her. It was those worthless pieces of paper that people expected other people to accept as wages and exchange for goods. Why, she wondered, would anyone hand over a coat or a chicken, if all they were getting in exchange was wrinkled pieces of paper? Back in the village, she had little to do with money, except for ceremonial purposes like paying the midwife for a birth or the priest for a funeral, but there, at least, you could put a gold or silver *krunar* in a little bag on a string around your neck and feel the weight and value of it. In America, even the coins seemed slighter.

With Marko's return, however, the value of the dollar rose sharply for Staramajka, although she still preferred coins to paper. It was a value measured in distance—how close could she get to the port of New York for one dollar? for five? for ten?—a value determined by the price schedules and timetables she'd had Frankie Tomasic collect for her at the train station downtown. Regarding steamship tickets, she was not so well-informed, although she had been talking to Mrs. Longinovich, who was in the midst of arranging passage for her mother from the old country. ("Are you sure she wants to come?" Staramajka asked Mrs. Longinovich. "Did you ask her?")

Within days of receiving the little black boots in the mail, Staramajka was after my father to write back. "Tell Marko the rest of you are staying here but I am coming home!" she said. "You know how to write that, don't you?"

My father knew how to write it. He had already started several letters, some in Hungarian and some in Croatian. He worked on them when he came home from the coke plant at midnight. I had seen him sitting at the kitchen table, writing with a pencil and erasing carefully and saving the paper to try again. He never got very far with any of them, not only because, like his brother, he wasn't much of a letter writer—the thought of catching Marko up on twenty years of family news must have been daunting in any language—but also because, unlike Staramajka, my father *had* believed for a very long time that his brother Marko was dead. It was hard, he discovered, to write a letter to a person you'd thought of as dead. Who could he picture reading his letter? The forty-two-year-old Marko who'd come back to the village was someone my father had never met, and the twenty-two-year-old Marko who said good-bye at the train station in Pécs when my father left for America—that Marko no longer existed. Even if he did, my father would not have known what to say to him. What could you say to the brother who went to war in your place? Thank you? Forgive me?

My mother came up with the idea of sending a family photograph instead of a long letter. Staramajka went with us to Gruber's Photography Studio on 27th and Forest Home and watched with great interest as Mr. Gruber arranged us, stiff and uncomfortable (at least I was) in our Sunday clothes. It took a long time. Madeline's boy kept wiggling and turning his head. We'd made the appointment for a Sunday so we could all be in the picture: my father and mother, Madeline and her husband John, her little boy Johnny, and me. Everybody but Staramajka. My mother said that it was stubbornness and superstition that kept her out of the picture. I thought maybe it was her teeth.

She only had three. One upper incisor and two molars. I had been trying to talk her into getting dentures for years already, ever since I learned in fifth-grade geography class about the Plains Indians, among whom loss of teeth meant death by starvation. Certainly my grandmother was skinny enough. I knew it was possible to buy teeth because of a sign in the storefront window of the Modern Dental Systems office I passed on my way to school. GUARANTEED HOLLYWOOD PLATE, the sign said. ALL PINK GUMS, UNBREAKABLE PEARL TEETH, $65 VALUE ONLY $32.50! The sign also offered FREE EXTRACTION OF TEETH WITH BETTER PLATES! and promised, *WE WILL NOT MAKE YOU GO TOOTH-LESS UNTIL YOUR BILL IS PAID!* When I first told my grandmother about the sign, she frowned and drew her lower lip up almost to her nose. "I got enough teeth," she said.

Now that her son was alive, she'd apparently changed her mind. "The last time I saw my boy, I didn't look like this, Georgie," she said. "I'm wondering where do we go to get them teeth you're all the time talking about."

The half-price sale was long over and the teeth she was suddenly interested in were going to cost more than our Sears bathroom—excluding installation—but this only seemed to strengthen her resolve. Eagerly, she asked me, "How will you pay for new teeth, Georgie?"

It was a difficult question to answer. Not that I lacked sources of income. In fact, I had several. I sold bullheads and snapping turtles to tavern kitchens. I gathered grain from around the emptied hoppers by the railroad tracks and sold it to an old couple on Stewart Street who raised ducks in their backyard. Occasionally, also, I gathered copper wire that could be reached through the fence around Milwaukee Standard Wire and Tube and turned over for a profit at the junkyard. For years I had saved my money, hoping to convince my grandmother about the teeth. More recently, though, I'd learned that one way to get a girl to talk to you was to ask her what kind of candy she likes. Another way was to take her and three of her friends to a movie. I now had less than ten dollars in the tooth fund, down from an all-time high of almost thirty. I had to tell Staramajka that I was sorry, but we couldn't get her teeth in time for the picture. She said, "Why should I be in the picture? He's going to see me in person with the Hollywood Plates."

My mother, who overheard this little conversation, cornered me later and asked, "What are these Hollywood plates?"

Caught off guard, I couldn't think of anything to tell her but the truth.

"Oh," my mother said, raising her voice along with her eyebrow so my father would hear. "First she buys all new teeth for her mouth and then she goes all by herself to Europe. Is that the way it's going to go?"

I have to admit that neither of those things sounded likely. Staramajka wouldn't even take the streetcar downtown by herself and she had never been to a dentist in her life.

My father held up both hands. "Let her dream," he said.

But Staramajka was no dreamer. Not since the time she talked my mother into taking on the orphaned Kaszube girl, despite neighborhood gossip about her deceased but still disreputable mother, had Staramajka shown such enthusiasm for a cause as she now brought to a variety of money-making schemes. She talked Mr. Solapek at the tavern on the corner into selling homemade baked goods for her: big, round loaves of bread for a nickel, foot-long *kolače* stuffed with walnuts or poppy seed for a dime, and family-size apple streudels that melted in your mouth for fifteen cents a piece. When my sister Madeline came home with freelance mending to do for customers at the laundry, Staramajka fixed the collars and cuffs of several shirts so skillfully that Madeline was obliged, by customer demand, to turn over all shirts to the woman who knew how to work the cloth miraculously back to a state of wholeness. (Missing buttons she sewed on for an additional penny a piece.) For work of Staramajka's caliber, people would pay as much as twenty-five cents a shirt, a price my mother found ridiculous. "I could buy a whole new shirt for fifty cents," she said.

Staramajka's most lucrative venture was the Harvest Bazaar at St. Augustine's. As soon as she heard about it, she gathered up every last piece of handwoven cloth that she had brought from the village—all those beautiful white and black and red striped tablecloths and dresser scarves that filled her trunk—

and she told me to sign her up for a booth to sell them at the bazaar.

"The money goes to the church, *Baka*." I should have spent more time explaining how this worked, but I was too busy with my own schemes, all of them aimed at getting a girl named Loretta Adams to dance with me at the Harvest Bazaar dance. At the moment, I was trying to look like Clark Gable, an actor I'd heard Loretta describe to her friends as dreamy. Clark Gable and I both had black hair and big ears. I figured it was a start.

"What are you talking about, Georgie?" Staramajka said. "Quit looking in the mirror."

I turned around. "You know. People bring things to sell at the bazaar, but they don't keep the money. They give the money to the priest for the church."

"Yeah, yeah," she said.

"Do you think I need a haircut?"

"What for?"

Sitting behind her piles of cloth at a little loom that she'd rigged up (it didn't work, but it was a crowd-pleaser all the same), wearing the knife-pleated skirt and the blouse with wide embroidered sleeves of her village costume, Staramajka was the hit of the bazaar, even without teeth. She sold out long before the booths offering *palačinkas* and *kolače* and crocheted items of every description, and while she was packing up her loom, the priest himself (not old Father Wojcek but a young fellow more recently assigned to the parish) came to thank her for her generosity and, for that matter, to introduce himself, for he did not recall having seen her at Mass. She gave him a steady, blank look—except for one moment when she saw me approaching and shot me a glance like an arrow across half the church hall, warning me not to interfere.

She brought home seventeen dollars and twenty-five cents from the church bazaar. We sat at the kitchen table when everyone else was at work, counting our resources to see if we had enough. We were close. I said maybe it was time to make a Modern Dental Systems appointment.

"Not yet," she said. She used her skinny arms to draw stacks of change toward her across the table like a gambler raking in chips. "But soon."

I DON'T REMEMBER how many letters the priest from Lukovišće sent us about Uncle Marko. Maybe there were only two or three, not counting the telegram. It seems like more because it took my father so long to read a letter to us, translating the priest's words as he read them from Hungarian into Croatian, the one language all of us understood. My father, like the priest, had gone to a school where village children were taught to read and write Hungarian. My mother learned to read Croatian instead, out of prayer books, although she spoke both languages (plus broken English). Her writing, such as it was, tended to combine the spelling rules of one language with the vocabulary of the other in a way that was intelligible only when she herself read it out loud. Sometimes Uncle Marko would write a note in Croatian, like the one with the boots, and other people—various cousins, mostly my mother's relatives—

sent news, too, especially when the news turned tragic, but most of Uncle Marko's story came to us in Hungarian, in fat envelopes stuffed full of thin paper veined with the priest's blue ink. My mother hefted the first one on her palm.

"This ain't a letter, it's a book," she said.

Staramajka made my father read all the letters to her over and over until she knew them by heart. When she reached the point of correcting or inserting details he tried to skip—it was at *Irkutsk* that they took Marko off the train, the Red Cross nurse was *Swedish*—my father would hand her the sheaf of tissue-thin sheets, smudged now and crinkled, and say, "You read it then." Judging by the hours she spent poring over the pages, anyone would have thought that she had taught herself to read Hungarian by memorizing the placement of each precious word. But she didn't need to *read* the letters anyway. Holding one in her hands was enough. It was an aid to meditation, like a rosary, helping her to imagine the mysteries, so sorrowful at first, of her son's long journey across the steppes.

MARKO KNEW RIGHT away that he was dead because he woke up in hell. Unlike the usual fiery descriptions (he later told the priest), it was a cold and muddy place, filled with moaning. In hell, Marko discovered, one could turn one's head, but the rest of the body was useless. Or missing. He tried to lift his head to see.

Is he alive? Vlad—talk to him.

Živiš? Čovek, živiš?

Mislim da ne.

What did he say?

He thinks not.

The language of hell was similar to the language Marko remembered from his time on earth (already it seemed long ago, that time when he walked about, looked at things, ate his mother's *kolače* and streudel—oh, with walnuts and apples!), but here the sounds of speech were shifted somehow. Or perhaps it was a problem with his ears that made the words of the boy who leaned over him, shouting into his face, largely unintelligible. A devil, Marko dimly supposed, with a boy's shape. He ignored it and it went away.

The next time Marko woke, he was lying face down on the floor of the stable behind a convent school in the Polish city of Lemberg, which had fallen into Russian hands. He didn't know any of that at first, but he felt the side of his face pressed into something—straw, by the smell of it. It prickled his nose and poked into his ear. This time, he found it was impossible even to lift his head, for a great weight pressed down on the middle of his back, pinning him to the ground. Suddenly he was aware of another sensation, a searing pain in his backside, as if someone was pushing a hot poker into his flesh, deeper and deeper, to the bone. He thought at once of his friend Pavo Jankovich, who had the blacksmith bend the end of an iron poker into the shape of a J to brand his twelve cows, a useless agony for the poor creatures in a village where all the people knew their cows by name. Pavo got the idea from a letter sent to him by his cousin in Texas. For payment of three laying chickens, Marko and his brother Josef had helped their friend brand his cows, leading them one by one to where Pavo stood, the iron rod in his hand, the J at the end glowing red. Their mother refused to eat a single egg from the chickens they'd earned with such cruelty. She warned them that hell would be their reward for helping Pavo Jankovich torture his cows.

But Marko was not, technically, in hell. A Polish surgeon was removing a bullet that had traveled through the thick meat of Marko's backside and stopped just short of the base of his spine. This was the Polish surgeon famous for telling wounded prisoners what lay in their future and begging their forgiveness for his part in it. "Tomorrow they will put you in a wagon," he told Marko the next day. "In the wagon they will take you to Kiev, to the train. For weeks at a time, you will ride on this train. Even if there is food and water, no one will help you get your share of it. Long before you reach the camp for which you are destined, you will be too weak to fight against disease. Instead of healing, as it has already begun to do, your wound will fester and blacken, the poison will enter your bloodstream, and this will end, after terrible suffering, with your death." At this point, as usual, the doctor was weeping. "It is completely unnecessary that this should occur," he said to Marko. "If you could stay here for even a week, maybe two, you would get well, I assure you. A slight limp, perhaps, and in the cold and damp you might ache a little, but you could return to your home one day, whole and well. Instead, you will die. I am sorry, young man. There is nothing more that I can do."

Marko was alert enough to wonder why the doctor was telling him this story about some very unfortunate young man. He wanted to ask how the doctor came to speak Croatian so well, when all around them voices babbled in German and Pol-ish and who knew what else, a confusion of tongues. But the surgeon had already moved on to the next pallet of straw on the stable floor. He was said to speak a half-dozen languages and he was destined, for his honesty and his tears, to end in a prison camp himself.

That Polish doctor knew what he was talking about. On the journey to Kiev, Marko bounced on a wagon bed covered with a layer of straw that grew thinner and thinner as the horses pulling the next wagon in line stretched their necks for another mouthful. He could feel first the bandages and then his pants soak through with blood. By the time they reached Kiev, he was such a gory sight that the orderlies loading the train put him in a boxcar with the most grievously wounded, the ones who were not expected to survive the journey.

For the first few days, before thirst and hunger (but espe-cially thirst) overcame him, he positioned himself near the wall of the boxcar and, lying on his side with his head on his hand, he spent the hours peeking out between the wooden slats, astonished first at the endlessness of wheat fields and then at the rolling, grass-covered plains. Compared to the narrow fields behind his village, this landscape appeared as infinite as the sky over it. It was June now, and the steppes were bright with flowers. Sometimes the train rolled by so slowly that he could recognize them: hyacinth, daffodils. The patches of color distracted him from his dry throat and throbbing back-side, at least for a while. His efforts to talk to his neighbors had met with groans or babbling or silence. He worried about the glassy stare of the fellow on his right. He tried to listen not to the moans and murmurs all around him but to the steady clacking and clattering that came from the tracks below. The sound made him think of the train station in Pécs and of his brother Josef boarding the train, Josef on the steps at the end of the car, one hand on the railing and the other waving his cap—a blue one, purchased for the journey to America. Usually, thinking of Josef made Marko wonder what kind of mistake had been made that left him heir to his older brother's six acres and the war that went with them. Now, however, thoughts of Josef filled Marko with a sudden flood of hope. What if this train were to stop in Pécs? What if the next time the door rolled back, the creamy brick station he remembered was out there? He could find his way home from the train station in Pécs! He and Josef could both go home together. How pleased their mother would be.

By the fifth day, it no longer mattered to Marko which way the train was going or where it stopped. He no longer noticed when the brakes hissed, and the rocking ceased, and the door flew open and air rushed in. Voices would rise then, grunts and curses, and bundles would fly over Marko's head into the light. (His glassy-eyed neighbor went out at the first such stop.) Sometimes, figures stepped here and there inside the car, and men still able to turn their faces upward and open their mouths like birds would be rewarded with a splash of water. Though Marko always turned his head and opened his mouth, the water bearers seldom came near enough to wet his tongue. The number of wounded in the car had dwindled, from more than fifty when the journey began, to fewer than twenty men.

Finally, at Irkutsk, near Lake Baikal, he had sunk so low they decided he, too, was dead. This time, when the train stopped, Marko was one of the first bundles that flew out into the light. He would have been consigned to a growing pile of corpses if the fresh air (and the flying) had not revived him a little. His moans attracted the attention of two women—a Swedish nurse from the Red Cross and, more important, that of her young assistant, a Russian volunteer from the far eastern city of Khabarovsk. It was to the credit of this young woman from Khabarovsk that, in spite of the half-dead prisoner's terrible condition and even worse stench, she already had an inkling, from the first time she wiped a layer of grime off his face, of the young man underneath it, a young man with cheekbones like carved ivory, his mouth distorted but tender, like an icon of the suffering Christ. (Marko was famously good-looking. You didn't want to get Staramajka started on her boy's blue eyes and black wavy hair, the straight and noble nose and perfect white skin.) The young woman from Khabarovsk wore her hair in a long black braid. She had almond-shaped eyes and burnished brown skin. Her name was Nadya Pitkin. She was a prosperous bootmaker's daughter and Marko's future wife.

THE FIRST TIME the priest from Lukovišće mentioned Khabarovsk in one of his letters, he described it as a city very close to the farthest edge of Asia, a place where the sea stretched eastward to America.

"I didn't know there was an ocean over there," my mother said.

✻

MARKO SPENT FIVE weeks in the hospital in Irkutsk. Nadya Pitkin came to visit every day. She talked to him about all manner of things—an argument she'd had with the Swedish nurse, another prisoner who had the same color eyes as he did, the cat who cried every night outside her window, the muddiness of the streets in Irkutsk at this time of year—things that would hardly be of interest to him even if he could have understood what she was saying, and yet her words made his head turn and his eyelids flutter and his unnerving blue eyes focus on her for as long as he could keep them open. Soon, his eyes were able to follow her every movement and he closed them only after she went away. She told him about her home. "Khabarovsk is built on three hills," she said, arranging her fists to show him, one, two, and here again, the third. "I live here," she said and pointed to a spot on her left index finger. "The whole city is overlooking the Amur River—here." She drew her finger through the riverbed along the heel of her hand. "Across the valley, you can see the mountains in China." She made her two hands into a mountain, fingertips together to form the peak. "The mountains are covered with trees. Trees," she said, and her fingers stretched out like branches. Marko thought she must be showing him a kind of dance. When she noticed that a nurse was watching her, she dropped her hands into her lap. "The mountains look blue in the mist," she said.

She wanted him to know from the start that, in Khabarovsk, all but the Sibiriak peasants were foreigners or descendants of foreigners—not only Chinese and Japanese but Polish, French,

German—everything you could think of. "You meet all kinds of people there," she said. "My father's people came from near Odessa in Ukraine, but my mother is from a village outside Khabarovsk, much older than the city." She didn't mention that her mother had died long ago. There was enough death all around them here. "My mother's people are true Sibiriak—descended from Buryat and Nanay—though not so wild as some." Here she raised her eyebrow in a manner Marko found endearing though he still had no idea what she said.

When he was alert enough to speak, she taught him to say a few words in Russian. They both were surprised (and pleased) as time went on to find some words that seemed the same, or almost the same, in his language and hers.

"*Da svidanja,*" Nadya said one evening after she'd brought him his bread and soup, having spilled only a little on the bed-clothes due to nervousness. She would have liked to stay and talk but she had other bowls to deliver.

"*Do viđenja!*" he said in reply, his smile resulting in another slosh over the rim.

"See you later?" she repeated in Russian.

"Until we meet again!" he answered in Croatian.

"They are almost the same," she said. "*The same, yes?*"

"*Da, da!*" he agreed with delight.

One day, toward the end of his stay in the hospital at Irkutsk, Nadya came upon Marko sitting on his bed, repairing a leather boot for the Swedish nurse with a long needle and an awl that he'd made from the tine of a fork. She clapped her hands and laughed, causing Marko to look up in surprise. Then he laughed, too. Nadya wrote her father immediately with the excellent news that she had found the right man to help him in the shoe- and boot-making business, a young man who had been injured in the war but was recovering nicely. Since he had to end up somewhere in Siberia—did she mention that he was a prisoner of war?—he might as well end up in her father's shop in Khabarovsk. He was from the Austro-Hungarian army, she admitted, but his village was Slavic so he could almost speak Russian already! She was going to do her best to bring him home.

In the meantime, she lived in fear of the day she might come to the hospital and find his bed—in the prisoners' ward at Irkutsk there were beds—empty. It was not only that he might be discharged at any time, though he was far from well, and sent to the camp outside Irkutsk. Prisoners were always being transported for no good reason from hospital to hospital, or even to schools and churches, to stables and people's homes. Sometimes a hospital inspection was impending, and rows of suffering men on the floors, lining the corridors or sticking out of closets, would not look good to Count or Countess So-and-So. Or perhaps the number of casualties reported did not coincide with the facts. Or maybe the hospital commandant had struck a bargain with the owner of a fleet of wagons to split payment for every transport ordered. No wonder the moves so often took place at night, when the sleeping citizens of Irkutsk would not hear the groans and cries of men whose bones gleamed through open wounds, or whose intestines spilled out of their bellies.

On the day Nadya found Marko's cot occupied by a different young man, one whose pallor made him look like a figure made of wax, she knew before she asked that no one would tell her what had happened to Marko. She spent that whole day searching through the makeshift hospitals, almost every school and stable, in all of Irkutsk. She found him at last in a crowded barn behind the church of St. Anastasia—he seemed to have a knack for ending up in barns—where he shared a narrow stall with two amputees, one of whom had been moved for the last time.

The second half of Marko's journey across Siberia was much more pleasant than the first. Only later did he learn that it was not fate, or even God's mercy, but Nadya Pitkin who had found a place for him on the train to Khabarovsk, not with the prisoners but in a third-class carriage for Russian wounded. He had a window beside him the whole way and room enough to lie on his stomach whenever his wound began to ache with sitting. Nadya sat with him for a while every day of the journey. (It was her duty, she told herself, to do as much.) She pointed out to him how, in August, the mountains along the shore of Lake Baikal were clothed on their lower slopes with alpine flowers. When the train lumbered into the first tunnel cut through the mountains, she felt him startle at the sudden darkness. She squeezed his hand. When they emerged again into daylight, his face lit up at the sight of her braids and her golden skin flushed pink.

A fortunate fact about the Trans-Siberian railroad between Irkutsk and Khabarovsk is this: There are forty-six tunnels cut through the mountains along the shore of Lake Baikal.

***

YEARS LATER, AFTER his return to the village, Marko spent many hours in the company of the priest who wrote the letters, walking with him through shady tunnels in the arbored rose garden outside the church in Lukovišće, or drinking strong coffee and scalded milk in the rectory when it rained, or sitting with him on the bench behind St. Anna's in Novo Selo (for the priest was shared by both villages), the two of them leaning against the warm stone wall and looking downhill toward the river. Sometimes, while they talked, Marko drew in the dirt at their feet a line that looped and curved like the path he had traveled from Khabarovsk to this sunny bench in Novo Selo. From where the line ended, at the tip of his toe, he sometimes drew another line, as if westward, a line that crossed the ocean and ended in America, in Milwaukee of Wisconsin in America, a place he could neither pronounce nor imagine. Once, on the map of the world that hung in the rectory—an old map colored with faded empires—the priest showed Marko that he and his brother Josef had wandered equally far from their village toward opposite ends of the earth.

Marko was deeply grateful to the priest for writing his fat letters to Milwaukee and pledged to him a lifetime supply of shoes in return. How much easier it was, Marko thought, to talk, to send words out into the air—where they disappeared in the smell of cut grass on the hill behind the church or mingled with the scent of beeswax and incense inside—than to sit alone and search for words to put on the paper that matched not only the sounds and pictures in his head but the tangle of feelings in his heart. He had tried to write. In the village near Tomsk, for example, where Fyodor started school, Marko sat down at least once a week and unfolded the wrinkled sheet of paper on which he had written: "Dear Ma, in case you don't know, I am alive. I got a wife and a son. We live near the city called Tomsk. We are well and"—here he hesitated—"happy."

That much he could write without trouble, aside from the confusions of spelling and an occasional Russian word slipping in. It was the next sentence that always stopped him. If he wrote what his mother wanted to hear: "We are coming home," adding perhaps, "someday soon," then he would have to return to the village, would he not? To his mother's pigs and cows. But if he wrote, "We are not coming home, we are waiting here in Tomsk"—or Irkutsk or Sibkray—"until the day"—which, even then, he knew might never come—"when we can return to Khabarovsk," if he were to write that—well, he simply couldn't write that. He had tried to explain to Nadya why he couldn't, but Nadya had never followed his mother secretly down to the Drava, where she went, she said, to be alone with God. Nadya had never seen his mother kneel, sobbing, on the bank of the river, a letter from his brother Joe in America pressed to her chest. Nadya had never heard his mother piteously calling his brother's name and asking God how, *how* had she sinned that her son Josef, blood of her blood, could leave his home and harden his heart against her?

"Don't you see?" Marko said. "If the Russians shot me, then *they* are the ones who made her suffer, not me. Let her hate them. Not me."

So he never sent a single letter, not from Khabarovsk, where the possibility of a different life was first revealed to him, and not from Tomsk, where they had to leave in haste one Sunday when a train of armored cars showed up to shell the village from the tracks, and not from Sibkray, where they spent three fine years, Marko making boots for rich kulak farmers and fancy shoes for their wives, until Stalin's hand reached far enough east to snatch the kulaks' grain "by any means," leaving Marko's business purged of customers. After Sibkray they moved south and west again (where else was there to go?) and Marko started telling Nadya about his village. He warned her not to expect too much—his mother was old, and unless his brother had returned, there was no one to keep the place in good repair. Marko thought he was ready for anything—the house burned to the ground, the whole village razed—but when they finally reached Novo Selo, the new wooden fence and the border of daffodils around his mother's garden took him by surprise. So did the Turk living out in the barn. And when they heard from this Turk that Marko's mother had gone to join Josef in America, the knot that had been growing in Marko's stomach as they neared the village rose to his throat for a moment. Then it melted away.

Marko told the priest that sixteen years was simply how long it took to cover six thousand miles, if you traveled like Gypsies in a horse-drawn wagon, and if you had to stop because winter was coming or your wife was about to give birth, or, as happened three times, because a desperate gang of bandit soldiers, White or Red, had helped themselves to your horses. Sixteen years was how long it took if you had to keep changing your route to avoid getting your belly slashed and stuffed with hay by angry peasants, or to cut a wide path around a city said to be littered with thirty thousand corpses, all dead of typhus, a rumor confirmed by your nose as you drew near.

But the journey home would have been much shorter, the priest remarked one afternoon, if Marko had traveled alone. The shadow of a stork returning to its nest in the steeple passed over them, and the priest looked up. He wondered aloud what kind of sorcery the Russians had used to keep Marko there, away from his home and his people.

Marko looked up, too, and saw Nadya climbing the grassy hill behind St. Anna's with their youngest daughter. Marie's shoulders barely cleared the tall grass, and she was laughing, tugging on her mother's hand, as they waded through it. They were probably coming to fetch him for supper. The priest was watching them, too. Marko's wife Nadya was no longer a young woman—the black braids wound around her head like a crown were threaded with gray—but she carried herself lightly, her back as straight as a girl's. "No sorcery, Father," Marko said. "Only charms. Siberian charms."

※

"*I ARISE, GOD'S slave Nadya, pray, go, making the sign of the cross, wash myself with cold spring water, rub myself with a fine towel, don my garments, girdled by the rosy dawn, protected by the bright moon, prodded by the many stars, and glowing with the glorious sun.*" Nadya looked down at Marko, who was stretched out on the ground under the birch tree, his head resting in her lap, the whole sky pouring blue into his eyes. "And now you," she said to him.

Marko closed his eyes to concentrate. In perfectly acceptable Russian, like a schoolboy reciting a poem, he said: *"I arise, God's slave Marko, pray to God, wash with spring water, pray to Michael the Archangel, and bow in every direction. I go, God's slave Marko, out through the doors, out through the gates—into the clean field, to Father Ocean."*

"You said it perfectly!" said Nadya. "We could be married tomorrow."

Marko opened his eyes. He propped himself on his elbows and looked down at the river. He could see the place where the new railroad bridge cut the silver ribbon of the Amur in two. "I have never seen the ocean," he said.

"You will," said Nadya. "One day, we can take the train all the way to Vladivostok."

They would have had to do it soon. Within the year, armored trains would be prowling the rails from Achinsk east to the sea, using villages for target practice, names like "The Destroyer" and "The Merciless" painted on the cars. For now, however, all that terror lay in the very near but unimaginable future. In fact, in the brief Siberian summer of 1917, if you were sitting, like Marko and Nadya, on the grass at the edge of a bluff in the far eastern city of Khabarovsk, the blue mountains of China across the valley at your feet, you might forget about the war for days at a time, until a glimpse of Japanese troops on Cadet Hill reminded you, or perhaps a drive past the prisoners' camp at the edge of town. The prisoners themselves, many of whom came and went in Khabarovsk on business of their own, were hard to distinguish from the usual crowd of foreigners, except in the matter of dress, where they were, as a rule, a little shabbier than most. And while it's true that in tea rooms talk of revolution floated like steam around the samovars—each morsel of news from Moscow or St. Petersburg either relished or worried over—still, the riots and barricades in those western cities were very far away. The irresistible unfolding of Russia's revolutionary destiny may have excited men like the shoemaker Pitkin, whose grandfather was a Decembrist exiled in 1825, but it was of little interest just now to Pitkin's daughter Nadya or to Marko, who lay back again in her lap. "Tell me that charm you used to bewitch me," he said. "The one your aunt taught you."

"Why do you want to hear that again?"

Marko reached up and laid his palm lightly on the side of her face. "So I'll know why I cannot bear to have you out of my sight."

"I warn you, Marko, every time I say it, the spell gets stronger."

"Good," said Marko.

Sitting up a little straighter, Nadya folded her hands on the top of his head in her lap, and began: *"Tsar Fire, Tsarina Spark, Smokey Smoke!"*

He interrupted with a laugh. "I hope the Commissar of Shoes in Khabarovsk doesn't hear his own daughter calling on the Tsar."

Nadya raked her fingers through his hair. She said, *"Fly, smoke, find, smoke, God's slave Marko in the open field beneath the white birch. His circle strike and twist."* Her voice dropped to a whisper. *"Remove his white shirt."* This part of the charm made her face warm and her heart race. *"Go into the white body, the lung, the liver, the hot blood, take him apart at the bone, at the joint, put in his heart a sad yearning, a painful pang, an inconsolable weeping, an unshakeable love."*

"No wonder I suffer," Marko said.

But there was more. *"Let his heart rush and rage, let his blood be troubled for me. Let myself, God's slave Nadya, be more beloved of Marko than the white light, more beautiful than the beautiful sun, more dear than his mother and father and all that he has ever known."* Here she saw something flicker across his face—a look she used to see more often. It meant that he was thinking of home—but with guilt? or grief? or longing? At that time, she couldn't tell. Marco sat up, pulling himself back, she thought, from a wide empty space in his heart. She wished she had stopped sooner.

Nadya didn't ask Marko very much about his part of the world, for every time she tried, she thought his face darkened a little, the smile in his eyes went out. Her father said she was imagining this. Pitkin seemed to have forgotten that his daughter was the one who brought Marko to Khabarovsk in the first place. He bragged about Marko, as if to convince her of his worth. "The boy can make anything out of leather," Pitkin said. "Even the Polish professor, Dyboski, says the boots Marko made for him are a perfect fit, and he never has anything good to say about Russian workmanship."

"Marko's not a Russian," Nadya pointed out.

"Yeah, well, Dyboski doesn't know that. It just goes to show what happens when the workers of the world unite!"

How much of who Marko was, and how he was, came from his isolation here, away from other young men who drank vodka until their noses ran and their teeth turned black, Nadya didn't know. It didn't matter. Marko's teeth were white. His hands were gentle. His voice was soft. *Let his heart rush and rage, let his blood be troubled for me.*

"I better get back to the shop," he said. "It's almost four o'clock. I think your father has a meeting with the Commissar of Teacups."

Nadya sat and watched him cross the park, limping slightly. Three times she whispered, *"Fire in front, water behind, a stone screen all around. Let my words be strong and clinging."*

❧

"WHAT'S THE MATTER with Marko?" my mother said. "How could he let his own mother suffer for all those years? Thinking that he's dead!"

"I didn't think he was dead," said Staramajka. "I never thought he was dead."

But why didn't he write? That's what everyone wanted to know.

"It's hard to write a letter in a wagon," Staramajka would say. "He probably didn't have a paper or a pen." Or, "Where could he mail it? What kind of stamp?" Or, "He was running away from the Cossacks. He couldn't stop and write a letter. What do you think, Georgie?"

I hated it when they both looked at me like that, my grandmother with her gums pressed together, her lower lip reaching almost to her nose, my mother with one eye squinting.

"Sounds like those Cossacks were a mean bunch," I'd say.

⁂

"I still think you could write and tell her that you are alive, Marko." That's what Nadya used to say, before she gave up trying to convince him. "At least you could tell her about Fyodor"—and later about Heinrich and Jelena and little Marie—"and about me." Nadya always feared that she was the real reason he didn't write. Perhaps he knew that his mother would not be pleased by a daughter-in-law with enough Nanay blood in her to give her eyes a different shape and her skin the burnished color of a Gypsy's.

The more years passed, the more impossible it was to write.

"By now she thinks I am dead," Marko would say, suddenly, as if he had been thinking about it all day.

⁂

SOMETIMES STARAMAJKA WOULD bring out the big guns, posing the question tragically: "How was he supposed to know we went to America?"

If he had been writing to the village, my mother said, the postmistress would have given his letters to the priest and the priest would have sent them to us.

"Is that so? Maybe she threw them away. She never liked me very much, that one."

"A postmistress does not throw away the mail," my mother muttered.

"In Russia, it was revolution going on," my grandmother said. "That could hold back the mail. Right, Georgie?"

"For sixteen years?" said my mother.

⁂

IN THE SNOWY spring of 1918, Fyodor Pitkin and his friends were still talking loudly about the *second* Glorious Revolution that rocked St. Petersburg in the fall. The first Revolution, which excited them so much the previous winter, had been only a warning tremor, they said now, a prelude to the cataclysm whose aftershocks had finally reached their city and shaken it, though rather gently, to its foundations. In Khabarovsk, no armed revolt was needed to put the Bolsheviks, both local and imported, in charge. Here, exiles and the descendants of exiles had been waiting for decades to organize committees and appoint commissars. Already the intelligentsia had been quietly replaced by blacksmiths and porters and street sweepers, and the bourgeoisie subtly encouraged to quit the scene, leaving their property behind. A red-nosed carriage cab driver was head of the Revolutionary Tribunal, and a tailor formerly known as Tobol but now named Krasnoshchekov presided over the Council of People's Commissars of the Far East. Marko and Pitkin had worked together to finish a fine pair of boots for the tailor to wear on the occasion of his installation as president.

During this same period, Marko's life had undergone similarly radical alterations. Thanks to one of those summer afternoons spent with Nadya in a secluded corner of the park—a summer afternoon that had stretched in Siberian fashion into a dusky evening that lasted almost till dawn—Marko was now a married man and soon to be a father.

He had just selected a medium-size awl from the tools spread in front of him on the counter when the little iron bell over the door rang, and a lanky fellow with shoulder-length hair entered Pitkin's shop. He was underdressed for the weather in a tattered brown velvet overcoat—an odd contrast with his feet, which were wrapped in furs in the peasant style— and he carried in the crook of one arm what might have been a pair of boots. His other arm was wrapped tenderly around an oblong leather case that he carried upright, like a baby, against his shoulder. The man reminded Marko of a character in a play that Nadya had taken him to see while her father, who did not approve of bourgeois entertainments, was in the countryside educating peasants.

"You are shoemaker Pitkin?" the character said in poorly pronounced Russian.

"I work for him," said Marko.

Next came a whisper. "You are then also prisoner?"

Marko frowned.

"Pole?"

Marko scowled.

Still the fellow looked hopeful. "You are citizen of the empire?" he asked.

"What empire?" Marko said suspiciously.

"Tell me. Where can one be finding the village from where you come?"

"North of the Drava," Marko said. "Near Pécs."

"In Austria-Hungary!" the other man cried. "Mein Gott, I am saved!" He plopped his boots on the counter. They leaned sadly against each other until he snatched one up, and the other toppled over. "You see how I walk," the man said, showing Marko the bottom of the boot. A papery leather sole surrounded an archipelago of holes.

"You need new boots," Marko said.

"This is news?" cried the man, shaking the boot like a chicken by the neck.

Marko lifted its fallen comrade to have a look. "If you leave them here, I can use them as the pattern to cut new boots for you."

"But at what cost?" the man implored.

Marko considered. The tattered overcoat might be misleading. A prisoner of war who had business away from the camp—someone like Marko, for example, who excelled at his trade—could make enough money to live quite well in the city of Khabarovsk, where supplies were not so scarce as in the west. Such a prisoner could also attract a dangerous amount of envy. Marko himself was careful, when he went out, not to look too prosperous, because a fine coat was no protection against the whims of a camp commandant encountered on the street or, these days, a commissar who liked to throw his weight around. A prisoner of war could lose his coat, his job, or his "freedom" in the twinkling of an evil eye. Pitkin had called Marko an old woman for worrying about this. "You are my son-in-law," Pitkin said. "Who's going to be jealous of you?"

"Fifty for the pair," Marko said to the man in the tattered overcoat.

"Kopeks?"

"Rubles!"

"To your own countryman you would make such a blow?" The man hung his head in despair, exactly as the actor on the stage had done.

"Well," Marko said, glancing at the leather case cradled by his arm, "perhaps you have something to trade."

The man hugged the case to his chest. "As soon be taking my feet!" he cried.

"You would have no need for boots then," said Marko. "What is so dear to you?"

It was a violin. The man in the overcoat introduced himself to Marko at this time as Heinrich von Steuben, first violinist in the finest all-Viennese orchestra the people of Khabarovsk had ever heard or would ever hear again, once the fortunes of war which had bestowed this blessing on them turned again and whisked it away. The orchestra was made up of prisoners, seventeen masterful Austrian musicians who played like thirty. They rehearsed in an upper room at the grammar school and performed two concerts a month. In the winter, the concerts took place in the school auditorium. When summer came, the orchestra would play in Chaska Chai, the park overlooking the river, the whole valley of the Amur serving as a fitting backdrop for the music. Heinrich von Steuben asked Marko how long he had been in Khabarovsk. Marko told him.

"And you never have heard the orchestra? You are not a Bolshevik, right?"

Marko said, "Let me see the violin."

Heinrich von Steuben looked at Marko a moment longer, appraising, and then he opened the case.

Marko was expecting gleaming curves, but the velvet lining was more impressive than the instrument. A dusting of resin coated the neck of the violin like a bad case of dandruff. The fiddle that Marko had traded away back in Kaposvar looked no worse than this one, he thought. The other man was gazing into the case with such a look as a man might give to a woman, his eyes traveling from the dusty scroll down the strings to the body of the violin, around the curves of its shoulders and waist, and then back up again.

"Play something," Marko said.

Heinrich von Steuben lifted the violin to his shoulder, nestling it there. With nothing more than the pressure of his chin to hold the instrument in place, he raised the bow again in his right hand and let it bounce on the strings, one after the other, listening to the shadow notes it made, while his free hand adjusted the pegs on the scroll. When he was satisfied, he stood for a moment as if he were poised on the brink of something, or perhaps considering some vista that Marko couldn't see. In that moment, Heinrich reminded Marko of the blind Gypsy who had taught him to play the fiddle in the village long ago, a man his mother knew. Marko braced himself, but whatever flood of emotion might have washed over him at this thought of home was dispersed by a flurry of notes.

Heinrich von Steuben's fingers danced like a spider on the fingerboard, his bow teetered over the bridge, it fluttered on the strings. Pitkin appeared at the top of the stairs when the music began, Nadya right behind him, peeking over his shoulder. Pitkin tugged at his pointed beard while Heinrich played, and he disappeared just as suddenly when the music was over, but Nadya remained. She had spent much of the past two months lying on her side in bed, trying to keep the baby from getting away from her, her aunt from the village said, as if the baby were a fish or a fox they were trying to catch. Nadya's aunt—a sharp-boned woman with tough yellow skin and squinting eyes—made frequent trips from her village to Khabarovsk, bringing concoctions for Nadya to drink and charms for her to mutter. When Marko asked what he could do to help, Nadya's aunt gave him a dark look, as if he had done enough already.

"Bravo!" Nadya cried, unwieldy but smiling at the top of the stairs. "Bravo!"

Marko looked up at her. Then he looked at Heinrich, who stood with his head bowed and his violin resting.

"I got an idea," Marko said.

The price they settled on for the boots was nothing more or less than music itself. Every Sunday morning, Heinrich von Steuben would come to the shop and play for one hour. During that hour, Marko would work on the new pair of boots. When the boots were finished, no matter if it took one month or two or three, they would call the account even, and Heinrich von Steuben would stride well-shod into the concert season of summer 1918.

Nadya was delighted with the arrangement. Last summer, her father had tricked her into signing up for the Young People's Collective, a group that worked in the fields on Sundays, and she had missed every single concert in the park. "I should have made you work in the fields *every* day last summer," Pitkin said sternly. Now Nadya's condition provided him with an excuse to agree to Heinrich's method of payment, though with an exaggerated reluctance that plainly showed, according to Heinrich, how much Pitkin looked forward to each musical installment. "Bolsheviks say it is bourgeois music we are playing," he explained to Marko. "This is why we make our concerts in the park. The people can't help but to hear. In this way, Bolsheviks can enjoy also, without the need to change their tunes."

Although he said nothing to Heinrich, it was Marko, not Pitkin, who had second thoughts about the arrangement. Marko had not foreseen how much Heinrich's visits would remind him of his own unsuccessful musical career under the guidance of the blind Gypsy. Like other small boys, Marko had walked with the Gypsy from village to village in the summer, holding his elbow and collecting his fees in an old tobacco pouch that resembled the ones Pitkin gave to his peasants. A coin or two often found its way into the boy's pocket, and even if the Gypsy had been less generous than he was, what small boy would not prefer a stroll and a country wedding to any of the chores that awaited him at home? The lessons were the painful part. Marko would have given back every coin he earned to escape the lessons. If only his mother had not found him a fiddle when he was eight or nine! His fiddle was too big for him at first—perhaps that was the problem, at first—but his mother had traded a piglet for it, so he carried it dutifully down the road to the place by the river where a whole caravan of colorful wooden wagons used to camp each summer in years past. Now there was only the blind Gypsy's wagon, painted with musical notes.

"Blind?" the old Gypsy would say (though Marko realized later that he was not so old). "What I see is the music!" He would tuck his violin under his chin, brandishing the bow without any tuning or tightening that Marko could recall, and all the while that he was playing he would describe what he saw. "Listen, Marko! See how this one snakes and whips about—and then stops—and rises slowly, like a woman waking from a dream? See how it swells and shrinks and turns the world dark, dark, darkness everywhere, oh yes *now* I'm blind but then—quick! Shut your eyes and see! Light welling up like water! Moonlight, Marko! Do you see it, do you? No? Ah, now who is the blind one, eh?" And the Gypsy's bow would swing from the strings to alight on Marko's shoulder or tap the top of his head. "Now this one," he would say, "whenever I play this one, the Brahms, dance number five, I see . . . not dancers. No. I see waiters."

"Waiters?" said Marko.

"Yes! Waiters," the Gypsy said as he began to play. "Waiters in fancy vests and black ties tight around their necks and their shoulders thrown back and their chests puffed out"—his bow moved smartly across the strings—"and their noses in the air, whisking about with trays piled high. I can smell the food, can't you? Roasted ducks and beautiful trout and whole pigs with apples in their mouths." Then the blind Gypsy would stop to listen while Marko's bow sawed back and forth through the music. One time he laughed and said, "When you play it,

Marko, I see the apples in the waiters' mouths instead! What do you think of that?"

It soon became clear to all that Marko would never play with sufficient skill the polkas and waltzes that his mother once hoped would more than repay the cost of his fiddle. He came to dread knocking on the door of the wagon where the Gypsy lived with his mother, an old woman that Marko had never seen. He dreaded even more his own mother's cheerful appearance at summer's end to hear what he had learned that year. She was there, sitting on a stool outside the wagon in her high-waisted skirt and apron and her white blouse with the fancy sleeves, on the day when Marko, a teenager now, played the first nineteen notes of Brahms's "Hungarian Dance #5" in so melodic and recognizable a fashion that a shuttered window flew open and an old woman's voice cried from inside the wagon, "Brahms! Oh, Brahms!" as if she had been trying all summer to guess the tune.

Marko spent the next three summers learning to play the rest of it.

He took his fiddle with him when the army called only because his mother had made a padded bag for it out of the beautiful white cloth with red and black stripes that she wove herself. The bag was not fiddle-shaped but round and gathered in such a way as to pull the woven stripes into circles, an effect that Marko found quite handsome until, on the way to Kaposvar, a soldier marching behind him had asked him why he wore a target on his knapsack. His mother often came to visit him in Kaposvar and never failed to ask for a song. She didn't seem to mind—or even to notice—that he always played the same one.

It was, she always said, her favorite. If other people were around when he began to play, they either wandered away or nodded their heads politely out of respect for his mother.

She wasn't there the night before his company left on the long, long march to the front. Marko went out that night with his two fellow couriers and, after sharing a bottle of brandy, allowed himself to be led to a shop they knew of that dealt in all manner of goods, no matter the time of night or day. There they convinced him, without much trouble, that in wartime there were far more sensible things to carry across Europe than a fiddle. They got three large tins of tobacco in trade and some excellent sausage made by the wife of the shopkeeper. Later, Marko wondered if his two fellow couriers were really so eager for tobacco and sausage, or if they wanted above all to be rid of "Hungarian Dance #5." He would have asked them, but they were both dead by then. In the end, he convinced himself that his fiddle was a casualty of war, like those two fellows, but he did not for a moment imagine that his mother would see it that way.

Marko had never revealed his musical past to anyone in Khabarovsk, not even Nadya, for fear that someone might produce a fiddle and ask him to play. He did put the violin up on his shoulder once when Pitkin and Heinrich were busy arguing politics upstairs. Another time, when Heinrich was playing, Marko forgot himself and cried, "I know this one!" They all looked at him, Heinrich pausing with the bow in the air over the strings. "I mean," said Marko, "that I heard it before. In the village. There was a fellow who played like you do. Well, not like YOU do, but he played that song." Because they were all still looking at him, Marko had added, "It was a favorite of my mother's. She called it 'The Waiter's Song.'"

That night, before they fell asleep, Marko clutched Nadya's hand in bed.

"Nadie," he said, "I am going to tell you something I never told anybody in this whole country."

"What is it?" said Nadya, her heart beating a little faster.

"Nadie, I am a fiddler."

"What?"

"I play the fiddle."

"Oh. Well, that's wonderful, Marko!"

"No, it ain't," he said mournfully. "I'm no good."

After making her promise that she would never reveal his secret to Heinrich or anyone else, he told her about the fiddle that he left in Kaposvar. "My mother would never forgive me if she knew," he said. "But I couldn't carry it all the way into the war."

"Is this why you don't write to your mother, Marko? I feel certain she would understand."

Marko said nothing. He hadn't told Nadya about the tobacco and the sausages.

WHEN HEINRICH AND Pitkin argued about politics, Marko had nothing to say. He found the finer points of Bolshevism, at least as Pitkin explained them, difficult to grasp. Mostly it seemed to be a matter of calling things by different names.

"Here's how it goes," Pitkin said one afternoon, having

recently returned from a meeting of the Council of People's Commissars of the Far Eastern Province of Khabarovsk. "We're not a shop no more."

"No more boots? We're making no more shoes and boots?"

"Of course we're making shoes and boots. We're just not a shop anymore."

"What are we then?"

"Association of Workers."

"What's that?"

"What we are."

"The two of us?"

"And Nadya. She keeps the accounts, so she's in it, too."

The iron bell over the door jingled just then and a customer came in, an old Buryat woman in a fur jacket and babushka who had come to pick up her husband's Sunday boots. "Good day to you, comrade!" Pitkin greeted her with a little bow. (He had forgotten himself there, he admitted later to Marko. After the Revolution, bowing was not required.) When she looked at him oddly, he straightened up and pounded himself on the chest. "Comrade, you are looking at the Commissar for Shoes in the Province Surrounding Khabarovsk!"

At first, the old woman was speechless. Then she said, "Are Leo's boots ready?"

It surprised Marko to find that Heinrich had different ideas from Pitkin about the Revolution. "I think they're making big mistakes," Heinrich said to Marko more than once as he wiped the snow off his violin case and set it on the counter. "Pitkin and that tailor and the driver of cabs, all that crew."

"What mistakes are they making?" asked Marko.

"With Czechs and Cossacks on the way, the Bolsheviks will turn their tails around and run," Heinrich said. "Pitkin and his friends will be finding themselves in a bad place, Marko, a very bad place. They will be left holding the bags."

Sometimes Pitkin startled them both by shouting at Heinrich from the top of the stairs, "What did you say?"

Heinrich shouted back, "I said the Reds will be running for covers."

"Is that what you think? Who said you're supposed to think? Just get up here and play. That's what you're here for. Play!"

Nadya was making very few trips downstairs these days. "I can't see my feet past my belly," she complained. Marko was working on a new case for Heinrich's violin, having finished his boots some weeks ago. The new case was Pitkin's idea. The old case, he said, looked like it had gone through a war, which, as Nadya pointed out, it had. To Heinrich, Pitkin said, "Why Marko thinks he needs to waste your time and his on all this fancy cutwork for a violin case, I don't know."

Heinrich wasn't fooled.

The baby was born in April. Marko did his part once again, which chiefly involved staying out of the way during the birth but also included throwing the right number of coins into the midwife's porridge (an odd method of payment, he thought) and sticking an army of new sewing needles like tiny spears into the wooden frame of the front door. This was to prevent a sorceress from entering the shop and doing harm to Nadya or the child. The baby was a boy, healthy and dark-eyed. The first time Marko held his son he was overcome by the squirming warmth and weight of him, the ribs and elbows, life so near the surface, complete in his hands. Marko carried him outside on the third night to show him to the stars, as required, but refused to unwrap him, in spite of the midwife's predictions of bad luck for the boy if Marko didn't do things right.

"His luck already is bad luck, poor little *kind*," Heinrich said when Marko sought his opinion on Sunday morning. "To be born in such a world as this one."

Marko did not mention to Heinrich that he was feeling very lucky to be alive in such a world as this one.

They named the boy Fyodor, for his grandfather. Pitkin was beside himself, and for days carried around two flasks of vodka (one a gift from Heinrich, the other from the cab driver who headed the Revolutionary Tribunal), raising toasts to little Comrade Fyodor all over town. True to his Bolshevik principles, Pitkin did not attend the christening that Marko insisted upon, which took place in the Russian Orthodox church of St. Constantine, with Heinrich as godfather and, as godmother, Nadya's aunt from the village. Wearing her traditional fur jacket and long flowered skirt, Nadya's aunt muttered charms to Father Ocean and the Heavenly Pike while the priest, whose beard could not hide his annoyance, poured water over Fyodor's head.

"She reminds me of my mother," Marko whispered to Nadya, who whispered back, "Everybody reminds you of your mother."

These days, that was true. Every woman with a babushka on her head who came to see Nadya (having gotten past the barricade of needles in the door) reminded Marko of his mother. Whenever Nadya or her aunt placed Fyodor in the arms of one

of these visitors so she could lean her face close to the baby, coo-
ing and clucking at him, Marko felt again the emptiness of his
mother's arms. At such times, he tried to picture taking his wife
and son back to Novo Selo, stopping the wagon in front of his
mother's house, that rooster of hers—could it still be alive?—
crowing its heart out, no matter the time of day. On the one
hand, there would be his mother's joy, beyond imagining. On the
other hand, there would be no shoemaker's shop, no park, no
orchestra, no plays or concerts (forbidden or otherwise), no
grammar school, not even a church with a full-time priest.

Lately, whenever Marko came around the corner and saw
Pitkin's shop window with its many panes of glass, the lamp-
light shining through it onto the stones in the street, he felt
something strange that was, at the same time, strangely familiar. It was something like the way he used to feel watching the
cows come home in the village, with the cowherd waving his
whip behind them. From boyhood, it had been Marko's job to
wait out front every evening, loitering with neighbors all up
and down the unpaved street, putting up with their good-
natured teasing and the premature matchmaking that Marko's
good looks and unexpected shyness tended to provoke. When
the herd drew even with his mother's house, two cows would
turn into the gate he held open for them, eager to be milked,
their udders heavy. Sometimes one of them would push her
huge head against his arm. They recognized him, those cows.
More than anything else in the village, they made Marko feel
that perhaps he had a place in the world.

Now, to his surprise, Marko had another place in the world.
It was here, in the shop in Khabarovsk, and it was better than

being recognized by cows. It was Heinrich playing for him and Pitkin counting on him and Nadya sending him downstairs every morning with a kiss and a cup of tea. On the day of his son's christening Marko was struck by this thought: someday, if he stayed here in Khabarovsk, the shop with its many-paned window would belong to his son. He was wrong about that, of course, but then he had always found the finer points of Bolshevism difficult to grasp.

In May, everyone was talking about the approaching White army. "What *army*?" said Pitkin with disdain. "Is that what you call a pack of lazy Cossacks, warmed-up tsarists and provisional government leftovers, not to mention that miserable legion of bourgeois-nationalist prisoner-of-war defectors?" The Japanese (and the newly arrived Americans) might call them allies, but the Whites were a mob of bandits, he said, undeserving of the name "army."

"Call them what names you want," Heinrich said, "they have driven the Reds out from Irkutsk."

When they got as far as Verkhne-Udinsk, east of Lake Baikal, even Pitkin's confidence wavered. One Sunday morning in June, he confessed to Heinrich his fears about whether the Bolsheviks would be able to hold their own against the Whites.

"Hold their own?" scoffed Heinrich. "Hold their own what?" He had learned a thing or two from Pitkin about wielding Russian insults. "Your commissar-in-chief the tailor already has left town and the rest are packing up their needle and threads before Cossacks get here and give Khabarovsk back to Mother Russia. They know that their time is running out. How is it with you, Pitkin? You are not worrying what will Cossacks think of your Association of Workers?"

"Mother of God," said Pitkin, tugging at his naked chin, the pointed beard having gone the way of his commissar's title.

Marko had just restored the old sign over the door that said BOOTS & SHOES, F. PITKIN, PROPRIETOR, when a young Ussuri Cossack named Kalmykov galloped unopposed into Khabarovsk with a letter in his pocket (no one knew from whom) that appointed him major general in charge of everything. A host of rumors preceded him—he had blown up schoolhouses full of children, he had dunked peasants through holes in frozen rivers and left them standing like statues in blocks of ice along the bank.

"Why would he do that?" asked Nadya.

"These are only rumors," Pitkin said nervously. "I heard also that he has horns and a tail."

"To make examples," Heinrich said.

"Examples of what?" asked Marko.

"What happens when Bolsheviks are hiding in your midst," Heinrich said ominously.

Pitkin decided to leave town later that week—as a precaution only, he said. He and Nadya and the baby would spend a little time with her aunt in the village. At first, Nadya refused to go. She would not be driven from her home "by a Cossack brat who probably doesn't know how to sign his name!" she said, but Marko prevailed upon her, for the baby's sake. And Pitkin's.

"It won't be for long," Marko said. "Just until we see which way things are going to go."

Marko stayed behind to keep the shop open. "Cossacks need plenty of boots," he said, hoping this was true. His Russian was so good by now that they all agreed he could pass for a local shoemaker. If questions *were* asked, Marko was simply a prisoner of war employed and then abandoned by a fellow whose politics he barely understood. That he happened to be married to the fellow's daughter was a fact that need not come to light, especially since the former cab driver who performed the ceremony had already burned all the records and left town.

"I can always sneak back to the camp," Marko told Nadya the night before they left. "If I need to."

In the morning, when Pitkin sat in the driver's seat of the droshky with the reins in his hands, Marko and Nadya kept up a brave front. (To admit their fear was to admit there was cause for fear, they each reasoned secretly.) "It's too bad we can't go with you to the concert next Sunday," Nadya said, standing beside the carriage while Marko nuzzled his face into the bundle of Fyodor in his arms. It was the first concert of the summer coming up, and in keeping with his new non-Bolshevik identity, even Pitkin had planned to go.

Marko lifted his face. "Do you think I would go without you?"

"Of course you will go!" she said. "Heinrich has something special they're going to play just for you."

"What do you mean, special for me?"

"That's what he told me."

"I won't," said Marko. "I won't go without you."

"We can all attend a hundred concerts when we come

back," Pitkin said from the driver's seat. "But for now, can we be on our way?"

Nadya climbed into the carriage and Marko handed the baby to her. She laid her hand on her husband's pale cheek and thought, *Fire in front, water behind, a stone screen all around.* He kissed the palm of her hand.

Marko watched the carriage roll down the alley behind the shop. It looked like the carriage of an ordinary family setting out for a drive into the countryside on one of the summer's first really beautiful days.

⚜

A REHEARSAL IS not a concert, Heinrich pointed out, and after giving the matter considerable thought for several busy days—for Cossacks really did need boots, not only new boots to be made but old boots stretched and repaired, saddlebags mended, belts and buckles set right—Marko was inclined to agree. On a rainy Friday, two days before the first Sunday concert, he closed the shop early.

From the bottom of the stairs at the grammar school, Marko could hear that Nadya was right about the orchestra: all the instruments playing together bore no more resemblance to the single voice of Heinrich's violin than the springtime roar of the river did to the sound of rainwater dripping from the eaves. (How pleased she had been, Marko remembered with a surge of longing, for coming up with such a clever thing to say.) He was late and sat down on the wooden floor just inside the room, half-hidden by the open door. The musicians were sitting on stools and chairs crammed between two tiled heating stoves. No one seemed to be looking at the portly fellow who stood facing the orchestra, one arm in a sling and the other waving a conductor's baton, and yet all but one of the wooden bows moved back and forth over the strings in unison—like sticks floating in the same current, Marko thought. They were playing a waltz, he knew that much. He leaned back against the wall and tapped his toes—ONE two three—inside his boots. Perhaps a half dozen other spectators leaned against walls or perched on windowsills. They all wore greatcoats in the Cossack style over makeshift military uniforms, and most of them never left off muttering to each other while the music played. Some turned their backs to gaze out the windows behind them.

When the waltz was finished, the muttering grew louder. The members of the orchestra were not pleased with the performance of one musician in the second row—the one whose bow had bobbed against the current. They waved their bows at him and complained while the Cossacks moved in closer, looking grim. Everyone was speaking German, of which Marko understood only a little, and Czech, which he understood a little more. It seemed that the offending violinist (who also wore a makeshift uniform) was taking the place of the man with his arm in a sling. Accusations were in progress. Members of the orchestra believed that the man with the sling had been assaulted last night not by an aimless gang of ruffians but by friends of this violinist. He denied it and accused the other musicians of acting superior because he was Czech and not an

Austrian like themselves. The violinist also said—and this was the charge Major General Kalmykov later chose to believe—that he happened to know which members of the orchestra had given a night's lodging to a fleeing Bolshevik some weeks ago. A sudden hush followed this pronouncement. Then the man with the sling cried, "The Czech lies!" and the chorus of shouts and grumbling rose again.

In the midst of all the agitation—bows quivering, hands on hilts—Heinrich spotted Marko by the door and waved his bow in greeting. It took three sharp raps of Heinrich's new heels on the wooden floor to restore a degree of order to the room. With some final muttering for good measure, the musicians returned to their seats and Cossacks to their places by the windows. Heinrich made a point of catching Marko's eye as the portly fellow raised his good arm and, still fuming, flung the orchestra into their next selection.

It was Brahms. "Hungarian Dance #5."

Marko was so impressed with the sound of the whole orchestra—an army of waiters, silver trays spinning like wheels!—that he hardly noticed the one violin plodding along in the middle of the music. (On many occasions he had dragged the tempo much more grievously himself.) But the other musicians were less forgiving. The man with the sling grew more and more agitated as the music continued. Using his belly to support his injured arm, he jabbed the other one like a fist throwing a punch, harder and harder, as if he could force the lagging violin to catch up to the rest of the section. Instead, the music fell apart. (This was very interesting to

Marko, to hear the individual instruments reemerging, all askew, from the sweep of sound.) The man with the sling cried in faulty Russian, "Impossible! Impossible!" Red-faced, he looked wildly around the room as if for something to throw—and then, swinging his good arm like a club toward the doorway, he burst out, "Dat peasant boy could easy be playing better dan you!" At this, the grumbling Cossack friends of the makeshift violinist leaped to their feet, and in a terrible moment of both clarity and disbelief, Marko realized that they were all looking at him—Heinrich with alarm, the violinist with anger and hatred, and his Cossack companions with something like blood-thirsty glee. He, Marko, was the peasant boy in question.

If he hadn't been sitting on the floor, Marko might have been able to escape, but hands were already pulling him to his feet and dragging him to the violin section. The angry violinist, his expression cooling to mockery and amusement, jammed the violin onto Marko's shoulder. A Cossack thrust the bow into Marko's hand and lifted his arm to balance the horsehair on the strings. Then they all fell back and jeered in Russian, "Play! Play!"

The last thing Marko saw before he closed his eyes and pulled the bow across the strings was Heinrich's anxious face.

He played the Brahms from memory—very badly, with wrong notes and woeful intonation and a tempo that alternately raced and dragged. Silence fell after the first three more or less recognizable bars, and by the time he had sawed his way to the end, the makeshift violinist (who really played much better than

Marko) had left in disgrace, his military escort dragging their heels behind him. The astonished silence went on for a second or two after he stopped playing and then the whole orchestra descended on him, hooting and clapping and cheering.

"How did you *do* it?" Heinrich shouted, throwing his arm around Marko's shoulders.

"A blind man taught me," Marko said.

❧

"HE PLAYED WITH the orchestra?" Staramajka said when my father paused in his laborious translation of the latest letter from Lukovišće.

"Not exactly," said my father.

"He played with the orchestra! That's what you said." She reached for the letter and looked the page over as if she could read it. "I know what song he was playing, too. The Waiter's Song." She laughed. We all looked at her. Staramajka didn't laugh very often. When she did, her face was transformed. Laughing, my nearly toothless grandmother became an elf or a wizened fairy, an ancient but merry being who had taken a moment from the other world where she belonged to make a brief appearance in our front room.

"'The Waiter's Song' is what he called it," she said. "That's not the real name, though. That's just what he called it. He had restaurant names for everything he played. 'Chicken Soup Concerto,' 'Goose Liver Suite'! Always he's asking me, What do you want to hear? I say, 'Chicken Soup,' if you please.

Mozart? he says. Too many notes, he says. So I say, What do *you* want to play? He says, Beethoven maybe. I say, 'Mushroom Sonata'? He says, Excellent choice!"

She laughed again, remembering.

⚜

BEFORE I HEARD about the blind Gypsy, I always thought that whatever Staramajka knew about music came from sitting next to the radio in our front room.

I remember the day my sister Madeline brought that radio home from the Beymors' mansion, where she worked. Mrs. Beymor had given it to her because the Beymors bought a better one. Madeline talked the chauffeur and a gardener into helping her transport it from the Gold Coast, north of downtown, to East Bay Street, at least a thirty-minute drive each way. And then those two fellows had to get it up the front hall stairs to our flat. If you wonder, Mary Helen, how she talked them into it, you would only have to see your aunt Madeline when she was young, and then remember that putting a big wooden radio on its side in the backseat of the Beymors' Packard meant that Madeline would have to sit up front with the two men. It was so hot sitting between them, she said, that she ruined her uniform by sweating dark circles under the arms.

Staramajka loved the radio. We all did. It was a cathedral-style Zenith, all wood, gold-flecked fabric over the speakers down the front. From the back, with all its tubes glowing, it looked like the setting for a Flash Gordon episode. Staramajka used to sit beside it for hours on end, listening to people talk. It didn't matter who: *Amos 'n Andy*, Jack Benny—but why did they laugh when he played his violin? she asked me—and later, FDR. In those days, Milwaukee had stations that broadcast in German and other languages, too. Staramajka enjoyed the Polish one because it sounded like Croatian. She could understand quite a bit. I tried to show her how to change the station, but she wouldn't dream of interrupting anyone while he was talking, no matter what language, and she got pretty agitated once when I cut off the announcer during a Kraft Food commercial. One Saturday while I was tuning through the stations, looking for the fights, I twirled the knob right past the opening notes of something that brought my grandmother charging out of the kitchen, yelling, "*Čekaj! Čekaj! Čekaj!*" which means "Wait!"

Reluctantly, I turned the knob back to the music.

"Liszt!" she cried. (At the time, I thought she meant "Listen!") She spent the remaining twenty-two minutes of the program bolted to the doorway, one hand clinging to the woodwork on each side, a dish towel flung over her shoulder, and her head cocked toward the radio. From then on, every Saturday at seven o'clock, everyone in the house was expected to maintain complete silence for one hour while Staramajka listened to a program called Kraft Music Hall. Brahms, Liszt, Schumann, Tchaikovsky, Beethoven, Mozart—I didn't know it then, but she recognized all the names. Staramajka was an active listener. She would grip the arms of the wooden rocker and lean forward until her head almost touched the speakers, and when the music ended, she would fall back limp in her chair. Sometimes, to concentrate, she listened from inside the tent of her apron tossed up over her head.

"I think she holds her breath for the whole hour," my sister Madeline said one night when we were helping my mother make frycakes in the kitchen.

Always keenly aware of what I was missing (the Saturday Night Fights were on the air), I said, "Nah. She breathes during the commercials."

Usually, my mother had no comment about Staramajka's listening habits. I realize now that she was probably glad to have an hour with my sister and me in the kitchen after supper, no Staramajka around to tell her or us what to do. That night, though, I guess my mother was tired of hearing us complain. She said, "Staramajka is not sitting next to a radio. She is by the Drava. She is listening to the blind Gypsy play. Do you remember that guy, Madeline?"

My sister, who was five when they left the village, did not remember a blind Gypsy. My mother looked disappointed.

"He was a *muzičar*—a musician," she explained. "He could play anything with strings. He could hear a song once and then play it, remembering every note. His family took him to Pécs and Szeged, down to Zagreb, and even up to Budapest, all over, other countries even. He would play the songs at the restaurants, from table to table, and people would give him money. They were Gypsies! He was their meal ticket, see. A blind boy!" She went on laying out round pats of frycake dough on the floury table for a moment and then, as if she'd made up her mind to share a real piece of news, she leaned over the table and said, "Staramajka ran away with him once."

Madeline and I gasped together: "No!"

"It wasn't like *that*," my mother said, clearly pleased by our reaction. "His whole family went to Pécs and she went with them. She slept in the wagon with his mother and sisters. They were going to hear a concert there, in a church. Staramajka tried to get her father to let her go with them, but he wouldn't, of course. So she left! Just like that. All the way to Pécs they went. For three days she was gone. Her father said no, so she snuck out in the middle of the night. She ran away! With Gypsies!"

I peeked through the doorway at Staramajka in the front room beside the Zenith.

Madeline asked, "How old was she?"

"Oh, fifteen, sixteen, like that. But she was already promised to your grandfather at that time. When she came back from Pécs, they were worried that he wouldn't take her anymore, but he did. He was quite a bit older than her, your grandpa. But such a nice man. And that nice new house he built for her. She told him she just wanted to hear the music and he says, All right, now you heard it. And they got married anyway. But she took a chance. Some men would say, Forget it."

I poked my thumb through a circle of dough to make the hole in the middle and tried to picture my grandmother in a wagon with Gypsies. That wasn't so hard. The hard part was imagining her fifteen years old.

My mother poked her thumb through a circle of dough and put it back down on the table. "A lot of Gypsies were musicians," she said. "It's something they can do without staying in one place. And they just got the talent for it. Staramajka said that when the blind Gypsy was young, some big shot from America heard him play at a restaurant in Budapest and said he was a genius. They sent him off somewhere when he was only a little boy—to Vienna or London or someplace, the big shot paid for everything—but then his mother got sick and he came home. Staramajka said it was the evil eye. She said somebody was jealous of him and put the curse on his mother."

We could hear the Kraft Music Hall taking a commercial break in the front room. "How did she meet this blind Gypsy?" I asked, very quietly, in case Staramajka could hear us now that the music had stopped.

"Oh, everybody knew him," my mother said. "His people always came back to the Drava for a few months, every summer. Staramajka said people in the village would wait and have their weddings and funerals when the blind Gypsy boy was there to play for them."

"How could they decide when to have their funerals?" my sister said.

My mother didn't know.

We thought it would be a delicate matter to ask our grandmother about the blind Gypsy (considering what our mother had told us), but Staramajka waved her hand as if there wasn't much to tell. "I went one time to Pécs in that wagon of theirs. I don't know how they can live in those wagons like that. No place to turn around." She told us about taking Uncle Marko to his lessons, lingering for a long time on the lovely walk along the Drava from Novo Selo to the Gypsy camp. She said that Istvan (she never called him the blind Gypsy) had tried to teach her how to play the cello. "Do you know what that is? Like a big fiddle? When we were kids, he taught me. And I taught him to swim in the river. He used to say he was the only Gypsy in Europe that knew how to swim."

My sister asked eagerly, "So could you play?"

Staramajka said, "A little bit." She smiled faintly. Not at us.

I said, "You never told us you could swim."

She shrugged. "Lotsa things I never told you."

❧

MY FATHER KNEW only the Hungarian word for "Gypsy," so when he got to *cigany* in the priest's letter, he looked to Staramajka for the Croatian. She raised her eyebrows and said, "That's Istvan he's talking about." My father waited, his finger marking his place among the words, but she had nothing more to say. After he finished reading, Staramajka took the pages, as usual, out to the porch.

"She's going to catch her death from cold," my mother said in the kitchen, although the weather was fine. She was reaching, on tiptoe, for matches on the shelf over the stove.

I said, "Maybe she'll see that blind Gypsy when she goes back to the village." I was the only one in the family who really believed that Staramajka would go back to the village. I used to get a hollow feeling, thinking about it.

My mother sniffed each burner and then straightened up. "Oh, he's dead now," she said, lighting a match. "They all died in the war."

"Except Uncle Marko," I said.

She stopped. The flaming match was like a tiny torch in the air. "Uncle Marko wasn't a Gypsy," she said.

❧

STOP!

THIS WORD WAS boldly printed, rather than written, across the top of a page in the letter my father was reading to us. It brought him up short, and he frowned at the page for a long time. The priest from Lukovišće had used the whole sheet of paper to warn in large letters that the event set forth in the pages to follow was too terrible a thing to be read to Marko's mother or his sister-in-law Agnes or his brother's children, who were, of course, Madeline and me. Uncle Marko asked specifically that only his brother Josef should read the rest of this particular letter.

Staramajka rocked furiously in her rocking chair while my father translated the priest's warning. When he was finished, she said, "Tch!" and told my father that if he, Marko's brother, could read the letter, then she, their mother, could certainly hear it, too. Not until she threatened to sneak the letter off to the Hungarian fellow who came around from time to time looking for knives to sharpen (he would be glad to read it to her, no matter how dreadful, in fact, the more dreadful the better with that fellow), did my father relent. He sent me from the room first. I went without protest, straight downstairs to the furnace, where I knew exactly which duct to press my ear to for optimal eavesdropping on each room upstairs. I was not happy to find my sister Madeline already down there, occupying the best listening post. At first she tried to lord it over me, being a married woman and all, saying she was going to tell my father and so forth, but then I guess she realized that, with her own ear to the ductwork, she was in no position to lecture me.

By the time my father finished reading the letter, my sister and I were glad to be down in the basement where we didn't have to watch our grandmother's face while she listened. We hardly dared to look at each other. We heard Staramajka's rocking chair squeaking more and more slowly as my father stumbled through the story until finally the squeaking stopped and we heard her groan, "God help them!"

WHEN HE FIRST saw the musicians in the street on Saturday, Marko thought perhaps he had his days mixed up. Were they going to Chaska Chai for the concert one day early? Or was today really Sunday? He hadn't heard the church bells. Yet the musicians seemed to be on their way to the park. Marko was disappointed. He had been looking forward to the way the musicians would greet him today when he came to the grammar school for rehearsal. Some of them would clap him on the shoulder, he thought, the way they did yesterday when he finished playing. Others would shake his hand. They would call, "Marko! Marko!" But now here they were, coming around the corner of Primorsky Street, carrying their instruments, apparently on their way to the park. He spotted Heinrich and lifted his hand to wave, but Heinrich did not meet Marko's eye as he marched on, his violin under his arm.

Not until the last of them came around the corner did Marko see that the Cossacks on horseback behind the musicians were not merely behind them, but driving them down the street. He cringed to see a Cossack sword smack broad-bladed against the back of the cellist, who had paused to hoist his instrument higher on his shoulder. The cellist was a pale and skinny fellow, younger than the others. The Cossack who dealt the blow was also young—a scrawny, sullen-looking boy of no more than twenty. He had long black hair, locks of it hanging like snakes to his shoulders. "Kalmykov!" Marko heard someone whisper. He tried to think of some harmless reason why Kalmykov and his men would be herding the orchestra down Primorsky Street toward the park—perhaps they were a guard or an escort—but when he saw Heinrich pull his violin from under his arm and stuff it deep into the hedge by the post office, dread filled Marko like sand filling a sack. Stumbling under the weight of it, he fell back and followed the strange procession into the park.

Cossacks pushed and prodded the musicians across the grassy space arranged for the concert, all the way to the edge of the precipice in Chaska Chai. When the musicians stopped, Kalmykov ordered them to spread out in a line along the cliff. From behind a tree, Marko could see Heinrich near the end of the line, next to the young cellist. Kalmykov ordered the musicians to put their instruments on the ground in front of them and to take off their boots. Most of them sat down on the grass to help one another. They were clumsy with fear. Tears streamed down the cellist's face, and when his hands grasped Heinrich's boot, Marko's fingers felt a jolt, so vividly did they remember the feel of the leather, every seam and crease and curve. Heinrich's new boots were too well-worked at the ankle to stand up stiff and straight like the other boots. Heinrich leaned them against his young friend's cello, where they slouched elegantly, black leather gleaming against the wood.

Kalmykov stood near the other end of the line with two of his lieutenants, watching the musicians help each other shakily to their feet. The three Cossacks laughed at something together. Still smiling, Kalmykov told the musicians to turn around, and while they stood facing the ravine, looking down but surely not seeing the river in the valley below, his men lined up behind them. Other people in the park—a young couple, an old man boldly wearing a red cap, a family with four small children, one for each parent's hand—stopped where they were on the path or the grass and stared. Kalmykov's men raised their rifles.

The musicians fell, one after another, like a fence collapsing. When the cellist fainted before his turn came, crumpling into a heap at the edge of the cliff, Kalmykov ordered a halt to the shooting. He made Heinrich and the French horn player hold the young man up between them before they were shot, all three together. When it was over, those who had not pitched forward into the ravine were pushed over the edge by Cossacks, and then, at a signal from Kalmykov, another group of men—among them Marko recognized the angry violinist from the day before—scurried forward to snatch up the boots and the instruments.

Heinrich's boots were the first to go.

⁂

I PROBABLY DON'T need to tell you that the shooting of the orchestra was the most terrible thing any of us had ever heard about. We were still reeling days later, when the telegram arrived. It was my mother who ran into the Western Union man downstairs on her way out to work and sent him pedaling away down the alley. No one else ever saw him. I don't know how the priest from Lukovišće, that long-winded soul, managed to squeeze into only fifteen words the unbelievable news that after surviving a journey of six thousand miles by horse and wagon across war-torn Russia and half of Europe, my father's brother Marko, our uncle, Staramajka's son, had been struck down by runaway horses and a wagon at the market in Szigetvar where he was setting up his shoe repair booth. Only two days past his forty-third birthday, Uncle Marko was dead again. This time it was final.

I didn't know anything about that telegram—there was always so much I didn't know anything about—until one day when I came home from school and found the house quiet as a tomb. This should have been no cause for alarm. My mother, who cleaned passenger cars in the railroad yard, usually got home after I did, and my father would have already left for the second shift at the coke plant. My sister Madeline and her husband had a place of their own now, so the only missing person was my grandmother, and she might very well be downstairs visiting with Mrs. Longinovich, something she'd been doing more and more lately.

I knew immediately that she wasn't downstairs. I think the fate of the orchestra had left me with a deep sense of foreboding about everything. The way my father selected his words as he translated that letter, the deliberation (and maybe disbelief) that put a pause between *raised* and *rifles*, between *halt* and *shooting* and *fell*, left plenty of room for your imagination to fill in the most specific and terrifying details. I kept seeing the last three musicians holding each other up, their fingers clutching at shirt fronts and jacket sleeves. It was so vivid in my mind that I wished I'd heeded the priest's warning not to listen in the first place, and now, in the silence of our upstairs flat, the feeling of dread that I'd been dragging around for days sharpened all at once into something that sent me scrambling to look for the cigar box hidden under my bed. I was certain that if the tooth fund was gone, Staramajka was gone.

There was no cigar box under my bed. I knelt there empty-handed for a moment. Then I heard footsteps thumping up the stairs. I raced to the door and caught my mother on the landing. She looked up at me, startled. "Georgie?" she said.

"She's gone!"

"No!" my mother said. "Do you think she saw the telegram?"

"What telegram?"

My mother pushed me through the doorway into the flat and pulled the door shut after us. "She must have seen it yesterday when it was in your pa's pocket. I told him not to leave it in his jacket!" She sat down heavily on the piano bench, took off her left shoe, and plucked from it a pale blue rectangle of thin paper, many times folded and slightly damp. I took it, unfolded it, stared at it. I asked, "What does it say?"

She told me.

"Are you sure?" I said.

"It must have broke her heart, Georgie!"

I looked down at the unintelligible words. "But it's in Hungarian," I said. "She can't read Hungarian."

"She would know what it was," my mother said, her shoulders

drooping. "She would wonder why we didn't read it to her. She would *know*."

All my life, whenever the subject of Uncle Marko had come up, Staramajka always said that she *knew* he was alive. She could feel it—she could feel him somewhere in the world. If he were dead, there would be a hole, an empty space, she said, inside her heart. Like a hole in a tooth or a hidden bruise, it would cause her pain. I wondered if she felt it now.

"But why would she go if she knew he was dead?" I asked my mother. "She wouldn't even get there in time for the funeral."

My mother looked startled again. She had very pale blue eyes—they seemed to get paler every year—and when she opened them wide it looked like a pair of lightbulbs really *had* gone on in her head. "You think she—*left*?" my mother said.

This seemed obvious to me.

"For the *village*?"

Where else was there to go?

My mother struggled to get a grip on the idea that Staramajka might have actually done what she had so long planned to do. There was someone knocking on the door downstairs, but we ignored it. The Serbs always answered the door downstairs. "Well," she said, "if she *did* go"—she was talking more to herself than to me—"if she really did go, she can't get far. She only had a ticket to Chicago. Isn't that right?"

"Frankie Tomasic went and got it for her," I said, in case my mother had forgotten who was to blame for that.

"So we'll go to Chicago, and get her!" my mother said. "We'll get Lenz to take us in his car to the train station. She don't know how things work. She don't know how much money all this is going to cost her. She don't have the money, that's all."

"She has the money from the bazaar," I said and added, since the knocking continued, "There's someone at the door downstairs. Do you want me to—"

"What money from the bazaar?"

I reminded my mother of the little loom and the Croatian costume and how Staramajka had raked in the dough. The person downstairs was rapping on the door with a stick or a cane or an umbrella. Maybe the Serbs weren't home.

"She's not supposed to keep that money! It's for the church!"

"I tried to tell her that, Ma. She wouldn't listen."

"Yeah, maybe you should try to tell me something once in a while. So how much money did she steal from the church?"

"Seventeen dollars and some cents."

"That's not enough to get even to New York yet, is it?"

I didn't know. Downstairs, the knocking finally stopped.

My mother paced fiercely across the room, causing the glass pendants that hung from the light fixture to tinkle and chime. Then she stopped and turned to me, all business.

"Georgie, you're gonna go down to Solapek's tavern and call the train station. See how much it costs to go to New York." My mother untied her apron and tossed it over her arm. "That crazy woman. Thinks she can get to Europe with seventeen dollars."

I said, "She's got more than that. She's got the money I saved for her teeth."

A burst of knocking followed this like a two-fisted drum-roll, not on the outside door downstairs, but upstairs, on our landing.

"For God's sake!" my mother cried as she pulled open the door, "who's there?"

It was Frankie Tomasic. Before he could say a word, she had him by the ear. She had to reach up, as he was almost eighteen and had eight or ten inches on her. "You!" she cried, giving his ear a twist. She and Mrs. Tomasic were such good friends they claimed disciplinary rights over each other's children and twisted ears at will. "Did you buy a train ticket for Staramajka?"

"She asked me to, she asked me!"

"When does she go? Did she tell you when she goes?"

"I don't know!" Frankie yelled, but when my mother gave his ear a tug he cried, "Tomorrow! She said tomorrow! Let go of me!"

My mother let go of him. "Then where is she now?"

"How do I know?" Frankie rubbed his ear and tried to regain the dignity owing to the bearer of important news. "What I came to tell you is you got company," he said. "He's waiting over at Solapek's because you people don't answer your door. He came in a *taxi*." Frankie paused significantly. "And he's blind!"

　　　　　　　　✤

MY MOTHER SENT Frankie Tomasic off to enlist the aid of Lenz and his Chrysler while I retrieved the blind Gypsy from Solapek's tavern on the corner. He offered me his arm to lead him down the street. When we reached the porch and I opened our front door, I found my mother waiting for us in the hall downstairs. She pulled me inside by the arm, leaving the blind Gypsy behind on the porch, and closed the door in his face. "I'm not going to let him in my house," she whispered. "He looks like a ghost, Georgie!"

"He's not a ghost, Ma," I said, although he had given me a start at Solapek's by taking my hand in both of his and saying, with that distant, almost otherworldly look the blindness gave him, "You are the grandson. Georgie." After he spoke, he smiled sadly, revealing a splendid set of all pink gums and pearl teeth, and he ruffled my hair.

I peeked out at him now through the window next to the front door. He was waiting patiently for us on the porch, an old man in a nice black suit with a black fedora in his hand, having just doffed it for my mother. His other hand rested on the head of a carved wooden cane. He had very thick white hair—a handsome contrast to his dark skin—and a neatly trimmed mustache. His eyes were the only odd thing about him. He kept them wide open, even in the afternoon sunlight, like the eyes of a person trying to see in the dark. When he spoke to you, they seemed to stare over your shoulder at someone who wasn't there.

"He's not a ghost," I said again, as I reached for the door, although I could see how, in a way, he was.

☙

LENZ THE TAVERN keeper was prepared to drive all the way to Chicago in search of Staramajka, but he didn't have to.

He found her downtown at the North Shore terminal, sitting primly on one of the high-backed wooden benches in the waiting room. On the platform, the hourly train was boarding—people streaming into the orange cars, looking out of windows under the broad maroon stripe that ran the length of the train—but Staramajka remained sitting on her bench, her hands folded in her lap and a rosary entwined around her fingers, as if she was in church. When Lenz asked her why she wasn't boarding the train for Chicago, she told him she was going to leave tomorrow. (The truth was, she had been trying to board the train all day.) When he asked her what she was doing here now if she wasn't leaving until tomorrow, she said, "I'm waiting." When he offered to bring her back in the morning so she wouldn't have to sit in the station all night, she said, "No thanks." Had she seen Lenz before he saw her, she would have bolted for the Ladies Lounge, which she would have to visit pretty soon in any case, but when he told her she had company waiting for her on East Bay Street—a blind man, Agnes said—Staramajka told Lenz, "His name is Istvan," and she agreed to come home.

❧

HE HAD COME to offer his condolences to Staramajka in person, Istvan told my mother while we sat stiffly in the front room. He, too, had received a telegram. He had remained in touch with the priest from Lukovišće—first old Father Klima and then this younger fellow—ever since he left the village in 1910. He worried about our family all through the war years, he said, and was glad to learn from the priest that we had come to Milwaukee when it was over. He himself lived in Chicago with his sister Irina and her family. It came out later that his nieces and nephews were all very musical. He had turned them into a string quartet plus vocals that was known throughout the Chicago area.

"In 1910 you left!" my mother said. "No wonder Madeline don't remember you. She was born in 1914. December." My mother was still a little pale but seemed to have gotten over her original terror of the blind Gypsy. I kept wondering when she was going to let him know that we had not yet told Staramajka that Uncle Marko was dead.

"It's terrible what happened to Marko," she said.

"Yes," he agreed.

"She was saving her money, you know, to go home for good."

"Poor Jelena," he said.

It was the first time I ever heard anyone refer to my grand-mother by her given name. Everyone I knew—including Frankie Tomasic and Chuey Garcia and neighbors like Mr. Solapek, people who were neither Croatian nor her grandchil-dren—they all called her "Staramajka" just the same. When the blind Gypsy said "Jelena," I knew he meant my grand-mother, but at the same time, as if I could see her in a sudden flash of light, I also knew that he meant someone else, a girl. This girl looked a little like my sister Madeline, and she was perched, against her father's wishes, on a Gypsy wagon rolling down a moonlit road.

When she got back from the train station, Staramajka greeted our visitor as if they had parted yesterday.

"Istvan!" she said, reaching out to take his hand. (She told me after he left that when you greet a blind person, you should always touch his hand or his arm to show him where you are.)

"Jelena," he said.

"You look good, Istvan!" she said, perhaps a little too heartily. "I mean it. That's a real nice suit."

"Oh, Jelena. Where can we talk?"

As she led him outside to the upstairs porch, I turned to my mother. "He thinks she knows about Uncle Marko!"

"I was going to tell him, Georgie, but there she was coming in the door!"

For the next hour or so, my mother and I stayed in the kitchen and watched them through the tall windows in the front room, as if they were a movie playing out there on the porch. They sat facing each other, one in each window like a pair of portraits in matching frames. At one point, through the window on the right, we saw Staramajka sit up straight and grip the arms of her chair. We thought that must be when he told her about Marko. "She's taking it pretty good," my mother said, and put her hand over her own heart. A little while later, we saw her rocking back and forth with her face in her hands, and we thought maybe *that* was when he told her, especially when he got up and leaned over her chair, as if to comfort her. When he straightened up, my mother took a sharp breath—he was very near the railing of the second-story porch—but he made it back to his chair. We saw Staramajka lean forward into his window frame, her face tilted up toward him. His hands moved over her features like the hands of someone searching for something he had dropped in the dark.

When a taxi beeped its horn downstairs, they came in, Staramajka in the lead. It was hard to tell anything from their faces. Staramajka's expression was strangely blank—as if she were hiding behind it—and of course there was no way to catch Istvan's eye. He took my mother's hand briefly while he ruffled my hair again and said something in Hungarian that made my mother's eyes widen. When I tried to follow them downstairs—directed by my mother's urgently pointing chin—Staramajka commanded me to "Wait here, Georgie!"

She came back upstairs a few minutes later, shuffled into the kitchen, and sat down across from my mother, folding her hands on the table in front of her, knuckly hands with prominent veins. When the silence grew unbearable, my mother finally spoke.

"It sure was something to see him at our door like that, wasn't it? Like seeing a ghost!"

Staramajka scowled.

"I mean, to see the blind Gypsy again after all these years!" my mother said.

"I don't know what you're talking about," said Staramajka. "Last time I saw Istvan was a little before Christmas, he stopped by."

My mother said, "He stopped by?"

"Yeah, his niece has some kind of business couple times a year in Milwaukee. She brings him along."

My mother looked at me to see if I was in on this. I raised my eyebrows to show my innocence. She turned back to Staramajka.

"Are you telling me that the blind Gypsy—I mean, Istvan!

—he has been coming to see you every year since we came to Milwaukee?"

"Couple years he didn't," Staramajka said. "His niece was traveling somewhere else."

"How come we never saw him?" I asked.

Staramajka shrugged. "You weren't home. They always take the same train, so he comes the same time. Today he came later than usual. I guess maybe he was waiting in the tavern for somebody to get home."

"What about Mrs. Longinovich?" my mother said. "Didn't she ever see him?"

"Sure she saw him. She answered the door when he knocked sometimes, with his cane."

"She never said anything to me about it," my mother said.

"Why would she say something to you?"

My mother and Mrs. Longinovich were not close.

"I still can't believe it," my mother said. "I thought the blind Gypsy was dead all these years!"

"You think everybody is dead," said Staramajka. She said it more like a sad fact than an accusation.

I said, "Everybody is, eventually."

My mother kicked me under the table then, but Staramajka didn't seem to notice. She said, "Istvan told me some bad news."

My mother and I both held our breath.

"He said Marko is not going to stay in the village."

"Oh?" my mother said, avoiding my eyes. "Where is he going?"

"Istvan says he doesn't know yet. Maybe Barcs or Pécs.

Maybe Zagreb. He wants to have a regular shop making shoes."

"Barcs is not far from the village," my mother said. Like me, she was wondering if the blind Gypsy had made this up, or if he had information that we did not.

"Marko wants to sell my house and the cows," Staramajka said.

"Oh," said my mother.

"He wants to go back someday to that place where she is from, the wife, but they have to wait because of all that bad business going on there."

"Oh."

"He is not going to stay home," Staramajka said. She looked desolate in the way that only Staramajka's sunken cheeks and deep-set eyes could make a person look. "Maybe that's why he didn't write to us."

If Istvan had been trying to take it easy on her, he had made up the wrong story. My mother and I could both see that. Whether Marko chose to leave the village, or whether he had left it already by means of a runaway wagon in Szigetvar, Stara-majka's dream of returning to her yellow house and a rooster crowing in the yard was gone.

"How does *he* know?" my mother said suddenly. If she had known what this question was about to unleash, she never would have asked it—certainly not in front of me. "How does the blind Gypsy know if Marko wants to leave the village?"

Staramajka only looked at her.

"All right!" my mother said, "Istvan! How does *Istvan* know this?"

"The priest told him," Staramajka said.

"The priest from Lukovišće? Why would the priest from Lukovišće tell *him* about Marko even before he tells you?"

"Maybe because the priest thinks Istvan is Marko's father." Staramajka said this very matter-of-factly, as if it wasn't something that would make my mother turn pale.

"The *priest* thinks Istvan is Marko's father?" my mother said. "Why would the priest think such a thing?"

"Oh, because Istvan confessed to him. Not to this young priest, to old Father Klima, I mean. Long time ago, before he left for America." She shook her head. "Now this young fellow knows the story, too, I guess. I'll tell you, if I had something to confess, I would go to Pécs, where nobody knows me."

The best measure of my mother's shock at this development is that she didn't think to send me out of the room. Instead, she said it again, turning it over and around, not asking a question but testing the idea: "Istvan confessed to Father Klima that Marko is his son." She waited for Staramajka to say something, but Staramajka was busy using her thick fingernails to groom the fringe on the tablecloth. It was one of the few that had escaped the church bazaar. Finally, my mother had to ask (and now I *knew* she had forgotten I was there), "*Is* he?"

"What?"

"The blind Gypsy's son!"

"No!" Staramajka said, indignantly, and then again: "No. Istvan only *wished* Marko was his son. I think that's why he worked so hard to teach him the fiddle. Always I would say, Istvan, if you could see Marko's skin, how white it is, or his eyes, how blue. I told him nobody is going to believe that boy is your son."

"You said the priest believed him."

Staramajka shrugged. "Maybe those priests don't know how it works with babies. Or maybe Father Klima was just being kind to Istvan. Maybe he didn't believe him at all, I don't know. Istvan thought he did."

"But *why* would—Istvan—claim that Marko was his son?"

"He wanted to take Marko to America!" Staramajka said, as if it should be obvious. "Josef, too, if I would let him."

"And what did he think their father would say to that?" my mother asked, amazed.

"This was long time after my husband dropped dead in the middle of them butchering that pig. Marko was sixteen already. Josef was almost twenty. I said no, Istvan, nobody's going to America from my family. This is our home. Four years later, Josef goes all by himself, no matter what I say, and now here we all are. What's the use?" My grandmother ran her fingers over the raised stripes of the tablecloth. "Istvan wanted to go to America ever since he was a boy, but you know, he was blind. How could he go by himself? They won't let him in, he said, a blind man who can't work the same as other men. I told him, Istvan, if they hear you play your music, they will let you in. But he didn't want to take a chance. He said he knew a guy who had a bad leg, completely crippled, but they let him in because he had three strong sons with him. That's why he told the priest that Marko was his son."

"But what about *you*?" my mother said. "What were you supposed to do if he took your sons to America?"

I was thinking the same thing.

"I was supposed to go, too. He wanted to marry me—old as

we were already. He wanted Father Klima to tell me to take my boys and go to America with him. That's what he wanted."

"Did Father Klima tell you to go?"

"He said maybe I should think about it. He said my husband was dead a long time, and now Istvan's mother was dead, too, and he didn't have nobody to cook for him or drive the wagon. He was all alone, a blind man."

"What about the other Gypsies—couldn't they take care of him?" my mother said. "I don't see why you should—"

"What other Gypsies?" my grandmother said bitterly. "They wouldn't have nothing to do with him. He was *magerdo*, like the Gypsies say. That's why he came back to the Drava with just his mother all those years. She stuck by him. When she died I don't know what would have become of him if Father Klima didn't help him find his sister in America. She wasn't going to let him come there either, he was *magerdo*, she said, but her husband, he said it was nonsense, so let him come, he's blind, what else can he do. Thank God for one American with a brain in his head. And the sister came to her senses, too, I guess, if she let him near her kids after all."

My mother said, "*What's* the matter with him?"

"He was *magerdo! Magerdo!*" my grandmother exclaimed. "It's Gypsy language. It means, I don't know how to say it in Croatian, like *dirty*. It means no other Gypsy can touch him or his things."

"You mean because he was blind?" my mother said.

"No, no," Staramajka said. "It had nothing to do with that." She sighed. "He was pretty mad at me when he left. Father

Klima had to find somebody from Lukovišće to go with him all the way to Chicago."

She looked desolate again. I figured she was thinking something like what I was thinking: that if she had brought Uncle Marko to America in 1910, he could have been making shoes on Mitchell Street all these years, instead of winding up in Siberia. And if he hadn't wound up in Siberia, he wouldn't have played Brahms for the orchestra, would he? And if he hadn't played the Brahms—that's what I was thinking.

Not Staramajka. She sat up straight in her chair.

"Why couldn't Istvan stay in the village?" she cried. "I would be glad to take care of him there! I would marry him even. Oh, but you know Father Klima didn't like that idea, that I should *marry* a Gypsy in the village. They didn't want a Gypsy living in my house with me, no—but we could both go to America if we wanted. And there Istvan was giving all those lessons to the kids, and playing! He was like a gift from God how he could play the music. A gift from God, and people throw it away!"

Staramajka fell back away from the table, exhausted by her outburst. She looked like a coat thrown over a chair. My mother, dazed, sat in silence across from her, no doubt thinking her own thoughts about the village. Without looking up, Staramajka said, "Istvan told me once he had a dream that he stepped off the boat and when his foot touched American ground, his eyes were opened and he could see. He knew it wouldn't really happen but he dreamed that it did. So I told him I had a dream that I was swimming all the way across the ocean and when I washed up on American ground, I couldn't breathe. Like a fish I dried up and died."

"Did you really have a dream like that?" I asked her, forgetting that they had forgotten about me. "Where you swam across the ocean?"

"No," Staramajka said. "I made it up." She looked surprised to see me. "Georgie," she said. "I almost forgot. I've got something to tell you. Guess what kind of teeth Istvan has in his mouth."

I didn't know what to say to that.

"They look pretty good," she said. "I never knew they were Hollywood Plates."

⁂

WHAT ISTVAN SAID in Hungarian as he shook my mother's hand good-bye was this: "Don't let Jelena send me any more money. My daughter says wait and see if she ever comes to Chicago. So I didn't buy those tickets yet." It was not his words but the fact that the blind Gypsy had her by the hand that raised my mother's eyebrows at the time, and so many stunning revelations and counterrevelations followed in the kitchen after he left that it took her another day to understand the significance of what he'd said.

"She had it all arranged!" my mother told Madeline and me that Saturday night. "He was going to buy her tickets for the ship and everything!"

Madeline whispered, "Was he going to go with her, do you think?"

No one had the nerve to ask her.

After the visit from Istvan, we all could see that something had changed in Staramajka. My mother said the steam went out of her heart. She gave her one-way train ticket to Frankie Tomasic—a promising development, I thought, if only he would use it—and before the week was out she let me make an appointment for her Free Extraction of Teeth with Better Plates. I was pleased. I told her that new teeth would give her a new lease on life. (That's what the Modern Dental Systems assistant told me.) With all the coins Staramajka didn't spend on a ticket to New York and steamship passage, we could afford to pay full price up front for the Hollywood Plate. ("Don't they have no cheaper teeth than that?" my mother said, though not in my grandmother's hearing.) A week after Istvan's visit, Staramajka was riding home in Lenz the tavern keeper's Chrysler, pale as a ghost, her mouth stuffed with gauze.

She was sitting in her chair by the radio, completely toothless now and not paying much attention to anything, including the mail, when another letter came. This one had been written by Marko himself the day before he died. ("Tomorrow we go to Szigetvar," he had written toward the end.) It was very sad and a little creepy—a letter from beyond the grave. My father read it to my mother and me in the kitchen, where Staramajka wouldn't hear. No one had ever told her about the telegram, which was weeks old by now.

The news the letter brought was old, too, after Istvan's visit. Marko wanted to open a shop in the city if he could—Szeged, he thought, or maybe Pécs. (Barcs, closer to the village, was not mentioned. On the other hand, neither was a return to Khabarovsk.) He had a buyer for the house and cow. There was only one cow. Shoes and boots were in big demand, he said. It was a good time to be a shoemaker.

The first thing he would do in his new shop, Marko said, was to make a nice pair of boots for each and every one of us, so we should all trace around our feet on a piece of newspaper and send it to him for sizing. If we could also measure with a string over the top of the instep and draw a line of that length on the same paper with the outline of the matching foot, he would be able to guarantee a perfect fit for all. We shouldn't forget to write the name of the person on each foot, too. The family picture we sent him would help him pick the best style for each of us, he said. He hoped to send a picture of his family soon, when he had the money from the sale of the house. In case we wanted to know, the children were called Fyodor, Heinrich, Jelena, and Marie.

"At least he could invite her to come and visit," my mother said and then crossed herself quickly, having spoken ill of the dead.

"She doesn't want to visit," my father said. "She wants to go home. My brother knows that." My mother and I didn't say a word. My father looked down at Marko's letter. "My brother knew that," he said.

❧

ON THE FIRST day after the free extraction of her three remaining teeth, Staramajka sat and sipped her soup by the radio in the front room. She didn't say a word when I changed the station, interrupting Fred Allen in midjoke so I wouldn't miss a single second of *Buck Rogers in the 25th Century*.

The next day, Saturday, I was in the kitchen with Madeline and my mother when seven o'clock rolled around. They were up to their elbows in dough, so they sent me into the front room to make sure the radio was tuned to Kraft Music Hall. Staramajka was sitting in the dark—she often listened to the radio in the dark ("Why waste the electric?" she said)—her face very faintly lit by the tubes in the back of the radio. I thought she was asleep, sitting there, but when I reached for the dial, her hand darted out to touch mine.

"Baka!" I said, my heart taking a leap. She was my grandmother and I loved her, but in the near-darkness it was not hard to see why she frightened little children. I told myself again it was a good thing that she was getting the teeth. "I'm just going to put the music on for you," I said.

I twirled the knob past a sudden swell of laughter and stopped at the sound of violins.

"How's that?" I asked her.

Staramajka put her finger to her lips. "Shoe man," she said.

We were already worried about her. It didn't seem as though losing three teeth should set her back this way. My mother was afraid that Staramajka might be giving up the ghost. "Are you hungry?" I asked her. "Do you want to come in the kitchen? Ma is making some nice—"

"Georgie!" Staramajka gripped my arm and looked over my shoulder. She pulled me closer with surprising strength.

"It wasn't because he was *blind*," she said.

I said, "What?"

"They don't care if he's blind. It was the *water*, Georgie, that was the trouble. They had all kind of rules about washing and keeping things apart. You would never put your whole body in the water, see, because the bad parts and the good parts would all be touching the same water, like that. How was I supposed to know that stuff? I'm not a Gypsy. He never told me nothing like that when we were kids. I didn't even know anybody ever saw us. I didn't know a thing about it till long time after I was married and I ask him, 'Istvan, what happened to the Gypsy camp? How come you and your ma are all alone?' That's when he finally told me." She shook my arm hard. "It was my fault, Georgie, and I never knew."

I didn't know what she was talking about, but I could feel in the back of my throat that I would be crying in a minute if she didn't stop. Or I might be crying in a minute no matter what. All of a sudden, I wished I had never heard of Hollywood Plate.

"And my boy Marko," she said. "I thought he forgot about me, but no. He was afraid to tell me, Georgie. He knew I was waiting for him to come home. That place he was? I'll tell you what. If there wasn't all that bad business with Bolshevitz and the orchestra, I think maybe Marko would never leave that place at all. Don't you think that's true?"

I did think it was true, but like Uncle Marko, I was afraid to say it.

She let go of my arm. "Now I have to tell you something very sad. My son Marko—" Her voice turned to air. She had to take another breath to say the rest. "He is dead."

She knew. "Baka," I said, "how do you know?" She only rocked back and forth in her chair. "Can you feel it?" I asked her.

"Yes," she whispered, rocking. "Here." She tapped her chest with both fists, a double mea culpa. "Also Istvan told me. He got a telegram."

"He did?" She had known all this time. "How? I mean, how did it happen?"

"A runaway horse and wagon," she said sadly in the dark. "Same exact thing as happened to your grandfather Wendell. Agnes's father. My poor boy. After all the trouble he went through." Staramajka looked at me, her eyes brimming.

My mother called from the kitchen. "Georgie?"

Staramajka gripped my arm again. "Don't say nothing, Georgie. They'll find out everything soon enough."

"Georgie!"

In the kitchen, I told my mother that Staramajka made me listen to the first movement of "Something Suite." By Schumann.

The third day, she stopped eating. My mother cried, "This is how they do it! They won't eat, they won't drink! It's a sin, I'm telling you!" Staramajka heard her from the front room and called, "Take it easy, Agnes. Bring me a bowl of soup." But she hardly touched it. All that day she sat, her shoulders a little hunched, as if she were listening, although the radio was turned off now, at her request. She had a look of concentration on her face, a look of readiness. This was how she must have sat in the train station, I thought, waiting.

On the fourth day, when I left for school, I kissed her on the cheek the way I always did. Later that morning, sitting in her rocking chair, she died. Mrs. Longinovich found her when she came upstairs to check on things while my mother was at work. She sent one of her boys after my mother and another after my father, and she helped my mother take care of everything, weeping the whole while as if it were her own mother whose clothes they changed and whose hair they combed. By the time they sent Mrs. Tomasic to school to bring me home, Staramajka looked calm and ready for the undertaker to arrive, her rosary draped around her fingers and her jaw tied up as if she had a toothache. The doctor said it was a stroke, but I knew it was a change of heart. She had decided to go home after all, and she didn't need teeth for that journey.

⚜

ISTVAN PLAYED AT the funeral. Watching him, I remembered something Staramajka said to me one time when she was listening to a violin solo and I was waiting to change the station. She said, "It's not so easy as it looks to play the violin. You have to hold it just so and keep the bones in your back, all those little bones, you have to keep them straight." She was gazing so intently at the radio as she said this that I looked, too, expecting to see a tiny person standing very straight inside among the tubes.

Istvan brought along the string quartet with vocals that he'd told us about, three middle-aged nieces and two nephews. It was nice of them to come, although I could have done without the singing by his niece. "The Waiter's Song" he saved for the graveside service at St. Adalbert's. Everyone's eyes were on the blind Gypsy while he played "Hungarian Dance #5," very slowly, in that minor key, and nobody's eyes were dry. He swayed slightly, bowing and dipping toward the grave from time to time, but mostly he kept the bones in his back very straight. You couldn't help but imagine Staramajka up there somewhere with Marko, listening to the Brahms, the two of them together at last and probably grateful, both of them, that Marko would never have to play it again.

☙

WHEN I WENT to the old country with my cousin Marie Sinyakovich in 1982, the young priest from Lukovišće, the one who wrote to us about Uncle Marko, was eighty-nine years old. We talked to him on a beautiful afternoon, sitting on a bench outside his church, which is where the woman arranging flowers in the sacristy said we would find him. He was mostly blind now, she said, and he liked to lean back against the warm stone wall and smell the climbing roses, his face turned to the sun as if he were one of them. The priest told Marie and me that he still regretted not sending a letter to my grandmother describing Uncle Marko's funeral, but he was afraid, he said, that the postmark would awaken hopes of a second return from the dead. ("That's ridiculous," Marie said in English. "He didn't get around to it, that's all.") It was an extraordinary funeral, he told us. Uncle Marko's wife Nadya cut off her long braid in front of everyone to bury it with her husband—a custom in that place where she was from. And Fyodor, the oldest boy, looked so much like his father that when he played the violin at the funeral people felt as though the young Marko they all knew had come back again, or maybe never left at all.

Marie and I visited Fyodor, too. He lived in a concrete high-rise in Pécs with his wife, a Hungarian woman whose name I can't remember now. Except for his teeth, Fyodor looked pretty good for sixty-four, which was two years older than I was at the time. He and his wife had both worked for many years in a factory that made ceramic tiles in the Turkish style, but like a lot of people they had another little business on the side, bartering goods for services. Fyodor's wife served us a lemon cake that he had earned that very afternoon by replacing the heels on a policeman's boots. "Ninety percent of the heels walking around this building came from my workbench," he boasted to Marie. The workbench was in the living room of their tiny apartment. We were using it as a counter for our coffee cups and cake. "Maybe 25 percent, I made the whole shoe."

After the lemon cake, Fyodor took a battered violin and bow down from the wall. The bridge, which was cracked, had been mended by winding a strip of leather around it, and one of the strings was missing.

"He's going to play 'The Waiter's Song,'" Marie told me while her brother tuned up. Fyodor said something else in Hungarian and she added, "This is the violin that belonged to our father's friend."

"Heinrich," said Fyodor helpfully, pointing to the violin. Then he swung it up onto his shoulder and played, on three strings, muted by the mended bridge, a tremulous "Hungarian Dance #5." He sang along, some words in Russian, harmonizing with the violin in a wobbly falsetto. It was something to hear. I got goosebumps.

In all the versions of my Uncle Marko's story that we heard in the village, and we heard several, the greatest point of con-

tention was Heinrich's violin. It had hung for years on the wall
of Nadya's house in Novo Selo (which was my grandmother's
house, people said, did I go there? did I see it?) long enough to
gather layers of mystery along with the dust. Some said that
Marko braved Cossack bullets to return that very night and
pull Heinrich's violin out of the hedge. Others claimed the violin materialized miraculously on Marko's back at some point in
his trudge across Siberia. In a variation on that theme, one old
woman told me that the violin appeared in the sky every night
of Marko's long journey and guided him home like the Star of
Bethlehem.

In Pécs, Fyodor told us that after the shooting, Marko
couldn't remember how he got from the park to Pitkin's shop,
and once there, he was afraid to go inside. Cossacks might be
waiting for him. He snuck back to the shed behind the shop
and hid under a wagon with a broken axle. He crouched there
a long time, shivering, not thinking straight, a frightened animal, his forehead pressed against the wooden spokes of a broken wheel. He kept seeing Heinrich at the edge of the bluff.
He kept seeing him struggle to hold up the boy beside him, the
way they both shuddered and tried to stand, as if a person
could resolve to stay alive no matter how many bullets
pounded into his heart. Lurking behind these horrors in
Marko's head, like a warrant of death, was the knowledge that
Pitkin's name was burned into the soles of Heinrich's boots—
on the arch just in front of the heel, where it wouldn't wear
away. It was only a matter of time before somebody led the
Cossacks to Pitkin's shop.

It took the sound of hooves on stone in the street out front to rouse him to his feet, and then how far had he gone toward the alley—ten steps? twelve?—before a voice snapped behind him, a voice that could only belong to a man whose sword gleamed below the hem of his greatcoat, a man whose rifle was braced in his hands.

"You! Stop right there!"

Marko stopped right there. He had no choice. His legs were made of water now, his gut was filled with water, all parts of him were dissolving where he stood.

"Turn around, please."

The "please" surprised Marko. It gave him hope. But no, he told himself. Maybe this was just another way to torment a man before you shot him in the head or kicked him over a cliff—first, you gave him a little hope. He turned around. The Cossack's rifle was in the crook of his arm. Marko was afraid to look at it. He could just make out the barrel in the dusk, pointing at the ground.

"Your name?" the Cossack said.

Marko told him.

"That is not a Russian name. Are you a prisoner?"

"*Da.*"

"Austrian?"

Marko tried to remember what Heinrich told him to say when asked about his nationality. *Be a Slav*, he'd said. *Mother Russia*, he'd said. Marko could almost hear his voice.

"Answer me," the Cossack said. "Are you a subject of Franz Josef?

Who are these Hapsburgs? You never heard of them.

Marko said desperately, "Franz Josef who?"

At this, the Cossack laughed, a surprising, hearty laugh that showed where his front teeth were missing. Marko was astonished to see how laughter could transform a man. When the Cossack's shoulders stopped shaking, he was a bony young man wearing a Cossack coat that was a little too large for him. The rifle under his arm was a violin.

"I heard you play at the school," the young man said.

Heinrich had given Marko no advice for responding to this.

"You were terrible."

Marko could not deny that this was true.

Then the young man made a clucking sound in his throat, and Marko saw two horses lift their heads sharply in the street. One of the horses turned and trotted toward them between the buildings. The young Cossack boosted Marko onto the horse's bare back. Then he handed up the violin.

"I used to bring my girl last summer to hear them play," he said. He put the reins in Marko's hand. "When you get where you're going, let my horse go, and she will come back to me."

Marko nodded. He whispered, *"Hvala."* The young man patted the horse's rump one more time, then gave it a slap.

Even Heinrich would have had to agree that Marko was a lucky man that summer night. He was lucky that it was not October or April or any month in between. He was lucky that he didn't drop the violin, and that he didn't fall off the horse, and that it was a fine intelligent horse, well-trained and kindly treated by her owner, easily influenced by the merest pressure of a knee against her shoulder. Marko was lucky that the village where Nadya and Fyodor were waiting for him was the first right turn off the road out of Khabarovsk, and that his lopsided seat on the mare's back had her looking for the first right turn that might lead to hay and water for the night. He was lucky that the peasant posted as a guard at the end of the village street had set aside the village rifle to have a smoke with Pitkin in the balmy twilight, and that the June sky stayed light enough for them to recognize him even on a Cossack's horse before the rifle could be raised. Pitkin shouted his name and Nadya, among others, came running, and Marko slid off the horse's back into her arms. He hid in the veil of her loosened hair.

When Fyodor finished telling us this story, Marie said, "Well, I guess there was one good Cossack in the world."

There was more than one, Fyodor said. Hundreds of Kalmykov's men mutinied not long after the shooting of the orchestra. Fyodor's mother Nadya had told him many times about watching those Cossacks thunder at full gallop down the road past the village on their way to Vladivostok, where they turned themselves in to the commander of American troops. The villagers hadn't known what to make of them pounding past in the moonlight, the red and white striped flag of the Americans waving here and there over their heads.

"Marie," I said, "ask him if Uncle Marko ever told the priest about this Cossack who lent him a horse." I was wondering why the priest from Lukovišće hadn't told us the story in one of his letters. We could have used a little glimpse of light in all that darkness. Marie translated my question for Fyodor, who shook his head. "I wonder why not," I said. When Marie passed that on to Fyodor, he shrugged and smiled in a way that reminded me of his grandmother. Marie translated: "Marko kept the horse."

⚜

AND WHAT ABOUT the Hollywood Plate? You're probably wondering about that, too. A card that said *Your Smile is ready!* came in the mail the day after Staramajka's funeral. When I told the Modern Dental Systems assistant why my grandmother couldn't use the teeth, she gave me a look like she'd heard that one before. She said that a lot of people had second thoughts about dentures, but once they got used to them, they usually decided they couldn't live without them. She put the teeth, grinning ghoulishly, into a little tin box with a lid shaped like a clamshell and told me that if my grandmother needed a fitting, I should bring her in anytime.

I didn't know what to do with the teeth. They had cost me sixty-five dollars, but even if they hadn't, I didn't feel that I could throw them away. I remember I walked three times back and forth past the Modern Dental Systems office before I got on the streetcar and passed by one more time, the tin box rattling on my knee. On the streetcar, there came unbidden to my mind the time that Staramajka tried to flush a fish head down the toilet. I had come home from school one day and found her hiding behind the bathroom door, her hand over her heart, and when I asked her what was wrong, she pointed without a word to the toilet.

Staring at me, glassy-eyed, its whiskers waving under the water, was the ugliest bullhead I had ever seen.

"Jesus, Maria!" I said.

"The fish, the fish," Staramajka moaned behind me. "He is stuck." She put a trembling hand on my shoulder and peered over it. The fish stared back at both of us. "I have broken the toilet?" she said.

"Maybe not," I said. "Maybe we can just—unclog it."

She watched me pull the fish head out—I had goosebumps all over, putting my hand in there and taking hold of its whiskers—and we both stood back to give it a trial flush. I remembered how Staramajka sighed as the water gurgled down with its sound like an old man clearing his throat. "Never flush a fish, Georgie," she said at last. "The guts go down. But the heads get stuck."

On the streetcar, I put my hand on the clamshell box to keep it from sliding off my knee.

Suddenly, my path was clear.

☙

I HAD TO break up the teeth with a hammer to get them down. They were dust, not dentures, by the time I flushed them. What I didn't know was that Staramajka's regular use of the toilet as a garbage disposal had led to a leak in the waste pipe that ran downstairs behind the wall of Mrs. Longinovich's kitchen. The leak had weakened the plaster and discolored the wall behind the stove where no one ever saw it until it was too late. Mrs. Longinovich was at the stove making dinner for her large family, staring at a crack in the wall but seeing other, finer things, when she heard the toilet upstairs give its final, fatal flush. The wastewater rattled down the pipe behind the wall in front of her, and then, before her very eyes, the crack in the plaster widened, a sudden network of tributaries branched out from it, and the whole soggy mosaic collapsed into her kitchen. Gray clods of plaster plopped into her steaming pot of chicken soup.

I didn't actually see it happen. While Mrs. Longinovich was uttering her first strangled cry in the kitchen, I was still kneeling on the bathroom floor upstairs, bawling my head off. Tears were dripping off my chin into the clamshell box, making the few stray bits of all-pink gums and pearl teeth glisten in the bottom. The empty space inside my heart ached and ached, just the way Staramajka said it would, like a hole in a tooth or a hidden bruise.

Meanwhile, miles away at St. Adalbert's, my grandmother lay in her lonely grave.

❧

WITHOUT KNOWING HOW she knew it, Staramajka understood perfectly the first two tasks of the dead: you had to forgive and forget. She got right to it.

She forgave her son Josef for bringing her to America and felt at once as if a long-shut window had been opened, light and air streaming in. She forgave him and Agnes both for burying her the way they did, not in the knife-pleated skirt and embroidered sleeves she'd saved so carefully, but in a navy blue dress that Agnes bought at Schuster's. She forgave Madeline for marrying an American boy. She forgave Agnes for the toilet and Georgie for the teeth. She forgave her husband—my old man, she used to call him, *moj stari čovek*—for insisting on helping to slaughter that pig and for standing too long in the hot sun beside the barn. He had died sprinkled with pig's blood, her *stari čovek*, looking up at the sky and thanking her—*hvala, Jelena, lepa moja*—for the two young boys who held hands at his funeral while Istvan played, the ocean already in his dark eyes.

She forgave Istvan for the ocean in his dark eyes.

She forgave Father Klima for bad advice and Father Wojcek for the Church in America, and while she was at it, she forgave old lady Begovacs and the postmistress in Lukovišće. She forgave that doctor, too, the Ellis Island doctor, who found the rash on Madeline's chest that Agnes tried so hard to hide and chalked a big white X on the back of Madeline's little black coat. She forgave Agnes and herself for merely screaming and tearing their hair as the nurses took Madeline away to Quarantine. She forgave the lady with the torch in the harbor, the one that Madeline could see from the infirmary window, for taking two whole weeks to answer a little girl's prayer that someday her mother (and grandmother) would be returned to her.

She saved Marko, her greatest challenge, for last, and was happy to discover that it was true: *He whose life was short can easily be forgiven.*

From the vantage point of eternity, Staramajka found, it was easy, even pleasant, to forgive everybody. Forgetting would be harder, she thought—in fact, she couldn't imagine it—but she understood (as we all will) that forgetting was necessary, too. It was like cleaning out an attic, or sorting through a chest of old clothes, a trunk full of papers, in search of something worth saving. Forgetting was the only way to get through it all, to sift through hours and days and years until you found the gray

morning or the sunny afternoon or the blue evening or the
darkest night when you were most truly who you are. This, she
discovered, was the ultimate task of the dead: not to burn or to
pray or to ask for your admission, but to search the years until
you found out who you were and are and always will be, for
good or for ill, world without end, amen.

Now there was nothing left for her to do but wait for her
true self to catch up with her.

If she had still been breathing, Staramajka would have held
her breath in suspense.

❧

*"GYPSIES! GYPSIES!" CHILDREN playing by the river are
first to see the wagons making dust down the road. They run back to
the village, crying, "Gypsies!"*

*The little mayor takes out his drum and picks up the cry, a strag-
gling queue of children behind him. "Gypsies!" To some, the word
means, Bar your doors! Lock up your cows, your horses! To others,
Bring your pots for repair! Wash your hands to get your fortune told!
Put on your shoes—or take them off—for dancing!*

*And what is she doing when she hears the cry? She's sitting at the
loom, which she does not enjoy, or punching down bread dough, which
she likes better, or learning not to tear the streudel, or sweeping the
yard or picking strawberries or planting grape cuttings, anything to
get her out of the woods, her mother says, to keep her away from the
river, at least for an hour or two. But where has she gone now? It
looks as if she caught her skirt on the weaving in her haste to escape.*

The shuttle is drawn down crookedly, threads billow loose in the breeze from the window that brought to her ears the cry that means one thing: hearing the music.

Oh, and perhaps one other: watching Istvan play.

✤

HE SHOWS HER how the cello needs to nestle between her knees, how the bow, pulled straight across, should bite the strings. "You need to eat more streudel," he says. Her elbows are sharp. Leaning closer, he says he can feel the vertebrae in her spine.

"What in my spine?"

"The bones, like little knuckles." He rubs his knuckles into her back.

"How do you know a word like that?"

"I know a lot of things. Like my name, Istvan."

"I know your name, too."

"But do you know it's Hungarian?"

"Of course I know that. In Croatian, you would be Stefan."

"Would you rather call me Stefan?"

"No, Istvan is fine. It's your name."

"Do you know how to say it in American?"

"I'm sure you will tell me."

"Steven."

"Stivn?"

"Will you come with me to America someday?"

"No."

"Why not? I'm going to be a great musician there."

"You are a great musician here, Istvan."

"Call me Steve."

"I will not."

⁂

"THE ONLY WAY for me to see you is to touch you," he says.

She throws back her shoulders and her chin juts forward, as if she is ready to take what's coming to her. She says, "Here is my face."

His fingertips skate across her forehead and around her eyes, behind her ears, down her nose, over her lips, across her cheeks and along the line of her jaw. They brush the ticklish places at the top of her neck, but she doesn't giggle.

"Stop!" she says.

He stops, then asks her, "Why?"

She shrugs—he can feel her shrug—and says, "It gives me a funny feeling."

"Here?" he says, running his finger lightly under her ear.

"No," she says.

His finger skims back toward her chin. "Is this where you feel it—your funny feeling?"

"No."

"Where then?"

She doesn't answer him.

"Far from here?"

"Yes!" she says, then "Stop." And "Why?"

He smiles at her—she can see him smile—and he says, "I don't know. That's just the way it works."

⚜

"THEN COME WITH me to Budapest," he says. They're on the wooden pier, dangling their toes in the water.

"Oh, no," she says, "not again. I got in enough trouble already."

"Why are you going to marry old Iljasic?"

"My mother says an old man makes a good husband. He won't bother me too much."

"What a thing to say! Do I bother you too much?"

"That's different. You're not a husband, you're—"

"A Gypsy?"

"A boy."

He leans closer but doesn't touch. He whispers, "And you're a girl."

She blushes. That is true. It's also true that the old man has a yellow house, newly built, and cows. His fields stretch all the way to the road along the Drava.

"I can't leave my river," she says and with her toe she sends a long arc of water splashing upward, showering them both.

"In Budapest there is a river."

"The Danube is so filthy you have to hold your nose on the shore."

"Who told you that?"

"You did."

"Perhaps I was lying. Gypsies are known for lying."

SHE'S THE ONLY one home at this time of day, not counting her grandson asleep in his crib, and she doesn't intend to answer the door at all, but the knocking goes on until she thinks it will wake the baby. So she pads down the stairs, barefoot, grumbling, and pulls the door open, her most formidable scowl in place. She knows him at once in spite of the American suit of clothes, the hat shading his eyes. He carries a violin under his arm and a white cane dangles from his wrist.

"What do you want to hear?" he asks her. "'Chicken Soup Concerto'? 'Goose Liver Suite'?"

SHE REMEMBERS SLEEPING in the wagon between his mother and his sister. Did she really feel something in the middle of the night, perhaps a little animal pushing its paws up between the floorboards? Or was it Istvan, underneath the wagon, whispering like the leaves? She remembers pressing her knuckles against her teeth so she wouldn't make a sound. It was Istvan, only Istvan, lovely Istvan, making it work again.

WHEN SHE WAS a child, she could swim like a fish—underwater—halfway across the Drava, holding her breath for so long that her older brother and her cousin Janos and her father himself had all run splashing into the river to save her at one time or another. Jelena always came up laughing from such rescues, propelled by her savior's hands around her waist or under her arms into the air, water spraying from her like a veil of silver, a rain of diamond droplets.

When she was ten and eleven and twelve, she assisted the engineer from the Ministry of Waterways, whose job was to monitor the river and maintain its banks. Starting from the little station near the village, she rode in a boat all the way upstream to the big bridge at Barcs. Who but Jelena would be happy to dive again and again under the water to see why the marking pole stopped at four or five feet where the depth should be eight or more? The engineer's wife called her Water Nixie and gave her little presents—some sewing thread, a bag of sugar—to take home to her mother.

Later, when the changes came upon her body, she would run to the river at the first spot of blood, disregarding all the warnings of her mother and her aunts and the other old ladies who called themselves *Teta* even when they were nobody's aunt at all. She would leave her skirt and blouse and apron and the hateful, bloody rags behind on the bank and swim away from the woman she was doomed to become, if half the stories *Teta* This and *Teta* That told her were true. She liked to swim against the current, upriver toward Barcs. The engineer told her that the Drava began in the mountains of Austria. Could she swim that far? she wondered. And downstream, he said, the Drava flowed by way of the Danube into the Black Sea, which crossed the straits into another sea, and another (he had told her their names but she'd forgotten them), all the way to the great oceans. Many years later she would grip the ship's rail and watch waves roil back across the Atlantic toward everything she left behind.

When she was thirteen, the river was the only place where her body felt at home. In the winter, she was an awkward stranger to herself, clumsy in boots and layers of wool. In the winter, she smelled like her mother and the *Tetas*. She smelled like blood.

She was thirteen the first time she came upon the Gypsy camp. It was midsummer. The water was warm and the banks thick with leaves. She might have been a half mile up from the village, swimming just below the surface, coming up for air from time to time, when she noticed the vibration in the water. Her ears felt it first, although she wouldn't say that she *heard* it exactly. At first, it was so faint that she wasn't sure it was anything at all. And then there was no mistaking it: the water quivering distinctly against her bare skin, as if the river were shivering. It tickled her. Up ahead she saw the pilings of a wooden pier— really they were saplings stripped of their branches and furry with moss. She would try to come up for a breath underneath it, just in case there was someone on the bank.

It was a good plan, or would have been, if she hadn't come up in the very spot where a bare foot descended from the wooden pier into the water. The ball of the foot met the bridge of her nose with enough force to dunk her in midbreath, which brought her bobbing back up again, coughing and choking, nose to toes, and not under the pier at all. The owner of the foot was saying something but the words were lost in her splashing and gasping. She was half-standing in waist-deep water at the end of the pier before she had enough air in her lungs to shake the water out of her eyes and see who the foot was attached to. She plunged back down into the water.

Leaning over the side of the pier with his hand held out toward the water was a beautiful dark-eyed, black-haired, brown-skinned Gypsy boy. Or perhaps a young man. At thirteen it was hard for Jelena to judge who was a boy and who was a man, especially through the wavy lens of the water. She would have to surface before she could swim away. She came up under the pier and coughed.

He leaned over farther so that his fingers touched the water. Long fingers, strong-looking hands, they were only inches from her face. "Are you all right?" he said, trying it first in Hungarian and then, when she didn't answer, in Croatian, both with no trace of a foreigner's accent. (Gypsies always know three or four languages, he told her, not counting the ancient one they speak among themselves.) He waited a moment, listening (she held her breath), and then he cried, "Say something! So I know I haven't drowned you—please!"

"Go away!"

"Thank God! Are you all right? Where are you? Under the pier? Let me help you." His fingers groped toward her.

"Go away," she said, moving back. The water was shallow here. He would see her as she swam away.

"Where did you come from?" he said. "Were you swimming?"

Jelena didn't answer.

"I wish I could swim. I didn't hear you because I was playing."

The vibration in the water! It came from here, from this pier, this boy. She said, "Playing what?"

"Mozart!" He sounded overjoyed to hear from her. She heard some scrabbling overhead on the pier and then he was holding a stick out over the water. "I was playing my cello, see? This is my bow. I love to sit down here and smell the water and feel the air stirring."

"I heard it," she said. It seemed unwise to say that she had felt it. "Under the water. What did you call it?"

"I call it 'Chicken Soup Concerto,' but that's because—"

"No. I mean what were you *playing*?"

"Oh! A cello. I'm playing my cello, see?" He tipped it toward the water so that she could see its neck and shoulders.

"It looks like a fiddle," she said. A very big one. With a deep voice.

"You like a fiddle better?" he said. "I like both. It depends on the day. Violin is sadder to me, even if I play very fast. Cello is wiser. It doesn't change so much from day to day. Have you never seen one before? Come out and I'll show you."

"No," she said, although her teeth were beginning to chatter and her arms and legs felt heavy. How could she make him go away?

"Did you swim here?"

"Yes."

"Are you naked?"

Her teeth stopped chattering.

"Where are your clothes?"

Her clothes were half a mile away, she thought, maybe more.

"I can get you something to wear. Come out." He ducked his head down over the edge of the pier, politely averting his eyes, at least, she thought. "Listen. I'll leave my cello here, at the edge. If I bring anybody back with me, you can push it in the water. I'll never play it again, I swear!"

Jelena would have liked to see that cello and to hear its music in the air (and also to feel it again in the water, although she didn't admit that part to herself). She was so cold now from squatting under the pier that she didn't know if she could make it back to where she'd started anyway. How had she gotten into this fix? She knew better than to come this close to shore. It was that music, she thought, trembling in the water. He had drawn her here with it. One heard about Gypsy wiles. Almost in tears, she said, "Please go away."

"Please," he said. "You can come out."

"I can *not*."

"It doesn't matter if you're naked." He seemed to enjoy saying that word, Jelena thought. She was about to say that it certainly did matter when he added, "I won't see you. I'm blind."

She stared at his handsome face which was upside down over the edge of the pier, his black hair sweeping the water.

"The only way for me to see you is to touch you," he said.

And the way he laughed at that moment—looking not exactly at her but past her shoulder, as if there were someone else, a fish or a frog perhaps, to whom he was confiding this little joke—made her want to throw her arms around him and his giant fiddle and pull them both into the water with her forever. The cello would float like a boat, she thought, and anyone can learn how to swim.

III

The Kaszube Girl

THIS IS THE story I wish I could tell my daughter now, if only I had the breath for it. I would tell Mary Helen that Staramajka had to argue long and hard to convince my mother that Kata—the Kaszube girl—should stay with us while Lenz tracked down her Kaszube relatives in Kenosha. Because it was late February—not long after Ash Wednesday—my grandmother made frequent references to the season of Lent, a time for penance, for fasting and abstinence, for putting away the player piano rolls and unplugging the radio. These sacrifices were low in penitential value, Staramajka said, compared to taking up the burden of the Kaszube girl, who was, my mother would have to agree, one of the very sinners Jesus gave His life to save. Staramajka was so persuasive that in the end my mother resolved not only to feed, clothe, and house the Kaszube girl, but also to earn extra points in heaven by transforming Kata into a model of piety and good grooming. "When her people come from Kenosha," my mother said, "they will not be scared to take her into their home."

Why would they be scared? Because by the time the Kaszube girl had reached the age of twelve, everybody in the neighborhood had a word or two to say about her. Older boys like Frankie Tomasic and Chuey Garcia, boys who had never so much as spoken to the Kaszube girl (because their mothers, like mine, wouldn't let them), told stories full of vividly imagined detail about what she would do for the right price in the gandy dancers' shack between the railroad tracks and the swamp. Other people shook their heads when they saw her going not to school, but to her mother's job at the Modern Laundry, where the foreman—a man named Putsz—kept her on in spite of her youth. There were those who hinted that the foreman kept the Kaszube girl—as, they also hinted, he had kept her mother—for talents that had nothing to do with laundry. I don't know if that was true. Kata herself never said a word to me about the foreman, except for one time when she described the villain of a story we were making up as "short and fat and hairy like Putsz."

I might never have spoken to the Kaszube girl either, if it hadn't been for my grandmother. When I was ten years old, Staramajka recruited me to accompany her on Sunday morning visits to the Kaszube girl's mother, who was hidden away at that time in the little frame house on Aldrich Street, hideously dying of cancer or leprosy or syphilis, depending on who told you the story. My job on Staramajka's mission of mercy was to carry the covered kettle full of bread and frycakes and pretend not to notice the way her hollow cheeks puffed in and out in exasperation when my mother called down the street after us, "Don't leave him alone with that girl for a minute!" I never let on, but my mother's warnings worried me. So did Frankie Tomasic, who lived around the corner on Hilbert Street and spent his days figuring out how to make the most of other people's grief. I hated stopping at the boardinghouse to pick up his mother's contribution to our kettle because Frankie was always there, hanging around. When he heard that Staramajka was taking me to visit the Kaszube girl's mother, he said, "I hear she's got no face."

I'd heard that, too. It was one of many rumors I tried not to think about as I waited on the porch steps behind my grandmother that first Sunday, the handle of the kettle carving a deep groove in the crook of my fingers while Staramajka knocked four times on the door. It was cold, but that's not why my teeth were chattering. I held my breath when the door finally opened just a crack, revealing mostly darkness but also a sliver of face and one blue eye.

"*Dobro jutro,*" Staramajka said.

The eye in the crack of the door widened. Staramajka pointed at me with her thumb like a hitchhiker. "That's Georgie," she said, also in Croatian. "My grandson."

There was a breathless pause after she spoke, as if the blue eye weighed her words, and then the door swept inward. The Kaszube girl stepped out into the sunshine. Her face was smooth and pale, her dark hair wild and curly, and her earrings—two coils of copper wire strung through washers and polished bottle caps—hung almost to her shoulders. She wore a dress that looked very complicated, full of flaps and layers, until you realized that she was wearing two or three dresses, one on top of the next, each one compensating for the missing buttons or ripped seams of another. Her lumpy shoes might have been a boy's galoshes once. To stop me from staring, Staramajka pulled the kettle from my grasp. She reached under the cloth, gave me a bundle of frycakes wrapped in a napkin and warned, "Don't come back for an hour at least." Then Staramajka stepped from the stoop into the gloom, leaving me alone with the Kaszube girl. Kata took my hand. My fingers thrilled.

She led me away without a word, and at the end of the alley behind Aldrich Street we plunged into swampgrass taller than I was. The dried stalks snapped and whispered as we pushed through them. When we emerged, we were in the railroad yard, not far from a tin-roofed building with two small windows and a door made of rough planks. It was the gandy dancers' shack. I had never been inside. Once, Staramajka tried to send me there to deliver the lunch pail my father had forgotten, but my mother wouldn't let me go, citing rough talk and possible goings-on. Now we made straight for the place. Inside, I found out exactly what the Kaszube girl did in the gandy dancers' shack between the railroad tracks and the swamp.

She read pulp magazines.

The shack was full of them: *Wild West Stories, Battle Ace Adventures, Dime Detective Mysteries,* and her favorites, the shudder pulps—*Terror Tales* and *Eerie Stories*—whose pages offered gems like "Mother of Monsters" and "Honeymoon in Hell." It seemed the gandy dancers bought new issues every week and passed them on to the Kaszube girl, stacking them up for her next to the door alongside an army of sledgehammers, their heads to the ground and sweat-stained handles in the air. She couldn't read all the words, but that didn't matter to her anymore than it did to the gandy dancers, for there were pictures. Shudder pulp covers featured ladies fallen limp across green-skinned villainous arms, their torn dresses sliding off their shoulders, their necks long and bare and about to be bitten or broken or slashed.

"Can you read?" she said. Her first words to me.

"Yes."

"English?"

"Of course!"

She selected an issue of *Eerie Stories* from the pile and handed it to me. On the cover, a swooning blonde in a sheer white gown was about to be halved by an on-rushing locomotive while several evil dwarves looked on. The Kaszube girl sat on the bench beside me, munching on a frycake and leaning close to see the pages, while I read aloud two stories, "Food for Coffins" and "The Corpse Came Back." Then I brushed crumbs from my lap while she struggled through "The House of Doomed Brides." We both were surprised to hear the bells of St. Stanislaus chiming the end of the hour.

I was back the next Sunday, and for I don't know how long after that, I risked eternal damnation on a weekly basis by spending Sunday mornings with the Kaszube girl. (My mother thought I was at Mass.) When we weren't in the gandy dancers' shack reading *Terror Tales*, we were sneaking off to Jones Island, where the old Kaszube fishing village used to be, to make up our own. This was in 1930 or '31, before the WPA landfill got underway, when Jones Island was still almost an island, only the narrow bridge of Bay Street connecting it to the mainland. The ruins of the village, already ten years abandoned by then, poked up here and there around the warehouses and the new sewage plant. I went fishing off Jones Island every summer, but going out there with Kata when ice still sparkled on the breakwater was like visiting a foreign land. She showed me the sights like a tour guide. Here was the very last pair of Kaszube houses on stilts, leaning drunkenly into one another, their unpainted boards battered by lake winds to a silvery gray. Here was the sturdy roof of Konkel's original open-air fish market, home now to a noisy population of gulls, and here, not far from the new sewage plant, was Felix Struck's red-brick tavern, one unboarded window in the back facing the breakwater, and the hulking skeleton of a loom inside. ("For weaving the fishing nets," Kata said.) She showed me the remains, nearly buried in lilac bushes, of a great hexagonal drying wheel. ("For hanging the nets," she explained.) We tried to use it as a torture rack one Sunday—it was perfect for "Mistress of the Damned"—but the old wood gave us too many splinters.

Wearing drapery capes of faded velvet that she had scrounged somewhere, we re-created Kata's favorite whippings and roastings from the shudder pulps. When we had enough of that, we acted out her embellished histories of the beleaguered Kaszubes, who had moved a whole village from the Baltic Sea to the shores of Lake Michigan, where they set up shop on a two-mile clump of mud and swampgrass, wave-washed and desolate. Nobody wanted Jones Island, Kata told me indignantly, until the Kaszubes got there and built the breakwater and the taverns and the houses on stilts, gradually transforming the uninhabitable into a piece of prime real estate too valuable to be left to a bunch of crazy Polish squatters who didn't know enough to pay taxes. The Kaszubes' eviction from the island in 1920—in truth, the end of a long drawn-out dispute over titles and deeds—was in our hands the high drama it deserved to be, complete with swordfights, torture chambers, spells, curses, spies, sabotage, aerial bombardments, and refugees drowning in the Kinnickinnic River.

Our histories often featured her father—played by me—a mysterious figure so long gone from Aldrich Street that no one among the neighbors remembered his name, if they had ever known it. Some, if you asked, would report having seen the man a dozen years ago, painting the house on Aldrich Street, trimming the grass. Kata remembered him, or claimed to, in scenes, like a character from a book or a movie. He was a dark-coated young man in the street, drinking beer from a bucket while somebody clapped and sang. Or he was dressed in a blood-spattered mackintosh, chopping the heads off lake perch at a wooden table, moving so fast that silver scales sparkled in the air around him. Whenever we did the house-on-a-barge scene (where the Kaszube girl's father pulls their threatened island home off its stilts and hauls it upriver to Aldrich Street), Kata made me wear a yellow rubber raincoat someone had left behind at the Modern Laundry. She was always falling off the barge in the middle of a hurricane, screaming, "Papa!" into the wind. Sometimes I was permitted to rescue her. Other times, depending on her mood, I would end up grieving over her life-less body, kneeling beside her in the yellow macintosh, so big it stood up around me like a tent.

"Now say, 'The last of the Kaszubes, alas,'" she instructed me, lying on her back with her hands folded across her chest.

"What about Lenz the tavern keeper?" I protested. "He's a Kaszube."

"*Say* it!" she said, and I did.

There were some things she couldn't make me say. I drew the line, for example, at *"lepa moja,"* which means "my pretty one." I told her I didn't care if her father used to say it all day long. *Lepa moja* also happened to be my grandmother's favorite term of endearment. When Kata said it (to show me how *he* said it), her *lepa moja* imitated Staramajka's tone of absent-minded tenderness so perfectly that she made me blush.

The most remarkable thing about my secret Sunday mornings with the Kaszube girl may have been how unremarkable they were. We were two children, playing. The rumor and innuendo that cast a shadow over the house on Aldrich Street did not darken the time Kata and I spent together, and whatever horrors might have awaited her inside the house—did her mother really have no face? I didn't ask, I didn't want to know—they never touched us either, until one rainy Sunday. It was the end of summer and cold along the lake. Or maybe it was fall already. We were huddled in a dry corner of Felix Struck's red-brick tavern, reading. All of a sudden, Kata put down her copy of *Eerie Stories*. She said, "I have this birthmark."

I said, "Okay," and waited for details.

She warned me that she wasn't talking about an ordinary birthmark. It wasn't brown or pink. It was iridescent blue and silver—a jewel upon her breast, a sign of royal blood. Why, if she had been born in the old country with such a mark, she would have had to marry a Polish count or maybe a duke or a prince! But perhaps it was as well that she hadn't been, she said, since everyone knew that Polish counts and princes were mostly vampires who locked their brides in coffins during the day and drank their blood by night. We sat, considering this scenario. After a while, I said, "So what happens next? You marry one of these guys?"

Kata looked at me. "What do you mean?"

"The Polish vampires—do you marry one?"

Her earrings trembled. "You don't believe me," she said. "You think I'm making this up."

I didn't know what to say. Every Sunday we made things up.

"I'm not!" she said. "It's true."

I accused her of deliberately locating this supposed birthmark where she couldn't show it to me. She threatened to show it to me anyway. I countered by claiming that she took the whole idea from "Art Class in Hell," where the vampire-artist brands his lovely victims near the heart, thus linking their fate with his forever.

"Those were tattoos, not birthmarks," she said, her bottle-cap earrings tapping and clicking dangerously.

"So?"

"So don't you know the difference between a birthmark and a tattoo?"

We both were guilty of mingling *Terror Tale* plots with what passed for history between us, so we left the matter unresolved, but I said to my grandmother later, "Kata says she has this birthmark."

Staramajka was at the stove, stirring soup. I expected her to say, "So? Everybody has a birthmark." Instead, she swung around and asked sharply, "What are you saying?"

I thought I must have used the wrong word. Staramajka felt personally betrayed whenever I gave any sign of being an American, and a lapse in Croatian vocabulary was one of the worst signs. I tried what I thought was "mole" instead of "birthmark," but that only made her more upset. She pulled the spoon from the soup and shook it at me. I was saved from a tongue-lashing only by the multitude of greasy spots the spoon had splattered across my white Sunday shirt. "Wipe your shirt!" she cried, whacking me over the shoulder with a wet kitchen towel, and then, "Go and change! Go!"

I had second thoughts about Kata's birthmark then—I had been thinking about it a lot, in fact—but I didn't get to ask her about it the next Sunday because of a startling incident that occurred in the middle of the week. The entire neighborhood was horrified—but not, some claimed, particularly surprised—when the Kaszube girl's mother, crazed one night by pain and despair, went after her only daughter with a knife. Kata fled down the street, her mother collapsed in the yard, and everyone else speculated. Those who needed to believe there was a reason for such terrible suffering took this opportunity to bring up old scandals—alleged visits from the foreman named Putsz, rumored affairs with various Kaszubes—that Staramajka called fairy tales. Possibilities arose in people's minds that were as tantalizing as the cover of a *Dime Detective* magazine. Perhaps, people said, the Kaszube girl's presence reminded her mother of offenses so unspeakable she dared not seek forgiveness. Perhaps the daughter was proof that her mother's soul was as twisted by sin as her face and body were deformed by her illness. One of the righteous even went so far as to scrawl with a lump of coal on the house of the Kaszube girl and her mother: "THE WAGES OF SIN IS DEATH." On the Sunday after the incident, I translated the scrawl for my grandmother. Her cheeks blew in and out in fury as she watched me help Kata rub the words off the weathered wooden siding.

After that, my mother would not allow me to involve myself in what she spoke of as the whole business, and my Sunday mornings with the Kaszube girl came to an end. Kata's mother lingered for a long time afterward, and my grandmother continued to visit her—sometimes Mrs. Tomasic went along— even though the poor woman's suffering seemed to weigh more and more heavily on Staramajka. All through the fall and winter, I caught only glimpses of Kata hurrying down the alley on her way home from the Modern Laundry or running through the railroad yard in the general direction of the gandy dancers' shack with her latest acquisition under her arm. Away from our charmed territory, we never spoke a word to one another, not until the day I saw her coming down East Bay Street toward our house, with Staramajka beside her and a little wicker suitcase under her arm. I knew then—we all did— that the Kaszube girl's mother had died at last.

※

THE FIRST THING my mother did was to post a guard at the door of the bathroom we shared at that time with the Serbs downstairs and set Kata up for a long soak in the tub. (Whether it was the Serbs or the Kaszube girl or both that my mother didn't trust, I never knew for sure.) The shapeless gypsy clothes went straight into the rag bag. My sister Madeline had quite the wardrobe in those days—castoffs of the rich ladies she worked for—so she provided Kata with three dresses and a pair of shoes that required only a little stuffing in the toes to make them fit. Of the dresses, Kata's favorite was a purple one with tiny pearl buttons all the way down the front. It was so far from shapeless that Staramajka warned my sister, "Your mother will not like the dress you have chosen for Kata."

My sister protested. "It's the one that fits her best."

"How it fits is what your mother will not like."

But my mother was too gratified by Kata's keen interest in devotional matters to notice the fit of her dress. The Kaszube girl took to religion immediately, with a fervor that surprised everyone but me. Even my grandmother raised an eyebrow at the long hours Kata was content to spend on her knees, contemplating the Sorrowful Mysteries of the Rosary with the help of Staramajka's illustrated prayer book and her carved ivory beads from the old country, the crucifix gruesomely detailed. Staramajka had initiated her into the Joyful and Glorious Mysteries as well, but these were much less interesting to the Kaszube girl than the Agony in the Garden, the Scourging at the Pillar, the Crowning with Thorns. Later, for a good-bye gift, Staramajka gave Kata the rosary to keep (it was *not* to be worn as a necklace), along with a Way of the Cross shrine that Staramajka won years before in a raffle at the Slovenian Lodge. The Way of the Cross shrine was a wooden box with a crucifix on top and a little window in front where the Stations rolled by on a colored scroll of paper connected to a little crank. (When I was a very small boy, I used to hide things in the hole where the crank was attached, forgetting every time that I couldn't get them out again.) By turning the crank, you could go from the First Station, where Jesus Is Condemned to Death, through all the falling and bleeding and dying, to the Fourteenth, where He Is Laid in His Tomb. Kata liked to roll the scroll backwards "to make him come alive again," she said.

The Way of the Cross was also her favorite church service. It was scheduled daily during Lent, and Kata loved everything about it: the flickering candles, the purple vestments, the filmy white gowns that the altar boys wore over their cassocks, the nails and thorns and thrashings, all leading up to the spectacular human sacrifice at the end. The first time we went to St. Augustine's, she couldn't stop staring at the life-size figure on the cross up front, above the altar. "How did they get him to stay up?" she asked me. "Wouldn't the nails tear right through?" To keep her quiet, I gave her a Way of the Cross prayer book from the back of the pew. She examined the cover—a picture of Jesus sweating blood in the Garden of Gethsemane—and exclaimed with pleasure, "It's the Agony in the Garden!" But she was not happy to hear that she had to stay in the pew while I got to wear a long white gown like the other altar boys—"It's called a *surplice*," I told her—and carry a smoking candle and follow the priest up and down the aisle until we all disappeared through a darkened doorway that led to hidden chambers behind the altar.

"How come you get to go backstage?" she complained.

"Shh," I whispered, though secretly I was pleased to be the object of her envy. I leaned closer and added, "Just be glad you don't have to get too close to Father Wojcek."

Father Wojcek was the priest with no nose, although, in

fact, he had about a third of one. The rest he had lost to disease, or to heavy shelling in the Great War, or to the sharp teeth of a dying lunatic who didn't like the way Father Wojcek administered the Last Rites. Several stories circulated among the altar boys. Whatever happened to the original, he'd had a new nose made of some kind of rubber, painted more or less the color of priestly flesh and attached to his glasses.

"Ever see him without the glasses?" Kata asked eagerly.

"Too many times."

Kata stared at Father Wojcek when we stopped near her pew for the Tenth Station, where Jesus Is Stripped of His Garments, but he must have looked disappointingly normal from where she sat. Taking her cues from the rest of the faithful, she knelt, stood, sat, genuflected, and bowed her head over the Way of the Cross prayer book. Then, when it was all over, the candles snuffed out and smoking and Jesus Laid in His Tomb, she got up from her pew and followed the little procession of priest and altar boys through the darkened doorway into the sacristy. I was pulling my surplice (not a gown) over my head, when I saw through the sheer white folds of fabric I was tangled in that she was out there in the hallway, looking around like a tourist, deep in the labyrinth of cabinets, cubicles, and other sacred places that were strictly off limits to the public. I ran out to catch her, but Father Wojcek had already come around a corner, his glasses in his hand, carefully wiping a lens with his handkerchief.

For a moment we stood in the narrow hallway and stared at one another—Kata and I at Father Wojcek and Father Wojcek back at us—all of us wondering what, if anything, to say or do about the fact that most of Father Wojcek's nose was in the hand that held the glasses, and in the center of his face was a glistening pink hole. Then Kata made a little sound in her throat, and Father Wojcek, the rest of his face flushed as pink as the membranous space where the left side of his nose should have been, spun around on his heel and made for the inner recesses of the sacristy, hooking his glasses over his ears as he went.

I pushed Kata out the side door into the late afternoon sunshine, where she balked and turned and said, with wonder, "I didn't know it could happen to men."

The next thing we knew, Father Wojcek wanted to baptize the Kaszube girl. This development pleased my mother no end but set my grandmother to scowling in a manner made all the more formidable by her lack of teeth.

Staramajka did not care for Father Wojcek, although he spoke both Polish and Croatian fluently and might have been some comfort to her if he hadn't made the mistake of trying to save her soul, which was my mother's idea. My mother told the priest that Staramajka had not attended Mass, confessed her sins, or performed her Easter duty in more than twelve years, ever since she stepped off the boat, in fact, all because she did not believe that the true Church existed in America. Father Wojcek said that this was blasphemy, that God was everywhere, but Staramajka stood firm. God might be everywhere, but she knew that His one true church was located on a hill at the edge of a faraway village, above the graveyard where my grandfather was buried.

Regarding the Kaszube girl, the old priest had made

inquiries—some of them while holding me by the ear with my nose only inches away from his rubber one—and he'd learned not only the identity of his intruder but also the prevailing neighborhood belief that she had never been cleansed of the stain of original sin by the saving waters of Holy Baptism. (No wonder the girl had been so brazen as to desecrate a sacred place, sneaking around where the altar boys were changing their clothes!) Recognizing an opportunity, Father Wojcek called on my mother and proposed to instruct Kata personally, if a little hastily, in the faith, so as to baptize her during the Holy Saturday service four weeks hence, while the rest of the congregation renewed their baptismal vows in the customary way. Father Wojcek liked to schedule at least one actual baptism on Holy Saturday—preferably a convert rather than a squalling infant—and Kata was his only prospect so far this year. Thrilled at having brought priest and heathen together in her own front room (imagine the penitential value of *that!*) my mother agreed.

"Do I have to take off my dress?" asked Kata, who sat on the piano bench and listened while they planned for her salvation. I spied on them from a crack in the kitchen door.

Father Wojcek, in my grandmother's chair next to the silent radio, looked alarmed.

"To go in the water," Kata said.

"Catholics leave their clothes on," my mother quickly explained. "You'll wear a beautiful white dress—isn't that right, Father?"

Father Wojeck nodded and pushed his glasses up higher. Being extra heavy, they had a tendency to slip.

So it was settled. My mother called me in from the kitchen,

and Father Wojcek bestowed on me the solemn duty of escort-
ing Kata to his office every day after the Way of the Cross—
taking care to avoid detours through forbidden territory. Then
we all knelt down to be blessed, the priest departed, and my
grandmother came in from her hiding place on the upstairs
front porch. She scowled as she shook out the cushion on the
seat of her chair.

My real job as escort, my mother emphasized, was to keep
Kata away from Frankie Tomasic and Chuey Garcia, who had
taken to loitering every afternoon in front of Solapek's tavern
on the corner. My mother devised a plan whereby Staramajka
walked Kata to the door of the church (but no farther) and
handed her off to me after school. I delivered her to Father
Wojcek. During her lesson, I waited in the vestibule, where I
often passed the time by rearranging the votive candles to spell
out my initials in tongues of flame. Kata always came out of
Father Wojcek's little office with her nose in the *Baltimore Catechism*, a green paperbound book of questions and answers that
she was determined to memorize from first page to last.

Personally, I enjoyed her zeal.

"Ask me these," she would say, handing me the open book,
and then she would take my arm to guide me down the street
while I asked and she answered, word for word. Already familiar with Fourteen Stations of the Cross and fifteen Mysteries
of the Rosary (three sets at five mysteries apiece), she now
learned the Ten Commandments, Seven Sacraments, Six Holy
Days of Obligation, and Seven Cardinal Sins, as well as the
mystery of Three Persons in One God, which could only be
contemplated, never understood. We practiced the baptismal

promises that Kata would make in front of the whole church on Holy Saturday, wearing a white dress that Staramajka had agreed to alter for the occasion, even though she was pretty sure that Kata had been baptized at St. Stanislaus when she was a baby. Staramajka thought she remembered the Kaszube girl's mother mentioning it. "The Kaszubes always get baptized at St. Stan's," she grumbled as she sewed.

"And do you want to be the one who tells the priest you know his business better than he does?" my mother asked.

Of course my grandmother wanted very much to tell the priest exactly that, but she bent over her work and said nothing while my mother signaled us to continue, and Kata, following my cues, renounced Satan and all of his works with an earnestness that brought tears to my mother's eyes.

⁂

I T   W A S   O N   the Fourth Sunday of Lent (less than two weeks away from Holy Saturday and still no word from the relatives in Kenosha, my mother was telling the neighbors nervously) that Kata asked me if I wanted to walk out to Jones Island with her. She said she had something she wanted to show me out there. I was surprised but much too pleased to ask questions.

We started off under a blue sky, I remember, Kata swinging a little velvet bundle at the end of her arm, just like the good old days, practicing catechism on the way. But it was April. By the time we reached Struck's tavern, the wind had changed and we ended up shivering on the steps. Kata dumped out her things and wrapped herself in the velvet cape. She had brought along four issues of *Terror Tales*, some kitchen towels, a metal flask, and a short-bladed knife of the kind used for cleaning fish.

"What's the knife for?" I asked her.

"Protection," she said.

"From what?"

Apart from the gulls and the gurgling of the new sewage plant, the Sunday quiet was complete.

"It's cold," she said. "Let's go inside."

We went around the back and climbed through the same window we'd used in the past to escape from pirates and sudden downpours. The tavern was one big room with a bar running the length of the longer wall, its brass rail still in place. Two locked doors on the opposite wall had always threatened to burst open at any moment, spilling who knew what horrors into our midst, and the broken loom and stretcher still hulked in the corner. Wooden boxes and bottles left by other visitors littered the floor. In the center of the room, exactly where we'd dragged it to take advantage of the natural spotlight provided by a large hole in the roof, stood a heavy wooden table. This was the Altar of Human Sacrifice. We used it in "Night of the Gnome." ("Guh-nome," we both said.) Kata told me to sit on the table, then hoisted herself up beside me. Almost a year had passed since the last time we sat there. She was thirteen now. I was eleven. My feet still didn't reach the floor.

"Georgie," she said suddenly. "I want you to baptize me."

"Baptize you?" I was even more surprised than I had been the time she asked me to tie her to the railroad tracks. "I can't baptize you."

"Father Wojcek says that anyone can baptize in an emergency."

"But this isn't an emergency."

"It could be a *conditional* baptism," she said. "Just in case."

"In case of what?"

"We don't even need holy water for a conditional baptism—although I have some." She held up the metal flask.

"But why not wait till Saturday, Kata? Don't you want to wear the dress and everything?" She had been trying on the white dress at least once a day for the past two weeks. Staramajka kept calling her *lepa moja*, and fussing with the hem.

Kata set the flask down, frowning. "I don't want to wait. I want to see if it works. Now."

"Kata," I said, "you can't *see* if it works."

She hopped off the table. "Wait here," she said.

She moved through the shadows to the bar, where she slipped the cape off her shoulders and spread it like a tablecloth. Then I remembered that she had something to show me. When she turned around again, she was unbuttoning the pearl buttons that began at the neckline of her purple dress and went all the way to the hem.

I said, "What are you doing?"

She said, "I'm showing you."

She walked toward me, slowly, and when her fingers reached the eighth button—I was counting—and her toes nudged the ragged circle of light around the table, she stopped. She folded back one side of the front of her dress to expose a perfect triangle of skin. "See?" she said, pointing to a spot on the slope of her small breast. There, before my eyes, was an iridescent blue and black and silver teardrop that did look, in the light from the roof, more like a jewel than a birthmark. I thought she would laugh at me when my breath escaped noisily, but she remained solemn. "You didn't believe me," she said, as she stepped back into the shadows. Her face seemed to be floating above the white triangle of skin, the birthmark a small, dark smudge in the middle of it. "You said I took it from a book."

"It was how you said you were betrothed," I said hoarsely. "To some prince or something. That's what I didn't believe."

Kata looked down at herself and touched the birthmark with the tip of her finger. I folded my hands in my lap. "That part wasn't true," she admitted. She took a step closer and the birthmark became a jewel again. "The truth is, it's a curse."

I pressed my folded hands into my lap.

"It's the mark of death," she said.

I recognized this line—I was sure of it. It was from the *Terror Tales*, not the catechism, but I couldn't think, under the circumstances, of which story. "Come on, Kata," I croaked.

She leaned into me, her eyes bright with storytelling, and whispered, "My mother had one, too."

The room had grown darker. "We better go," I said desperately. "It looks like rain."

She did laugh at me then, quietly at first. She turned her back on me, laughing, all her scorn and disappointment bubbling up out of her until she could hardly button her dress, until she was laughing so hard she was almost crying. All the way back to East Bay Street, while I walked in embarrassed silence, Kata kept sniffling and giggling, as if she couldn't help herself. She left no doubt that my usefulness to her was at an end.

IT'S TRUE WHAT they say about old people, how we remember things. Who knows why? Right now, all of a sudden I'm remembering my grandmother in our kitchen making streudel, it must be seventy-five years ago. Staramajka had an apron with a pattern of little bears stealing honey from little beehives that made a big impression on me. Her apron pockets were always lumpy with marbles that she wouldn't let me play with ever since she'd caught me rolling one around in my mouth. She wore her babushka low on the forehead and tied in the back. She sprinkled ground walnuts and sugar on dough spread out so thin that you could see the red and black stripes on the tablecloth underneath it. Once, she was getting ready to roll the dough up into a long tube when a fly landed on the walnut filling near my end of the table. Staramajka was busy with her edge of the dough, making sure it didn't roll up fatter at one end than the other, her fingers moving back and forth like somebody playing a streudel-dough piano. She didn't see the fly, but I did. I got a really good look at it, my eyes being at tabletop level in those days. The fly, like her, suspected noth-ing. It was rubbing its front legs together thinking boy-oh-boy I'm gonna eat like a king! And in the meantime Staramajka's roll of streudel dough was coming closer and closer, like a cartoon steamroller. She was only two inches from that fly before it finally wised up and flew off.

"Jesus, Maria!" she cried. "Now I gotta throw the whole thing out!"

I told her, "No, no, Baka, the fly stayed right here all the time," and I drew a square in the air over the dough to show her how little had been sullied by the fly. I must have been four years old, maybe five. She looked at me then, her lips pressed together over very few teeth, and I realized that I'd made a mistake, but she didn't say anything about it. She reached over the top of my head for the silverware drawer and rattled around in it until she found the right knife to cut out the offending square of dough. Then she patched it with a piece from the edge. As if it was yesterday, I can see her fingers pinching the dough together. As if I was still standing there in the kitchen, I can see it.

But I'm not confused. I know I'm not standing in the kitchen. I know I've got more wires and tubes coming off me than lines on a float in Macy's parade. You probably think I had a heart attack or something. Wrong. You'd never believe it to look at me, but I punched a man at the mall today. Or maybe by now it's yesterday. In the Emergency Room, when we first got here, my daughter was afraid they were going to charge me with attempted murder. I could have told her that aggravated assault was more likely—manslaughter if he kicked the bucket—but she was in no mood for technicalities.

"Dad, you practically killed that guy! You broke his pace-maker!" she said.

"It didn't break," I said. I could still talk then, in the Emergency Room. "It just stopped for a minute."

I didn't mean to hit Frankie in the pacemaker anyway. The shoulder strap on my oxygen tank slipped and threw me off. I meant for him to take it on the chin.

"But why, Dad?" Mary Helen kept saying. "Why did you hit him?"

If I had known that this would be my last chance to give her a straight answer, I would have done it. I would have tried to explain. I would have told my daughter about the way certain moments in your past expand as you get older, how your memories of them take over, displacing other memories, who knows why? Before you know it, those moments are filling up the empty spaces of the present, too—and there's always a lot of empty space in the present—until they're so much bigger than their original size and relative importance in your life that who you are seems to have begun right there, sitting shoulder to shoulder, say, on a bench in the gandy dancers' shack or in the shell of a tavern on Jones Island, with the Kaszube girl pressed against you for warmth and to see the pages, her lips moving silently as you read the words.

I didn't tell my daughter any of that. I said, "Some people deserve to get belted." It's true.

It's also true that some people think if you've got a tube down your throat, then your ears don't work either. Since I graduated from ER to ICU, I've heard a lot of things that I know I'm not supposed to hear, like the doctor talking to Mary Helen about my condition. Congestive heart failure, he says, due to massive sodium intake. And Mary Helen talking on the cell phone to her sister in California. The burritos again. They can't leave them alone.

"I didn't *let* him eat those burritos, Aggie. He's a grown man. He knew how much salt—Yes, Aggie, if he had put a loaded gun to his head, I would have tried to stop him. There's a big difference, in case you haven't noticed, between a loaded gun and a sausage burrito."

I heard all of that. I heard Kata, too. I wasn't expecting *her* to show up, that's for sure. "Just let me see him for a minute," she said to somebody out there. "Please. I've got something to show him."

"Are you immediate family?"

"It's very important," she said. "You want to let him die thinking bad things about people? About his father? How can you want that?"

❧

I HAVE TO tell you, I wouldn't even have known that Kata was back in Milwaukee if she hadn't sent me a sympathy card (this is six years after my wife died) with a return address at the senior citizens' high-rise over on Lincoln Avenue. The fellow she married years ago in Kenosha—Rudy was his name, a welder by trade—had long since passed away. When she first came back, I wasn't on oxygen around the clock yet and I could still drive my car, so I called her up. We got reacquainted. I guess you could say that was my first mistake. In the meantime, Frankie Tomasic was hauling her all over to craft fairs and antique malls, sharing his booth with her so she could sell her sweatshirts with the fancy leaves and snowflakes and things sewn on them. When Frankie started furnishing her apartment with "antiques and collectibles," I decided it wouldn't hurt to show her something I could do. My second mistake.

For the record, I took up stained glass back in the early eighties, a long time before every other Tom, Dick, and Harry started doing it. I had been moping around after my first double bypass, regretting my choice of early retirement over a desk job in the Traffic Bureau. Then my wife Carol suggested a class at the community college. It didn't take me long to outfit every window in the house with a rainbow or a butterfly or a hot air balloon. Suncatchers, they were called. Carol used to say that walking through our front door on a sunny day was like stepping inside a kaleidoscope. I gave it up when she died, put all the stained glass in the basement, where I wouldn't have to look at it. All those pieces are still down there, hanging on the pipes like suits on a rack.

My daughter always thought it was a shame that I'd given up my hobby just when I needed it most, so she was delighted to help me move my workshop from the basement into her old bedroom last summer. I started without a plan, laying down red bits of glass from an old kit I never finished, and then deciding they were bricks. I'd never worked without a store-bought pattern before. I must have been inspired. Once the red bricks turned into a tavern, the fish market rose up like magic next to it, silvery slivers of glass heaped up to look like fish. Pretty soon crooked houses were marching on stilts through lilac bushes complete with bunches of purple flowers that my daughter mistook for grapes. "Grapes?" I said to her.

"Maybe you need glasses." I put in a drying wheel, too. My daughter thought it was a giant spider's web. By the time I was through, there was even a little guy in a yellow raincoat, specks of white gull flying over his head.

Finished, it was as big as a window. I got it framed professionally and called AAA Glass to arrange delivery. That was mistake number three.

When Kata saw it leaning against the patio doors in her apartment with the sun shining through Felix Struck's tavern and painting her carpet red, she started to cry. I had known her since she was twelve, on and off, and it was the first time I had ever seen her cry. She stood there in front of it, exclaiming over every detail, noticing the gull and the lilacs, which she did not mistake for grapes. I was sitting on the ugly plaid sofa that Frankie had given her because he couldn't find anybody blind enough to buy it. Finally she came and sat down next to me. With the light coming through the stained glass on her white hair and her white sweatshirt, she looked like a masterpiece of many colors herself. She put her hand on top of my hand. "Georgie," she said, "I can't take this wonderful thing from you."

"Why the hell not?" I said, a little breathlessly. My portable oxygen tank was in my lap.

"Because me and Frankie?" She hesitated. I had no idea what was coming. "We're getting married," she said.

I swear the room darkened. Either the sun had gone behind the clouds or I needed to turn up my oxygen.

"What the hell for?" I wheezed.

"I knew you wouldn't like it," she said. "But I didn't think you would take it *too* hard. Considering."

How could she marry Frankie Tomasic? It was like announcing that you were going to marry Al Capone. I said, "Considering what?"

"You know," she said. "The whole other thing."

"What other thing?"

Kata looked at me, a strange expression on her face. "I thought you must know it by now," she said.

"Know what, Kata?"

"*Somebody* must have told you."

"Told me what?"

"Oh holy mother," she said. She stood up. There was no slow unfolding at the hips, no favoring of creaky knees—she just stood up. Kata is very limber for a person her age. I'm constantly amazed by what she can do. She paced back and forth in front of the patio doors, then stopped and looked out over the top of the stained glass. From her twelfth-floor living room, Kata has a view of the lakeshore that includes the thumb of land they still call Jones Island. She can count the oil storage tanks down there, row upon row of them, as white and round as layer cakes. On a clear day she can see the sewage plant at the end of where the harbor bridge used to be. She turned around suddenly. "Georgie," she said, "remember my baptismal certificate from St. Stanislaus? Remember Staramajka showed it to you? She told me that she showed it to you. That's why I thought you knew. All these years, I thought so."

I looked at her. I felt as if I had taken a wrong turn somewhere. Sometimes low oxygen does that to you. "What does this have to do with anything?" I asked her.

"Don't you remember whose name was written on my baptismal certificate? In the space marked 'Father'?"

"No," I said. I didn't remember any name. I didn't remember a space marked "Father."

"No? Don't you remember anything about it at all?"

"I remember it said *Illegitimate*." Immediately I regretted saying this, although it was what I remembered.

Kata only lifted her chin. "Georgie," she said, "*your* father's name was written on my baptismal certificate, in the space marked 'Father.'"

What was she trying to say? "What are you trying to say, Kata?"

"I've said it." She threw her shoulders back and the silver snowflakes on her sweatshirt turned colors in the light from the window. "Your father and my father were the same."

"Are you crazy?" I said.

"That makes us brother and sister, Georgie. On our father's side at least."

"Wait," I said. "You want me to believe that while my mother was stuck in Europe during the war, my father and your mother were here in Milwaukee, fooling around?" I ran out of breath toward the end of this sentence, but Kata read my lips.

"They weren't fooling around!" she said indignantly. "They fell in love. They woulda got married if they could."

Now I stood up. My little oxygen tank looked very far away down there on the couch.

"Do you have this—certificate?" I was wheezing again.

"You think I'm making this up?"

"Do you have it?"

"No," she said. "It got lost."

I said, "Hah!"

It was a lot of air to waste on a single syllable. I sat back down—a little harder than I intended although I wouldn't have called it falling—on the couch. I had always thought of the Kaszube girl's mother, when I thought of her at all, the same way I thought about the doomed and twisted creatures in a *Terror Tale*. She was "Mother of Monsters" (no offense to Kata). She was "Mistress of the Damned." She was "Honeymoon from Hell." The Kaszube girl's mother and my father occupied entirely different regions of my mind. Their worlds did not intersect. Kata sat down beside me.

"Georgie," she said. "It's not like you think. They were young, both of them. My mother told me the whole story."

"Yeah, I *bet* she did."

I said this breathlessly, too, but with so much scorn, like poison, in my voice that Kata called a cab for me.

We haven't spoken since, except, of course, very briefly, right before I punched Frankie.

✻

MAYBE I *WAS* asking for trouble, getting my daughter to take me to the mall. I knew the Christmas Craft & Antique Fair would be there. Kata had put me on the mailing list for a postcard. I don't know which was worse, that postcard from Tomasic's Antiques & Appliques or the wedding invitation, which was a color photocopy, 8 by 10, of the happy couple standing on a dock in Key Largo with a large fish hanging between them. (I guess they did the honeymoon first, which is not a bad idea at our age.) On the back of the picture Kata printed by hand: "A December Wedding, Knights of Columbus Hall," followed by the date, the time, and "No presents please." I was surprised Frankie let her put that on there about the presents. I had already sent a wedding-type card to Kata, inviting her and Frankie to enjoy my stained glass masterpiece in good health or else to throw it out the window, what did I care.

I did not attend the wedding.

But I did go to the mall (mistake number four), half thinking that Frankie might have decided to sell the stained glass, in which case I could get it back if I was willing to pay an arm and a leg. The last thing I expected to find for sale in their booth was the Way of the Cross shrine that my grandmother gave to Kata so long ago. I knew they were getting rid of things ("When two hearts become one, the apartment gets crowded," the printed postcard said), but it seemed wrong: Christ crucified towering over a red-and-green-covered table full of wooden radios. Blood that looked like red nail polish dripped from His head and hands and feet. I think they spruced Him up for the occasion.

"Jesus Christ, Frankie," I said when I saw it.

"That's right," said Frankie. He was wearing a Santa Claus hat over his speckled head.

I put my sausage burrito down on the table and reached for my checkbook. Frankie named his price.

"A hundred and fifty dollars?" I said.

He blew some dust off the crown of thorns. "You get what you pay for, Georgie."

While I was writing the check, Kata showed up with a couple of coffees. She offered me one but I declined. At least she had the decency to look embarrassed. When she saw what I was buying, she leaned over and turned the little crank to scroll through the Stations, making it squeal like a fingernail on chalkboard, scrolling frontwards, then backwards. Making Him come alive again. You could see that she was having second thoughts. Then she stopped turning the crank. She put her coffee down and tilted the whole box thing back and forth. It made a sound like marbles rolling around inside. "There's something stuck in it," she said, hunching over to look. "I can't get past the Fourth Station."

I said, "Where Jesus Meets His Mother?"

Frankie looked annoyed. He didn't know the Fourth Station from a fifth wheel.

Kata straightened up. She said, "I changed my mind, Frank." She calls him Frank. "I don't want to sell it."

"Are you kidding?" he said.

"Give Georgie his check back." She picked up the shrine, which was heavy and awkward, resting the crucifix against her shoulder. Frankie was so afraid of losing that hundred and fifty bucks that he said, "Wait!" and grabbed her arm. That's when she dropped the thing. It broke—not just the crucifix but the whole wooden box and the glass window. The scroll fell out, torn to pieces, and a handful of marbles rolled away under the table. Then Kata stooped down to pick up the pieces, and the glass must have cut her hand. It was the second time I had ever seen her cry. So I punched him. Who wouldn't?

✥

WAY BACK THEN, when we were kids, I blamed myself, at least in part, when Kata took up with Frankie Tomasic, but Staramajka believed—correctly, as it turned out—that Kata had been cultivating Frankie all along, as a kind of backup, in case the Catholic Church in America let her down.

Things changed after my last trip to Jones Island with the Kaszube girl. In the middle of Holy Week, Frankie and Chuey disappeared from their usual spot in front of Solapek's tavern, and my mother decided that it was safe now to let Kata run errands for Staramajka while I was at school. There was a lot of Easter baking and egg decorating going on at the time. But my mother was wrong. By Holy Thursday, I had intercepted two notes, snatching the folded bits of butcher paper from messengers who appeared to be part of a whole network of bribed and threatened little Serbs in Frankie Tomasic's service. "Soo Line boxcar," one of the notes said. "Neer Soowidge plant," said the other one.

I didn't squeal on anybody, but the Serbs must have told Frankie the jig was up, because on Good Friday, he and Kata abandoned secrecy and came boldly to church together. I spotted them from the sanctuary during the first reading of the Passion. They were in a pew near the back, behind the rows of children and nuns. When Frankie had the nerve to come up for Communion, I glanced up at the vaulted ceiling to see if the stone angels were about to let it drop. I also tried to decapitate him with the paten when he knelt down and stuck out his tongue at Father Wojcek, who mumbled "Corpus Christi" and heedlessly put a host on it. I couldn't tell if it was the close-up view of Father Wojcek or the gold plate I was pressing into Frankie's windpipe that made his eyes bug out in such a satisfying way.

They left after Communion. I saw them slip out the side door next to the confessional. When it was finally over, and every last penitent had come up to kiss the feet of the crucifix (something Kata would have enjoyed, I couldn't help but think), I hung up my surplice and trudged home. The dark and silent front room—shades still drawn in observance of the suffering Christ—dashed any slim hope I had of finding Kata there. Only Staramajka would be at home, I thought, in her room, on her knees, filling the hours from noon to three with Sorrowful Mysteries to make up for not going to church on Good Friday.

"Georgie?" I heard her call. "Is that you?"

My grandmother was in her room, but she wasn't praying the rosary. She was sitting on her bed with Kata's wicker suitcase lying open on the floor at her feet, a *Terror Tales* in one hand, and in the other, the "Way of the Cross" booklet Kata had stolen from church. Staramajka kept glancing from Jesus languishing in the Garden in her right hand to the maiden fainting in chains in her left. I could tell by the thoughtful look on her face that she was seeing them both through new eyes. She looked up and said, "Come in, Georgie, come in. I want you to read to me."

"But these are Kata's books," I said.

"Of course they are Kata's. She is not here. Now read."

I took the open magazine she offered and began to read in the middle of a page. It was the usual stuff—an unfortunate bride baring her long, white throat to her corpse-like captor.

"No, no," Staramajka interrupted. "Not in English."

"You want me to *translate* 'Brides of the Undead'?"

"Clear your throat and read," she said. "In Croatian."

I gave it a try, struggling for a long time with *vulnerable*—a word I had looked up in the dictionary at school—and finally offering *easy to cut*, which was certainly not right but the best I could do. My grandmother listened, her forehead drawn together fiercely, a single glistening tooth biting into her lower lip. I stumbled through until I got to the part where the ghoul, his face a grinning mask of evil, prepares to initiate his bride into the ways of the undead by plunging his dagger into her heaving breast, when I stopped and looked up. "Baka," I said, "why do you want me to read this stuff?"

She scowled. "I want to know what is Kata doing with that bum Frankie."

I was afraid that I knew. Shamefaced, I told Staramajka about the last time I went out to Jones Island with Kata. I mentioned her strange baptismal request, but left out certain details, such as the exact location of her birthmark and her offer to show it to me.

"Ah," Staramajka said, sighing. "Yes. Her mother had such a mark."

"She *did*?"

"Right here," my grandmother said, and reaching across the

suitcase full of shudder pulps, she touched a place on my neck. I pulled back. She sighed again. "But I don't think Kata wants a baptism from Frankie Tomasic—that's not it."

"She thinks it will wash away the birthmark," I said.

Staramajka looked sad. "I don't think she does, Georgie. Not anymore." She handed me two pieces of paper that had been lying in her lap. One was neatly folded, the other crumpled and smoothed out again and ragged where the bottom of the page was torn off. "I found them in her books," Staramajka said. "I was afraid this would happen."

The folded one was a note from Father Wojcek to my mother, expressing on rich vellum paper in the church secretary's professional handwriting Father Wojcek's regrets that the resplendent Holy Saturday baptism could not take place as planned. I read the note to Staramajka, translating the best I could. She only shrugged. The other sheet was more important. It was the top part of a certificate of baptism from St. Stanislaus, bordered with angels and filled out in blue ink by a bolder hand. Two items on the form leaped out at me: Kata's full name—Katerina Ludmilla Budzik—and next to it, the unmistakable *Illegitima*. I must have had a look on my face as I read it, for my grandmother said gently, "Who are we to judge these things, Georgie? Maybe her father was an old Kaszube who ran away. Maybe he was some other kind of bum. What difference does it make?"

I said, "It made a difference once."

Staramajka raised an eyebrow.

"You know," I said. "When Kata's mother chased her with a knife."

My grandmother scowled. "You think her mother was try-ing to hurt her?" she said. "Because Kata was a bastard?"

"That's what everybody said."

"Tch!" said my grandmother. "What everybody said. Every-body is nobody." She leaned closer to me. "I will tell you what happened that night, Georgie. When poor Anica went after her own flesh and blood with a knife, by then already she was not right in her head anymore. But she was not trying to hurt her daughter. Oh, no." Although there was no one else in the house to hear us, Staramajka lowered her voice. "She was try-ing to save her, Georgie, to cut it out of her."

"Cut what out?" I asked in growing horror.

Staramajka threw her hands in the air, scattering shudder pulps. "The birthmark!" she cried. "The mark of death!"

I sat back on my heels and stared at my grandmother. Sud-denly we both knew, with dreadful certainty, what Kata wanted Frankie for.

❋

I GUESS WHEN you're eleven you're bound to find a girl's birthmark much more interesting than anything written on a piece of paper. The birthmark turned out to be a red herring (although it was, in fact, blue and silver—I can vouch for that). What I should have been paying attention to was her baptismal certificate. About that baptismal certificate so much more could be said. There were important details that I might have wondered about at the time, like the names I saw in the space for godparents. Alois Lenz (the tavern keeper) was one of them, Ludmilla Tomasic (Frankie's mother) was the other. Where were they, I might have asked, when Father Wojcek and my mother were busy making plans to baptize the Kaszube girl? Why didn't Mrs. Tomasic—who was my mother's best friend in Milwaukee—confirm Staramajka's theory that Kata had been baptized years ago at St. Stan's? Why on earth, I should have wondered, would Lenz and Mrs. Tomasic keep this secret from my mother? Most important, I might have noticed what was missing on the form. It was the part with places for the names of the Kaszube girl's unfortunate mother and her mysterious father. I might have asked my grandmother if she knew what happened to the part that was torn away. And if she had seen it, I might have asked her whether or not a name was written in the space marked "Father," and if there was a name, I might have asked her if he was anyone she knew.

But never in a million years would I have thought to ask my grandmother if she was hiding something in the pocket of her apron on that Good Friday, something she had torn off and stuffed there when she heard me at the door. Later, when Kata was leaving for Kenosha and Staramajka had me carry the Way of the Cross out to the car for her, I saw the round, white end of a roll of paper peeking out of the dime-size hole where the crank was attached to the workings inside the box. I tried to dig the paper out with my fingernail, thinking that I'd give my marbles one last shot at freedom, but I ended up making whatever it was fall into the box, where no one would ever find it even if Staramajka had wanted her to. For sixty-some years, I never gave that rolled-up paper another thought.

The only thing Staramajka ever told me about the Kaszube

girl's father was that I should never, ever, ask Kata who he was. "Does she even know?" I said once, not long before Kata left for Kenosha, when I was still feeling the sting of her scorn. My grandmother looked wounded by my question. "Don't ask her," is all she said. And I never did.

⁂

KATA DIDN'T COME home after the Good Friday service. Everyone went looking for her. I made several quick tours of the railroad yard, stopping twice at the gandy dancers' shack, and I even hiked out to Struck's (near the "Soowidge plant") at dusk, but I didn't find her. When my father came home from the coke plant close to midnight, he went with a lantern to check the empty house on Aldrich Street. On his way back, he saw a light in Lenz's tavern. ("Open on Good Friday?" my mother exclaimed, although it was Holy Saturday by then.) Pa stopped to ask if the old Kaszube knew where Kata was. Lenz hadn't seen her, but he offered my father an illegal beer and some good news he had received only that morning from his brother with the fishing boat in Kenosha. "My brother talked to Anica's people yesterday." Anica was the Kaszube girl's mother. "They said they would take the girl."

My mother wept in frustration when she heard. Then my sister called sharply from the upstairs porch and we all rushed out there, thinking she had seen someone in the yard or the alley below, but it was the full moon my sister wanted us to see, rising huge and almost blood-red above the roofs that hid the lake from view.

⁂

"DAD," MARY HELEN said. She obviously thought that my ears didn't work either. "I JUST TALKED TO KATE TOMASIC. FRANK'S WIFE."

They say nothing can pierce your heart like words that fall from the lips of your own child. I cringed, and at least she reduced her volume.

"They gave him a new pacemaker, Dad, and he's doing fine. It's not that big a deal, replacing a pacemaker, Mrs. Tomasic says."

Mrs. Tomasic, she says. Another arrow.

"And Dad. She wants to come and see you—whoa! Take it easy."

That's just one drawback of being on a heart monitor: there's no way to hide your true feelings.

⁂

THE RED MOON my sister called us out to see was high and white when I opened my eyes and saw near the foot of my bed a featureless figure in a long nightgown, her fine white hair released from the topknot she wore during the day and a scarf pulled tightly around her shoulders. "Wake up, Georgie!" she was saying. I held my breath until my grandmother's face emerged, all eyes and hollows, from the darkness.

"What is it, Baka?" I finally thought to whisper.

"Your friend Garcia," she said. (She would not call him

Jesus, not during Holy Week.) "He is throwing things at the house. He will wake up everybody. Hurry!"

I sat up, pulling on my pants while another shower of dirt hit the window. Staramajka put a bent finger to her lips and led me through the house to the front door, which she opened very quietly. She pulled my jacket and my father's long black coat off their hooks.

"Baka," I said, snatching her sleeve as I followed her down the stairs. "Where are we going?"

"To get Kata," she said grimly.

Outside, I ran to the end of the front porch and looked down the narrow canyon between our house and the next. "Chuey!" I whispered as loudly as I dared.

Chuey stopped in the middle of his windup and stumbled toward us. As he reached the porch, he gasped, "He's going to kill her!"

Staramajka leaned over the porch rail. She grabbed Chuey's ear and hissed, in English, "Where *is* she?"

"Struck's!" he cried, and broke away. I watched him disappear, running, through the yard and into the alley.

Staramajka was already on her way down the porch steps. "*Hajdemo!*" she called to me.

"But Baka—"

She turned to look at me fiercely. "What now?"

"You're wearing a nightgown."

She wrapped my father's big black coat around her and said again, "Let's go!"

We hadn't even reached the corner of Bay Street before we

saw a caped figure heading toward us, leaping and running, the cape flapping wildly behind it.

"Jesus, Maria," Staramajka breathed and pulled me back into the shadows between two houses.

It was Frankie. He flew past, his face as white as the lining of the cape he was struggling to unfasten as he ran. It dropped to the pavement practically at our feet and Frankie ran on, crossing the street and melting into the darkness on the other side. When my grandmother picked up the cape, I could see under the streetlight a dark spot on the lining.

"It's Kata's," I said.

Staramajka hung it over her arm.

The moon lit the rest of our way to Jones Island, where we hurried past Konkel's old fish market and two new warehouses, until we were so close to the sewage plant that we could hear— even over the sound of the lake only yards away—the swish of the water through the sluices. "Rivers of shit," I heard my grandmother mutter. On principle, she had no word for sewage plant. When at last we reached our destination, Staramajka climbed the steps of Felix Struck's tavern as matter-of-factly as if she had a drunken husband to retrieve. She rattled the doorknob.

"There's a window in the back," I said.

"Go," said Staramajka. We went around. She held the crate steady under the window while I climbed up and in.

"Kata?" I whispered, as soon as my feet touched the floor. There was no answer. Keeping my back to the wall, I peered into the sandy nooks and crannies of the place. Moonlight, pouring through the hole in the roof, made a silvery pool in front of me. Beyond it, the broken loom crouched like a giant insect, and in every corner, darkness did its usual tricks, shifting and gathering into shapes that disappeared as fast as I could turn my head to look at them. "Kata?" I said again, a little louder. When my grandmother rapped on the window behind me, I almost screamed.

"I'm going around to the door," she called up to me. "Let me in."

Staramajka found her. She was curled up on her side under the Altar of Human Sacrifice, hugging a bloody dish towel to her chest. Next to her, crumpled on the floor, was the other velvet cape, the white lining spattered with more dark stains. I knew at once that she was dead—what other fate was worthy of so much blood and moonlight? I looked away. My grandmother said sternly, "You are a foolish child," and I turned back to her again.

What I saw, to my astonishment, was Staramajka reaching down with one hand—the other still held Pa's coat shut over her nightgown—and pulling Kata to her feet. "Enough of foolishness," my grandmother was saying. "Now we go home."

It may have been the influence of the season, but for a long time afterward, I thought of the Kaszube girl as having risen from the dead.

❧

SOMEHOW SHE TALKED her way into the ICU. Maybe she bribed the nurses with customized sweatshirts. Or maybe my daughter was scared—who could blame her? So was I—and wanted company. You can bet that nobody asked my opinion. Even on a ventilator it's possible to blink twice for NO.

"Your color is good," Kata said to me. "That's one thing about these machines. They pink you right up." She picked up my hand, IV needle and all, and laid it on hers. I give her credit for that. "Don't worry," she told my daughter. "I've seen all this tube and wire business before."

Mary Helen had been making dashes to the restroom and the nearest vending machines, certain that any terrible thing that was going to happen would happen while she was gone. (She was right about that.) Kata talked her into taking a real coffee break. "And don't drink that crap from the machine either," she said. "They got much better down in the cafeteria."

As soon as my daughter was out of sight, Kata dug into her purse and pulled out a wrinkled scroll of paper. She unrolled it and held it up for me to see. The paper was ragged at the bottom and networked with creases. It trembled in her hand. "Do you see what this is?" she said. She sounded excited.

I squinted at her. My glasses were in a drawer next to the bed. Kata opened the drawer. She held the glasses up and breathed on the lenses, buffing them on her red sweatshirt before she put them on my nose, still warm. The left ear piece was poking inside my ear instead of over it, but she didn't notice. I closed one eye and made out fancy words flanked by a pair of angels on the top of the paper.

"It's my baptismal certificate, Georgie. From St. Stan's. Do you see? I found it today when the Stations of the Cross broke."

I was astonished. Could it still be that same day?

"Just today I found it!" she said. "Staramajka must have hid it in there."

She held up another piece of paper that looked equally frail. She showed me that the torn edge of this piece matched the torn edge of the other. "Do you see?" she said, leaning closer. "Do you understand?" She let the first piece of paper roll back up and fall to my chest and she moved the second one closer, trying to hold it steady in front of my face. She whispered, as if she was worried the nurses might hear, "Do you see what it says?"

In a space labeled *Parentum* was her mother's name: Anica Katerina Budzik. Below her mother's name was another, in angular writing that differed from the pious hand that had filled out the rest of the form. Josef Iljasic. My father's name.

"Do you see?" she said. "What I told you before?" She waved the strip of paper. "Do you see? Your father's name is right here. Staramajka didn't want anyone else to see it, I'll bet—especially you. So she tore it off and she hid it in the Stations of the Cross."

It was at this point that something peculiar began to happen to the top half of the baptismal certificate that had dropped from her hand down to my chest. It was getting heavier. I could feel the weight of it through my hospital gown. At first I thought Kata must be leaning on me, but no, she was standing beside the bed with both hands on her second precious piece of paper, holding it up like a lottery check. She was still talking, but I could hardly make out what she was saying, the weight on my chest was growing so fast that I wasn't sure I could stand the pressure. I hoped she wouldn't let the second piece of paper fall next to the other one, but pretty soon she did. It landed on my chest like a slab of concrete. My head felt wrong, too. Kata must have seen something in my face. Or I might have made a noise. All of a sudden she was leaning over me, cradling my head in her hands.

THE WAY THE doctor explained it to my daughter, sometimes you just can't win with sodium: too high and you drown (especially if you've got poor heart and lung function in the first place like I do), too low (or too rapid a plunge from previously sky-high levels) and your brain and spinal cord can swell up. Either way, your heart can go haywire. Or, as in my case, all of the above.

After the excitement died down, I couldn't move, not an eyebrow. Whether connections were permanently broken, the doctor couldn't say. My pupils responded to his little flashlight, but I wasn't doing any flinching, no matter how hard he pinched or pricked or tried to startle me. (It sounded like maracas he was shaking next to my ear, but I couldn't turn my head to see.) Nobody could tell if I was conscious or not. My blood gases weren't looking any better either, in spite of the ventilator.

"It's not your fault, what happened to Dad," my daughter told Kata. They were down there at the foot of the bed, in chairs the staff had brought in for them. "It wasn't anybody's fault."

"I just wanted to tell him about his father," Kata said. Her voice was thick, as if she had been crying. "Things I should have told him a long time ago, things my mother told me. But I hardly got a chance to talk. Right away his eyes started bugging out."

"I still don't understand why Dad hit your husband in the first place." Mary Helen sounded as if she had been crying, too.

"I don't know," said Kata. (She certainly did know.) "Maybe Georgie is a little jealous even yet."

"Jealous about what?" said Mary Helen.

"About me. He had a pretty big crush on me, you know."

"When you were kids, you mean?"

"It's possible to have strong feelings at that age," Kata said. "At any age."

My daughter stood up and looked at me then, hoping, I think, for a sign of strong feelings. Or any feelings. Her face was so mournful that I might have been dead already.

"My sister should be here by now!" she cried. "And where is my son? I've left messages for him everywhere. Even at the tattoo place—I don't know what else to do. Where *are* they? Why don't they come?"

Kata offered her a folded paper napkin pulled from the sleeve of her sweatshirt. Mary Helen said, "Thank you," in a wobbly voice and made use of it. She sat down again, still dabbing at her eyes with the napkin, and said, as if to show that she was back in control, "What were you going to tell Dad about his father?"

"It's a long story," Kata warned.

"I never met my grandfather," Mary Helen said. "He died before I was born."

That was all the encouragement Kata needed. She would never have a more captive audience. My daughter and I were in for the long haul.

※

"MY MOTHER'S NAME was Anica," Kata began. "Nica for short. It's spelled with a 'c' like 'Monica,' but the sound is 'tz.' Neetza."

Mary Helen dabbed at her eyes with the napkin. "Like 'pizza,'" she said.

"My mother was a Kaszube," Kata continued. "She was born on Jones Island when the Kaszubes still lived out there. She spoke Polish with German mixed in. Croatian she learned later—that's why I speak it, too, a little—and also perfectly good English from when she was a little girl in school. They took the kids to Milwaukee for school. Sometimes in a boat.

"When my mother was a kid, she worked with her father, mending and drying nets, smoking fish, all that stuff, because *her* mother died when she was born. She did that until the old man lost his fishing boat. My mother said people tried to tell him not to go out that day, a storm was coming, but he wouldn't listen, he was drinking. It was lucky—sort of—that he didn't drown. The bad part was that somebody *did* drown. My mother's cousin from Kenosha. He came to work on the old man's boat, but it turned out that the cousin liked to drink as much as his uncle. He was only a teenager, like my mother, and he was leaning over the side in that rough weather when he fell overboard. The family couldn't forgive the old man for what happened. That's one reason why, years later, when she had all her troubles, they wouldn't have nothing to do with her, even when it wasn't her fault. So many bad things happened to my mother that her own family didn't help her. They were afraid they'd catch bad luck from her, I guess, and then later, they were afraid they'd catch her sickness."

Kata was silent for a moment. The ventilator clicked and sighed.

"People can be very cruel when they're afraid," my daughter said.

"Yeah," said Kata. "After the old man lost his boat, he got a job from Lakeside Fuel Oil and Coal—you'll see what came of that—and my mother got work in boardinghouses on the mainland, in Milwaukee. She must have been sixteen or seventeen. First she just cleaned and washed clothes, then she cooked and served meals, and so forth. By the time she was working for Mrs. Tomasic on Hilbert Street, my mother knew how to practically run the place. She was an expert on bugs. The worst thing about a boardinghouse in those days was the bugs. Roaches, fleas, lice, bedbugs—you couldn't get rid of them with all those people coming and going. Mrs. Tomasic was tearing her hair out until my mother came along with her recipes for stuff to paint on the woodwork for scaring away ants and roaches or to put in the wash water for wiping out fleas and lice on the sheets. Word got around. People would come looking for rooms in Mrs. Tomasic's boardinghouse just to get rid of their fleas! I wish I knew all the recipes my mother could make—I don't know where she learned them—but by the time I was old enough, she was too sick to teach me. People thought our house on Aldrich Street was some kind of dump, but it wasn't. It didn't look too good from the outside, but inside it was clean as a whistle. Georgie's grandmother helped with that, and so did Mrs. Tomasic. She said it was the least she could do, after all the help my mother gave her, way back when.

"Mrs. Tomasic—that's Frankie's mother—she had her hands full in those days with her new baby and a dead husband. Mr. Tomasic was killed before Frankie was even born, in an accident at the leather-tanning place where he worked. They were emptying a big vat of something and Mr. Tomasic, whose English wasn't good, thought the sign said STAND HERE. Really it said STAND CLEAR. He had gone all the way back to Europe to find a bride, so when he was killed, his family wanted Mrs. Tomasic to marry one of his brothers, after they spent all that money to bring her here. At first she said no—she'd had a hard time with giving birth to Frankie and she wasn't eager to get herself in that position again—but eventually she gave in. She had five more little Tomasics, and then the second husband was electrocuted in the Milwaukee Railway strike. I was in Kenosha by then, but we read about the strike in the papers. Mrs. Tomasic didn't marry anybody else after that. She must have thought, enough is enough."

"I don't blame her," said Mary Helen.

"Apart from her and baby Frankie, the people who lived in the boardinghouse were workingmen, foreign born. My mother's languages came in very handy. Between her and Mrs. Tomasic, who knew Slovenian and Croatian and a little Italian, they had most of the men covered. A lot of the languages were pretty similar. My mother said people would talk two, three languages at once, each one speaking what they knew best but mostly understanding each other. Some of the men in the boardinghouse had good jobs at International Harvester and Pfister Vogel—that's a factory, too—but some were only day laborers. Joe Iljasic was one of those."

"Joe—that's my grandfather?"

"Yeah. And he was also a gandy dancer in the railroad yard."

"What *is* a gandy dancer?"

"You don't know? It's a guy who pounds on the rail with a big sledgehammer to make it straight. Now they do it with a machine. Joe worked for years doing that. He used to leave those magazines for me in the gandy dancers' shack, where they ate lunch and things, him and the other men. Magazines with scary stories I liked. I used to go there and look at them. Georgie went, too, sometimes." Kata's tone had changed, as if she were smiling down there at the foot of the bed. "Your dad ever tell you about that?"

"No."

"Oh, he should have. I wish he did."

Kata sighed pointedly. Neither of them said anything for a moment, giving me ample time to feel the weight of everything I should have done and wished I'd said in my life. Then she continued.

"Joe was always hoping that Harvester or somebody would hire him for a regular job with benefits like the company doctor and days off with pay. That's how my mother convinced him to sign up for English lessons. She said it would help him get a regular job and eventually it did. My mother taught English to Georgie's dad, and Georgie pretty much taught me how to read when we were kids. With those scary magazines. What goes around comes around I guess is true, at least to some extent."

"What about my grandmother?" said Mary Helen. "Was she living in the boardinghouse, too?"

"What—you mean Joe's wife Agnes? Oh no, no, no. She was still in the old country. That was the way with a lot of the men in the boardinghouses. They came to America to make money and then they sent it back home to their families, or else they worked to bring their families here. Like the Mexicans do nowadays. Same thing. During the war—this was World War I, remember, before me or your father was born—a lot of people ended up like Joe and his wife Agnes, separated for years. Agnes didn't come to Milwaukee until 1920, the year Georgie was born. I don't know if they could have come sooner. Travel was not so safe, after the war. I do know that Joe's mother—we called her Staramajka, you know that word? like Grandmother?—she really hated Milwaukee. All she wanted her whole life was to go home to her village, but she never saw it again."

A nurse came in and checked all the monitor lines and the IV—they were being extra careful now. Kata waited. After the nurse went out again, she said, "My mother met Georgie's father in 1917. That's the part Georgie don't believe, but it's true. That was a crazy time in Milwaukee, my mother said. Half the people here spoke German back then. When the war first started, a lot of them were rooting for Germany. They had dances to raise money for German widows and orphans and everything. If it was up to Milwaukee, I think the United States would go in on the side of Germany if they had to get into the war at all. But nobody wanted to get into the war, my mother said. They were having peace parades and everything, just like the sixties for Vietnam. Then America declared war on Germany—that was in 1917—and all of a sudden you couldn't say '*Guten Tag*' anymore without getting yourself in trouble. And Joe Iljasic, he wasn't in much better shape because where he was from—that was Austria-Hungary—they were on the same side as the Germans, right? That's why my mother and Mrs. Tomasic both told Joe that even though he didn't speak German and his name wasn't German, it was more important than ever for him to learn to talk like an American."

❧

THEY USED TO linger at the table after Sunday dinner, Kata said, Mrs. Tomasic on one side with the baby in her lap and the *Milwaukee Journal* spread out before her, Joe on the other side with his book. Anica would gather the plates in a leisurely way, balancing a stack on her forearm and stopping from time to time to peek over Joe's shoulder at *English for Foreigners*. Joe had borrowed the copy from a fellow who taught lunchtime classes at International Harvester, where men could earn raises for learning to say things like, "I hear the starting whistle" and "It is time to go into the shop." Joe was working on Lesson Two.

"I hear da vist—" he said and paused. "I hear da—"

"Whistle?" Anica suggested.

"Give me the book," Mrs. Tomasic said. She let the baby slide off her lap to sit on the floor. With her finger she marked the place on the page and said, "Go."

"I hear da fife minute vistul," Joe said.

"Whistle," said Mrs. Tomasic, leaving only a little "v" in her "w."

"I hear da fife minute—vwhistle."

"Good!" said Anica.

"What then?" Mrs. Tomasic prompted.

Joe frowned.

"It is time . . . ?" she hinted.

He tugged at his mustache.

"To go into the shop," Anica whispered.

"Oh, Joe!" said Mrs. Tomasic. She handed the book back to him. "You oughta come with me down to night school," she said. "They got better lessons there." English was serious business for Mrs. Tomasic. She bought a *Journal* every Sunday and carried it around for the rest of the week, following her teacher's advice to practice reading every chance she got. "At night school, they gonna teach you more than when the whistle blows."

Anica agreed. "They'll teach you hello and how are you, what's your name, everything."

"I don't get no job for hello how are you," Joe said in Croatian.

"*English Only* at the table," Mrs. Tomasic reminded him as she folded her newspaper. She stood up and tucked little Frankie under one arm, leaving the other hand free to hold the paper. At the kitchen door, she stopped and turned around.

"'Carp Sales Friday at Second Ward Market,'" she read to Joe and Anica by way of good-bye. "Seven cents a pound!" Headlines and advertising were her specialties.

Now only the two of them were left in the dining room. Anica tapped the next sentence in Joe's book with the tip of her finger. He could feel her skirt brushing his elbow. He squinted at the page and said, "I vork on—on—"

"Until?" said Anica.

"Ontill! I vork ontill da vwhistle blows to—?"

"Quit," said Anica.

"Kvit?"

"Quit. It means finish, kaput, the end."

"Oh, sure. Quit. I work until da whistle blows to quit," he said, whistling past each "w."

"And then?"

"I go home!"

"Right! See?" She leaned over the book again. Her sleeve— or maybe her apron—smelled faintly of soap and starch. "Here it says, 'I go home.'" She looked up and down the table. "As soon as I get all this washed up, then *I* go home."

Joe gave his mustache a quick brushing with the back of his index finger—two strokes to the left, three to the right—a sign that he was coming up with something to say.

"I gonna help you," he said finally, "vwit da table."

Anica set down the stack of plates and looked at him. "Sometimes you speak pretty good English, Joe."

Joe was pleased to hear her say it. He was pleased about nearly everything in those days. The first night that he spent in Mrs. Tomasic's boardinghouse, Joe thought he must have died and gone to heaven. For more than a year he had been sleeping in shifts in an upstairs flat with a family from the village back home—a family overflowing with daughters and sons, cousins and nephews, spouses and children, the head count exceeding the bed count times three. Joe would come home from work in the morning to sleep in the bed that three little girls left empty (and sometimes damp) when they got up for school. When his work schedule changed, he had to move to a flea-infested roominghouse on Canal Street, where the proprietor rented his bed to any fellow off the street who wanted it during the day. At Mrs. Tomasic's boardinghouse, Joe shared a green-wallpapered room with two other men, but the bed was his own. To Joe, the narrow mattress, clean white sheet, and vermin-free blanket were accommodations worthy of Paradise.

The young woman who had done her best to explain in some kind of Polish Mrs. Tomasic's rules for meals and use of the bath compared pretty favorably with his idea of an angel, as well. It wasn't only that Anica sang like one while she worked. On the very first day, Joe admired the delicate way she showed him to the bathroom, where a steaming bath that smelled like vinegar awaited him. He never told anyone that he was shocked at first—perhaps this was not the kind of place he thought it was—but then, thanks to Anica's tactful behavior, he understood. It was the standard antiflea procedure. After providing him with a towel, trousers, shorts and shirt, she had stood discreetly outside the door, waiting for him to hand forth his own dirty clothes. These she had not thrown away or burned, as Joe feared she might. Instead, she washed and pressed them and left them folded on his bed the next day, having repaired a hole at the knee of his trousers and sewn five buttons on the shirt! When he came home from work and found them there, he caught Anica with her arms full of linens in the hall—she and the Slovenians were the only ones he understood in those early days—and he showed her the shirt and trousers. Whose were they? he asked her. She said they were his. He thought she must have misunderstood his question. She laughed and told him to take a closer look. Sure enough, inside the collar band was the red and black cross that his wife had stitched into all three of his shirts to mark them as his own. When Joe turned to ask, with some concern, if there was any extra charge for laundry, Anica was already gone. He heard her singing on the stairs.

Mrs. Tomasic's boardinghouse also gave Joe his first experience with hot, running water, and after a few weekly baths in the white porcelain tub with feet like the claws of an eagle, he began to wonder how his poor wife Agnes had managed to sleep beside his unwashed self through the two winters they had spent as husband and wife. In the summer, at least, he had bathed in the river.

"Well, she never took a bath in a tub either," Roman Jagodzinski pointed out to him one Saturday when Joe came upstairs, scrubbed and glowing. This was true, and made Joe picture his wife bathing in the wash house behind the kitchen, where he had sometimes caught a glimpse of her with her blouse folded down to her waist. (His wife Agnes was a very modest woman.) He thought about watching her dip a cloth into a bucket and rub it against a cake of hard lye soap before she used it to scrub her neck and chest and under her arms. He remembered how she lifted her breast with her hand—but per-haps this was not something for him to be thinking about while sitting here on his bed under the eye of young Roman Jagodzinski. Joe had many reasons to feel guilty about Agnes, but of all the ways he had wronged her—coming to America, leaving her with his mother, letting the war rise up between them, and worse things to come—he always felt the sharpest pang of guilt for being cleaner than she was.

The only thing Joe didn't like about Mrs. Tomasic's board-inghouse was English-Only-at-the-table, a house rule she had decreed in part to help the men learn the new language, but also to make clear whose side her establishment was on when it came to the war in Europe. As far back as 1915, when Milwau-kee newspapers were still printing banner headlines that announced German victories—"Lusitania Sinks!"—with more excitement than regret, Mrs. Tomasic already knew which way the wind was going to blow.

Her situation was a little more complicated than most. While other boardinghouses in Milwaukee tended to attract residents of a single nationality, sometimes from a single city or village, Mrs. Tomasic's place appealed to the cleanest types from any country. Living under her roof in 1917 were four Germans, five Poles, two Italians, and four Slavs, including two Slovenians, and Joe Iljasic, her newest boarder, who spoke Croatian more than anything else. As proof of their loyalty—and hers—to America, she required the men to gather in the parlor in clean shirts and brushed trousers every Sunday night for a lesson in American History provided by one Mrs. Simon, a Milwaukee schoolteacher with prematurely white hair and military posture. Mrs. Simon made the rounds of several South Side boardinghouses each week, dispensing civic knowledge under the auspices of the Milwaukee County Americanization Committee and the Wisconsin Women's Club. Mrs. Tomasic had provided two local policemen with gifts of apple streudel and homemade *šlivovice* in hopes of being chosen for the program. She ensured good attendance among her boarders by serving walnut *kolače* and coffee with cream in the parlor every Sunday night.

Now, in principle, Joe Iljasic was not opposed to learning English, nor to eating *kolače* and drinking coffee with cream, but he lived in such terror of being asked a question (or three) by Mrs. Simon that he couldn't enjoy the refreshments, which he consumed continuously in an effort to keep his mouth full at all times. He didn't know that she would never call on him to answer her questions, which she asked in groups of three for pedagogical reasons known only to herself, because she couldn't pronounce his last name. Italian names were her forte. This is why she called on poor Tony Corrao at least twice every Sunday, no matter how far he positioned himself from her reserved seat in the parlor's only fully upholstered chair.

"So, Mr. Corrao," she typically began, rolling the "r" and straightening her shoulders in a way that caused the buttons on the front of her ample gray jacket to stand at attention. Immediately, Tony Corrao would set his coffee down on the chair between his legs and wipe his hands on his pants, rubbing them up and down his thighs as if he had a cramp there. Last Sunday she had begun by asking him to name the first president of the United States of America.

Tony, who had his own solution for unpronounceable names, replied promptly, "George da Wash."

"George Vashington he means," said one of the Germans, a man named Erich Schultz.

"Atsa what I say," Tony protested.

"And who is president now?" Mrs. Simon asked him, shooting a stern look at the German.

"Mr. da Wils."

Erich Schultz said, "Pff." The rest of the men, Joe included, slurped their coffees tactfully. Mrs. Simon frowned. "That's Mr. *Wilson*," she said. She tried again: question number three. "And could *you* be president, Mr. Corrao?"

"Excuse me please, I got pretty good job at Harvester," Tony said, and everyone took another loud sip of coffee.

Even more distressing for Joe than Sunday nights with Mrs. Simon were the Saturdays beforehand, when Mrs. Tomasic made dinner itself contingent upon participation in a study session aimed at improving the men's performance the following day. Anybody who wanted to advance from the soup to the fried pork or chicken had to practice English Expressions for Everyday Conversation under the guidance of Anica, whose Jones Island English was just as good as Mrs. Simon's, at least to Mrs. Tomasic's ear. Unfortunately for Joe, Anica had no trouble at all with his last name.

"Mr. Iljasic!" she liked to say, causing everyone to look at Joe expectantly.

No matter how many times she called on him this way, Joe's face always flushed. He did much better with English on a one-to-one basis. Not wanting to break his concentration at such moments by looking at Anica's face, he fixed his gaze on the white collar of her dress. She had a diamond-shaped birthmark on her neck, about midway between her collar and the line of her jaw. From where Joe sat, one chair away from Anica's place at the head of the table, the birthmark looked dark blue, almost iridescent. When she tilted her head, it seemed to be part of the small golden hoop of her earring.

"Mr. Iljasic," she said again, startling him once more. His eyes darted from the collar to her face. "Tell us. Where are you from?"

Joe stroked his mustache, left side, right side, left again. "From village," he said finally, "by name of Novo Selo. In *magyar*—in Hungarian, is Totujfalu."

"Very good!" Anica said. "Do you have family there?"

"Yah."

"No one-word answers!" said Joe's roommate Roman, a Polish boy of eighteen, already naturalized, who spoke excellent English himself. Roman Jagodzinski had made his own way in the United States since he was twelve, when he lost his father to a meal of spoiled beef on shipboard that nearly did the boy in, too. To this day, Roman ate slowly, tentatively, fearful of contamination, even at Mrs. Tomasic's table—one of few places he would eat at all—and he was as skinny as a stick. Rules were important to him. "You have to say more than one word," he reminded Joe.

"I got mother," Joe said, "name of Jelena. In English is Helen." (Mrs. Tomasic had told him that.) "I got brother, name of Marko. My father, name of Josef like me, he is dead."

"And a wife!" Roman said. "You got a wife."

"And I got a wife," Joe said. He found it even harder to look Anica in the eye as he said this—although he found it hard to look her in the eye at any time, perhaps because her eyes were the same bright blue as his, and looking at them was like looking in the mirror that Mrs. Tomasic had hung in the bathroom so the men could shave themselves properly. Back in the village, Joe's wife Agnes had blue eyes, too, a lighter, smokier blue that turned to gray when she was unhappy. He imagined that by now, after almost three years with no way to get word to each other, his wife's eyes must have no blue left in them at all. When a chance comes, you have to take it, Joe had told her before he left. It may not come again.

Everyone was looking at him now—except for Roman, who turned to Anica and asked, "What happened to question number three? You only asked two. Joe needs another question."

Gently, Anica asked him, "What is your wife's name?"

"Agnes," said Joe.

Roman began to bristle. Joe spoke up again.

"My wife, her name is Agnes."

⚜

ON THE MORNING the letter from Agnes arrived, Mrs. Tomasic was at the Second Ward market on 8th and Mitchell, waiting with hundreds of Polish women to purchase her share of carp and suckers for seven cents a pound. Unlike Roman Jagodzinski, who sorted the mail in her absence, Mrs. Tomasic would have recognized at once the significance of a letter that came from the old country, apparently by way of the moon, if the condition of the envelope was any clue. Roman was far too interested in burning Erich Schultz's latest issue of *Germania* in the sink, page by page, to pay much attention to the series of postmarks, so many they almost covered Joe's latest address. He put the battered envelope out on the table with the rest of the mail. Joe discovered it there when he came home from the railroad yard and took it to his room without saying a word to anybody, mortally afraid of what the contents might be.

The letter was short—just four lines written in his wife's curious combination of Croatian words and Hungarian spelling. When he finished it and was absolutely certain that he had read the news correctly, he ran out into the back yard where Mrs. Tomasic and Anica were putting chunks of ice in a washtub lined with fish. He waved the letter in the air. "Look! Look at this!" he cried. "I'm a father!"

Anica and Mrs. Tomasic both dropped the ice chunks they were holding and, shaking their cold and fishy hands dry, they hustled Joe inside the house, kissing his cheeks on the way. Inside, Mrs. Tomasic washed her hands and broke out the *šlivovice*. Raising their glasses, the women said, "To mother and child!" and Joe said, "To my son!" He took a drink and added, "Or daughter!" He put down his glass and asked the two women, "Do you think it will be a boy or girl? I know some men they say, give me a son, but for me, a daughter would be welcome, too, a little girl. Jelena we'll name her, for my mother." He threw the letter and envelope into the air, watched them float back down to the table, and lifted his glass again. When he put it down, it was empty, and both women were looking at him.

"You mean the baby isn't born yet?" said Anica.

Joe's expression changed.

Mrs. Tomasic put down her glass and wiped her hands again on her apron. She picked up the envelope. "Joe!" she said after a moment. "This letter was mailed in 1914." She showed him the postmark. "See this here? It's three years old!"

"Really?" He took the envelope from her. "That took a long time to get here."

"Don't you see what that means?" Mrs. Tomasic said.

It meant, Joe thought, that he had done his wife Agnes a grave injustice thinking ill of her, even for a moment.

"It means your baby must be almost three years old by now!"

Joe stared at Mrs. Tomasic, then at Anica, then down at the letter on the table. He pictured the village of Novo Selo, the muddy street, the midwife—a whiskery woman named Gospođa Dragovich—hurrying through the mud. Joe knew that Agnes didn't care very much for Mrs. Dragovich, who also told fortunes and diagnosed illnesses by melting the wax from a person's ear. Agnes's mother had lost three babies, all of whom died in the hands of *Baka Draga*, as other people called her. (Agnes called her *"Baka Vraga"*—Devil Granny—though not to her face.) He watched Mrs. Tomasic pouring more brandy into the tiny stemmed glasses.

"Do you think everything came out right—that Agnes is well, and the child?" he asked as she handed him one of the glasses.

"Oh, I'm sure of it," said Mrs. Tomasic, crossing herself quickly. Then she picked up her glass and raised it again to the health of mother and child. Anica did the same.

Joe raised his glass and then lowered it slowly. His fingers on the stem were, like the rest of him, very still. He was thinking—suddenly they were all thinking—that his wife Agnes might be three years dead. He sat down slowly on a kitchen chair and looked up at the two women.

"Do you think, if she was—if it went wrong—that I would feel it, that I would know it somehow?"

Neither Mrs. Tomasic nor Anica knew what would be the right thing to say. Anica did not mention that her own mother had died when she was born. Finally, Mrs. Tomasic crossed herself again and told Joe how her mother had felt the passing of her father—a ferryman who drowned in the Sava—as a chill that did not leave her until her husband was pulled from the river and dressed in dry clothes for burial. She asked Joe, "Did you feel any chills lately?"

"Not that I remember," he said. "But it would be three years ago I should have felt it, no?"

They looked at one another.

"Oh, this is nonsense!" said Anica. "Your wife is alive and well and you are a father, Josef Iljasic. I can feel it in my bones."

"Oh yeah? Do you feel a boy or a girl in your bones?" Joe asked her. They laughed and drank their brandy.

Later that evening, Joe was sitting on the porch, rereading the letter from Agnes, when Anica came out the door, going home. He got up. Something anxious in his face, as well as the letter in his hand, made her say to him, "Walk with me," and together they walked down Hilbert to Homer Street. When they reached East Bay and their feet turned toward Jones Island, she asked him about his wife. "What is she like?"

"Agnes is a good woman," Joe said, careful to speak in the present tense. This was hard to do, not because he was speaking English but because he had been away from her now for almost twice as long as they had been man and wife together. "I'm sure she makes very good as mother," he said, although for the life of him, he could not picture her with a child—their child—in her arms. He was glad now that he had left her with his mother, who was good at keeping babies alive and who would be so grateful to Agnes for giving her a grandchild that the many differences between them would have no doubt melted away. Of course, Joe's brother Marko could be married by now and also a father. Unless he had gone into the army. Agnes had said nothing about Marko. Three years to get a letter through, Joe thought, and she writes only four lines.

"What does she look like?"

"Who?"

Anica laughed. "Your wife!"

"She is—short." Short and round—but not fat, Joe thought—where Anica was tall and too skinny, the ladies in the village would say. He added, "And she is light."

"Light? Do you mean her skin is light in color?"

"Yes, light skin. Also light hair, light eyes—blue."

"Let me see your eyes, Joe," Anica said.

He held his breath while she leaned toward him. "Joe," she said, "I think it's a blue-eyed child you have waiting for you in your village."

"Same like you!" said Joe.

WHEN AGGIE ARRIVED at the hospital later that afternoon or evening—who can tell?—there was so much weeping
and gnashing of teeth that Kata stood up to make room for my
daughters' grief. "I just knew I was going to be too late, I knew
it," Aggie kept saying.

Kata bent over me and whispered, "I'll be back."

My daughters sat and wept together over my cold feet,
lamenting birthdays of mine that they had missed, visits they
should have made, phone calls. Aggie regretted—as well she
might—that her twin boys had grown up in California, tragically separated from their grandfather. Mary Helen regretted
the burritos I ate at the mall. Aggie was sorry that she hadn't
been around more to help when Mom was sick. Mary Helen
said (not very honestly) that no one blamed Aggie for that.
There was a fresh round of tears. Eventually, though, they settled down, reduced to sniffling and the blowing of noses.
When a nurse came to the doorway, they both looked up at her
expectantly. She flicked my IV tube, touched a few knobs and
switches, and when she left, Aggie said, "So who's the old lady
in the elf outfit?" (Kata wore matching red sweatpants with her
autumn leaf sweatshirt.) Mary Helen explained.

"The other guy's wife? What's *she* doing here?" said Aggie,
sounding indignant. "What is she talking about?"

"I think it's something she wants Dad to hear."

"Mary Helen," Aggie said, more gently, "Dad can't hear."

"How do you know? They say sometimes people in a
coma—"

"Look at him."

They looked at me. Mary Helen started crying again. "I

wish Robbie could have gotten here. Dad was always so crazy about Robbie." Aggie put her arm around her sister.

I hoped Kata would get back before they decided to pull the plug.

꙳

MAY 1917 WAS a particularly difficult month for Mrs. Tomasic and her lodgers (Kata said when she returned, bearing bagels). Two of the men—German-born cousins who worked at the leather factory and had, in fact, pulled what was left of Mr. Tomasic from the contents of the fatal vat—showed up drunk for supper one evening. They had come from the court-house by way of six different taverns, including Felix Struck's place on Jones Island, after their final applications for citizen-ship had been denied. Only a year ago, with a little help from Anica, Erich Schultz had won five dollars from the *Milwaukee Journal* for his third-place entry in the "Why I Love America" contest. Now that war had been declared, both Erich and his cousin Walter were suddenly enemy aliens, or alien enemies, the two men could not agree in their drunkenness on which way the judge had put the slander. Instead of sitting down to celebrate his citizenship with a nice dinner of fried fish, Erich Schultz had splashed what remained in his bucket of beer all over the dining room table, singing "God Damn America" (in English Only) and setting off a fight with Roman Jagodzinski. When Joe tried to take Erich Schultz aside to calm him down, Schultz broke two house rules at once by spitting on the floor and growling in Polish, which he spoke as well as he spoke

German, "What's the matter with you, you crazy Hunkie? You're gonna be the enemy alien, too!"

Overhearing this, Roman Jagodzinski had picked up a chair, intending to hit both men over the head with it—patriotism preceding friendship in Roman's heart—but somehow he had swung and missed and cracked his own kneecap with the tip of the chair leg, ending both the fight and Roman's hopes for a military career. Only yesterday, down at the South Side Armory, he had consumed thirteen bananas, a large box of crackers, and a half-dozen glasses of water in a vain effort to meet the weight requirement for enlistment. Despite having spent the rest of the day upstairs with a bucket beside his bed, Roman had been planning to eat hearty for a week and try again.

"*Dumkopf!*" Erich growled as they lifted him, cursing and sobbing, from the floor. "We haf probably saved your stupid life."

"It ain't just the war, it's the heat makes everybody crazy," Mrs. Tomasic said later in the evening, after the enemy aliens had carried Roman to the Emergency Hospital on Windlake Avenue and brought him back with his leg in a splint. She fanned herself with a section of the newspaper she had been reading. "Ninety degrees in May! It's like the end of the world is coming. Look at this." She poked the paper. "In here it says a guy shoots himself because he can't get rid of the hiccups."

"No!" said Anica. She was sitting on the other side of the table, attempting to reassemble Mrs. Tomasic's favorite bowl from the old country—another casualty of the afternoon's hostilities.

"You sure you got the words right?" Joe asked. He was standing by the back door, looking out, with his hands in his pockets, worrying about his future.

"What do you mean, do I got the words right?" said Mrs. Tomasic. "It says right here." And skipping over the words she didn't know, Mrs. Tomasic read: "'Ray F. Garvey, 37, salesman for the Milwaukee Casket Company, while visiting under—'" She frowned. "Undertaker! you know, like Schurell on Mitchell Street? 'While visiting undertaker in' someplace—" (she did not attempt "Sioux City, Iowa")—"'shot himself through the right temple.'" She tapped the side of her head to show them where.

Joe, who had come around to look over Mrs. Tomasic's shoulder, pointed to a different headline. "What does that say?"

"'Fate of Balkans Still in—'" The next word was "Balance," but Mrs. Tomasic didn't recognize it, so she offered a reasonable, if unphonetic, substitute. "Trouble," she said. "Fate of Balkans Still in Trouble."

"And that?" Joe touched the smaller headline under the first.

"What?" said Mrs. Tomasic. "The number? It's five. You know the numbers, don't you?"

"Five what?"

"Five—million, it says."

"What else? More than one word is there."

Reluctantly, Mrs. Tomasic read, "'Five million already killed in Europe.'"

Joe straightened up. He walked toward the door.

"I think that's talking about soldiers, Joe," Mrs. Tomasic called after him. "Not—" The back door closed behind him. "Not people."

⚜

"I TELL YOU what, Anica," said Mrs. Tomasic the next Sunday. "I ain't risking my life no more to buy fish in that mob on Eight Street. Mrs. Simon can't come for lessons today. Let's go out to Jones Island."

While Anica got the coaster wagon ready for the baby, Mrs. Tomasic went looking for Joe. He had been hiding out ever since he found out that when the United States got around to declaring war on the Austro-Hungarian Empire, he, too, would be an enemy alien. A walk by the lake would be good for him, Mrs. Tomasic thought. She knocked on the door of the room he shared with Roman and Tony Corrao.

"*Da?*" came a voice from inside.

"Is that Joe?" she said through the door. She used Croatian, too.

After a tiny pause, he said, "I'm sleeping."

"Are you decent?"

Bed springs squeaked. "Yeah, yeah, come in," he said.

He was sitting, rumpled and sweaty, on his bed. The other two beds were neatly made (Roman was resting his leg downstairs, where it was cooler), and sunlight poured in through the window.

"Whew, Joe! How come you shut the window? You're gonna die of the heat."

"Too much noise," he said, but he didn't protest while she propped it open with a stick. The breeze stirred the apron over her dress.

She turned around, dusting her palms. It would take some talking to get Joe to come along. She would have to choose her arguments carefully.

"You want to walk out to Jones Island and buy some fish?" she said.

Joe looked at her, scratching his chest.

"Anica is coming."

Joe walked in the middle, pulling the wagon, with Mrs. Tomasic on his right and Anica on the left, their skirts flapping briskly around their ankles, each one carrying a tin bucket in one hand and holding onto her Sunday straw hat with the other. Halfway there, Mrs. Tomasic untied the scarf from around her neck and wrapped it, like a babushka, over her hat.

In May the narrow isthmus of Bay Street should have been underwater this close to the lake, but the spring had been so dry and hot that the road was rock hard where it wasn't covered by cinders. As they got nearer to their destination, the road turned to sand, and they encountered a few strolling couples. The women nodded politely and the men doffed their caps, and one of them—a tall fellow with a well-dressed woman on his arm—greeted Anica by name.

"Who's that?" Joe asked.

"Auggie Wolf," Anica said. "And his wife Marta."

Mrs. Tomasic peeked around Joe and winked at Anica. "That Marta don't look too glad to see you."

Anica made a long-suffering face.

"That fellow Wolf used to be sweet on our Anica," Mrs. Tomasic explained to Joe, who turned around to get another look at him.

Blindfolded, they could have followed their ears and noses to Konkel's open-air fish market. The roof was covered with gulls and the gulls were screaming their objections to the nets draped over the open sides of the structure from the roof to the ground, protecting tables redolent with fish. Behind each table stood a child with a fan made of leafy branches to discourage flies. A score of women, some in aprons and babushkas, others in elaborate hats, examined piles of perch and crappies, red lake crabs, whiskered bullheads, and more. Joe pulled the wagon toward the opening in the nets.

"Wait!" said Anica, laying her hand on his arm. "We're going this way."

They skirted the fish market, moving very slowly over the hardened ruts in the street, past a wooden building with round windows like portholes and a name—GOV. ANTON KUBIAK—in gold letters over the door. It was the kind of door that swung back and forth without stopping, a good thing for the stream of men and boys bearing buckets either full of foam or newly emptied, depending on whether the bearer was on his way in or out. At one point, Joe had to stop and take a detour around a man in the street with a bucket to his lips and his head thrown back, oblivious to everything but the beer flowing down his throat and the front of his shirt in approximately equal measure. To Joe's surprise, Anica stopped and said something in the man's ear. He shrugged her off. He was a grizzled old fellow, rather damp in the pants as well as the shirt, and Joe thought she would do better to give him a wide berth. He was about to tell her so when Mrs. Tomasic snatched his sleeve.

"It's her father," she whispered.

Joe stared. He knew nothing about Anica's life on Jones Island. Every morning she showed up in Mrs. Tomasic's kitchen in time to serve breakfast—no need to ring a bell or blow a whistle to announce that it was ready, not with Anica in the kitchen singing polkas or dirges in Polish or German, depending on the weather and her mood. Usually, she was still there—sewing or hanging laundry in the yard or mixing up her concoctions—when Joe came home between first shift, in the railroad yard, and second shift, usually at Harvester or the coke plant. Only on Sundays was he there to see her walking down Hilbert to Bay Street after dinner was over and the dishes put away, on her way home. Sometimes he walked with her, turning around when the road changed from cinders to sand. It was impossible for him to picture Anica—clean and smooth Anica, her collar and apron ironed and starched—coming home to a fellow like this. Did she make him supper? Did she wash the beer out of his shirts and trousers? Mrs. Tomasic tugged on Joe's arm just in time to keep Anica from catching him while he stared.

"To Struck's!" Anica said when she caught up with them again.

They approached the red-brick tavern from the back, where two men stood at a long wooden table with a mountain of fish at one end. One man chopped off heads and neatly gutted the fish, then tossed the entrails over his shoulder to a shrieking, swooping flock of gulls. The birds caught most of his offerings in midair. The rest of the fish he slid down the table to the man beside him, who gave it a slap, scrape, scrape, scales flying like a shower of sparks, until a final slap of his knife on the tail sent the fish somersaulting into a half barrel at the end of the table. When the barrel was full, two boys delivered it to a woman tending a row of cauldrons that hung over open fires behind the tavern. The boys moved fast, for the men went on cleaning and scraping without pause.

"This is the place," Anica said. From inside, a concertina could be heard, playing at a frantic tempo. She took the buckets and rolled the wagon under a lilac bush. Then she gathered her skirt with her free hand and started up the steps, Mrs. Tomasic right behind her, little Frankie in her arms.

"We're going in?" Joe asked, hesitating behind them. Even in Milwaukee, he had never heard of women in a tavern. Also, he wished he had changed his shirt.

Anica looked over her shoulder. "It's the Feast of Mary Magdalen today," she said. "Everybody does what they want!"

A curly-haired man with a folded sleeve where his left arm should have been met them at the door. He held it open with his foot and greeted Anica very enthusiastically, taking the buckets off her hands.

"What about the fish?" Joe shouted to Mrs. Tomasic. He looked around, but Anica had already disappeared. Had she gone off with the one-armed man?

"You'll see," said Mrs. Tomasic. "Look." She pointed with her chin. Anica was standing on something that raised her waist-high above the crowd. The man with the concertina stood beside her.

The price of a two-gallon bucket of perch (a fine fish which would have cost them at least twelve cents a pound at the market, Mrs. Tomasic told Joe) was four Kaszubish songs—two mostly in Polish, two in German—and a grand finale of "America, the Beautiful," in English. People sang along, especially with "America," but Anica's pure soprano rose above the rest. When she finished, amid cheers and clapping, the men near the front handed her down from the bar and the concertina skipped into a polka. Joe fought to make his way to the front, where Anica, dancing with the one-armed man, pointed him out to Felix Struck, the owner, and before he knew what was happening, Joe—"Joe! Joe!"—was handed a bucket of Struck's own brew—an old German recipe. After drinking a fourth of it, Joe felt as if he'd known these Kaszubes all his life. After drinking another fourth, he danced a polka with Mrs. Tomasic and the baby. By the time that dance was over, Joe's head was spinning. People kept calling "Joe!" and handing him the bucket of beer—somebody was refilling it—and before long he had completely lost track of Anica and Mrs. Tomasic. Then somebody gave him a plate and he ate perch and potatoes drenched in butter, spitting out the little fishbones and seeing before his mind's eye the sparkling scales and the flying entrails and the gulls snapping up a headless silver perch as it tumbled through the air. He ate it all before he felt his head turn heavy as a brick and he knew exactly what was going to happen next.

How he got outside in time he would never know. He had barely finished depositing a stomachful of beer and boiled fish under the lilac bush when he heard someone calling his name.

He stood up, the ground tilting under his feet, and reached for a branch to steady himself. Anica cried from the doorway, "There you are!" She had been tasting a little homemade German brew herself. (Everybody does what she wants on the Feast of Mary Magdalen!) Joe forced himself to take a few steps and met her halfway between the lilacs and the tavern, a spot where the cooling lake wind came unimpeded over the breakwater. The wind pressed hard enough at Joe's back to feel like a great hand holding him gently upright in spite of his spinning head. The concertina poured a waltz out the windows above them.

Anica grabbed his hand and dragged him up the steps. "I saw you dancing, Joe!" she said. "Now you have to dance with me."

It was a sobering experience. The moment her hand touched his shoulder, all the numbing influence of the alcohol dried up in an instant and he was left with every nerve on alert. He fell behind the beat and Anica leaned close to his ear to count, "*One* two three. *One* two three." This did not help his coordination. He tried not to breathe in her direction. He didn't realize until the next day, while he was bringing a sledgehammer down against the side of a rail in the switching yard, the echo of the blow ringing in his arms and fingers and teeth, how much he must have hurt her feelings when the dance was over and he said, dizzily, "Ain't it time to go?"

❧

WHAT DO I know about my father?

He was Joe to Lenz and Mrs. Tomasic, but to my mother he

was Josef, with an English "J" and an "s" like "z." To Staramajka—her "J" like a "Y" in Croatian—he was Josef or Josip or, in rarer moments of affection, Joza.

I called him Pa.

He smoked a pipe. When he came to Milwaukee as a young man, he knew from the start (though my mother did not) that he had come to stay. He confessed this to me in a whisper not long before he died. His lungs gave out on him, too. He didn't last as long as I have—he was barely sixty—but he had both tobacco smoke and coal dust clogging up his alveoli. He let my mother name me George, after a favorite uncle of hers, when I should have been Joseph like him. He worked two full-time jobs. Except on Sundays, I hardly ever saw him. I knew his presence mainly by the lingering smell of his pipe.

My father was wiry and small. I used to think I looked like him, only I got taller than he ever did and my eyes are brown. He had blue eyes—all right, blue eyes like Kata's. They were especially startling when he came home from the coke plant at midnight with his face dusted black. Usually, I was asleep by then, but once in a while he brought two or three coal-blackened men home with him to sit in the back yard after midnight, drinking home-brewed beer and eating sausages my mother made to feed her family, she said, not my father's drunken friends. On those nights, I could look out the bedroom window and see the glowing bowls of their pipes floating and bobbing in the dark down there like orange fireflies.

Once, my mother took all of my father's clothes and dumped them out on the sidewalk in front of our house. I don't know why. Maybe my sister knew. I never asked her.

My father liked to swim, but only on his back. It was said that he could swim on his back the whole length of the breakwater from South Shore Park to Jones Island, by kicking only, while smoking his pipe and reading the newspaper. On Sunday afternoons, if the weather was hot and he wasn't working, he and my mother took us sometimes on the streetcar to the unguarded beach beyond South Shore. Ma would sit under a tree at the edge of the sand and make my sister hold my hand the whole time we were in the water. Pa would swim out toward the breakwater. It didn't look like swimming. On his back, with his arms at his sides, he looked like a small barge propelled by the motor of his feet. He could pick his head up out of the water and sight down his chest and legs through the V his feet made to look at us, left behind on the shore. My mother was always under the trees with her rosary, praying him back in.

There was the time I lost sight of him. "What's the matter with you?" my sister cried when I squeezed her hand, and when I found him again, bobbing like a log out there, I staggered to stand my ground, the sand eroding under my feet with each wave, until I saw him float ashore many yards up the beach. I wrenched my hand from my sister's and ran, keeping my eyes on my father where he lay half in and half out of the water, resting from his long swim. Unwilling to look away even for a second, though the sun on the water was scalding my eyes, I could hardly see by the time I reached the spot, and what I did see filled me with horror. My father had been transformed into a tree, his limbs draped in seaweed. Each wave coming in lifted him like a breath.

I don't know how old I was when that happened—five or six or seven. Afterward, for a long time, I had dreams about it, my father floating ashore as everything but himself. Most often he was made of painted wood, with one hand gripping his pipe and the other a snarl of seaweed. He bore a marked resemblance in these dreams to the statue of St. Joseph perpetually gripping his carpenter's square and a lily in the front of our church.

I have been dreaming about him in here. One dream is a lot like the old one. He washes ashore blackened like burned wood. In the other, he comes walking up the street, looking like himself, carrying a suitcase. When he opens the suitcase, it's like a door opening. Inside there's only darkness, a sliver of face, and the one blue eye.

⁂

IT WOULD HAVE been hard for Joe to say exactly when walking Anica home from the boardinghouse became a Sunday habit—not all the way home to the rickety porch of the house on stilts where he might run into the old man Mrs. Tomasic called her father, but at least to the end of Bay Street. Often, while they walked, they played a game of pretending to choose which of the houses they passed was one that Joe or Anica would like to buy. Today they were on Aldrich Street, several blocks out of their way, but then they often took detours. To look at different houses, they both said. They were in front of the second house from the corner of Aldrich Street and Lincoln, when Joe stopped and said, "So what do you think of this place?"

Anica tilted her head to one side, considering. The house was small and a little weather-beaten, but the angles looked square, and what she could see of the windows and doors seemed trim and solid. There was a small porch with a built-in bench on one side. The house looked vacant—no curtains in the windows, no signs of life.

"It needs painting," Joe admitted.

"Well, sure," said Anica, "but it wouldn't take much to paint it."

"Too small you think?"

"I didn't say that." She walked on to look at the side of the house. "The yard goes back pretty far, and there's a nice big window on this side, must be the kitchen. Looks like a bedroom upstairs, too."

Joe shaded his eyes to look up at the window under the peak of the roof. The house faced east—"That's the best way," Anica told him—and the sun was sinking behind it now.

"It's only attic up there," he told her. "But place for two rooms. Two bedrooms, I'm thinking."

Anica laughed. "How do you know it's only an attic?"

He wanted to say, "Can't you see how the sun is coming right through the place from the back window to the front?" but all he came out with was "See the sun?"

He pointed. The upstairs window was lit from behind with reddish gold light. If it weren't for the sun setting, Joe thought, the fiery glow would be alarming.

"It could just be the door is open between two rooms up there, so the sun comes through," Anica said.

"It's an attic," Joe said. "Come on. I'm gonna show you." He pulled a key chain from his pocket and held it up for her to see.

"You've got the key?" she said. "Where did you get the key?"

Joe had kept his face from breaking into a grin for as long as he could. Now he laughed. "Why not a key to my own house?" he asked her.

"Your own house?" Anica said. She looked less pleased than Joe had expected her to be, more wary. "You bought a house, Joe?"

"Nine hundred dollar I paid. Mr. Westphal at Harvester, he wanted one thousand for the big yard, but he took my money because I have cash."

Anica had already turned to walk down the street. "I better get going home," she said.

"You don't want to go inside and see?" he called, following her.

She stopped and glanced around, up and down the empty street. "Joe," she said. "That's for your wife Agnes to do."

"Agnes is not here."

Anica continued down the block. "All the more reason I shouldn't be."

He stared after her for a moment, then ran to catch up. "Wait," he said, and when she didn't, he took hold of her arm. She stopped and looked at his hand on her sleeve. He let go. Suddenly, he felt ashamed and unjustly accused. His embarrassment and indignation swelled into anger.

"What?" he said. "You think I got my mind in the gutter? I wanna show you, that's all."

It was the wrong thing to say. He knew it before she turned on her heel and strode away from him, knew it before it came out of his mouth. Where did he *get* such a word as *gutter*? And in English yet! He was not even one hundred per cent sure what it meant, by itself, although the meaning of the sentence in which it played a key role was all too clear to him—and to Anica.

At supper the next day, he asked Roman about the word. How bad was it? he wanted to know.

"You said *that* to her?" Roman shoveled another dumpling into his mouth and pointed to Joe's plate with his elbow. "No wonder she didn't give you any chicken. All you got there is cabbage and dumplings."

It didn't matter about the chicken. Joe was too miserable to eat. Anica had served an entire meal to the table of fifteen men without once looking at Joe, much less speaking to him.

Big John Borkowski, a man whose size made him impervious to the jokes of others as well as oblivious to their feelings, said in Polish, "Just be glad she didn't pour your coffee in your lap!" Most of the men who heard him laughed, a couple of them hesitantly, not quite sure what they were laughing at. Only Joe and the Italians refrained, Joe in his sorrow and the other two because they understood no Polish at all and knew it was more than likely that they themselves were the butt of any given joke.

Joe could not have predicted the consequences of the terrible thing he had said to Anica. He understood why she was angry with him—how could she not be? Even before he got back home—after a joyless solitary tour of his property on Aldrich Street—he had resolved to apologize to her. What he did not anticipate was the desolation that stopped his breath in his throat when she saw him coming and quickly turned away, or when her eyes passed over him as if he were invisible and then lighted with warmth on somebody else—Mrs. Tomasic or Roman or little Frankie, or the cat. It was as though she took the air out of the room when she left.

Then, for two days, she didn't come to work at all. Not knowing where else to turn, Joe begged Mrs. Tomasic to talk to Anica, to tell her he was sorry, he didn't mean it the way it sounded, not at all.

"So you bought a house," Mrs. Tomasic said. She was mixing up some of Anica's antiroach concoction in a Mason jar. Eight jar lids—one for each room in the house—were lined up on the table in front of her. Mrs. Tomasic thought it just as well that Joe Iljasic assumed he was the reason for Anica's absence. The truth was that Anica's father was commemorating the anniversary—or, more accurately, obliterating the painful memory—of his life's greatest loss: his fishing boat. Anica stayed home to keep the old man from getting into drunken fights or otherwise hurting himself and to cover for him at Lakeside Fuel Oil, where he worked as a deliveryman.

"If you would only talk to her," said Joe.

"If you bought a house, that means that you don't plan to return to your village after all." Mrs. Tomasic lifted the jar to her nose and sniffed.

Every day Joe wondered how much of his village would be there, after the war, but he said nothing about this now. "You could tell her how sorry I am. Or how stupid I am. Tell her I don't know what I am saying, in English."

Carefully, Mrs. Tomasic began to fill the jar lids with the brown potion. "I wonder what your wife will think of coming to America for good," she said.

Joe tugged at his hair. "What else can I do but tell her that I'm sorry?"

WHENEVER THE OLD man had too much beer to be trusted with a wagonload of kerosene, Anica would dump him into bed, pull off his shoes, hitch up the horse they borrowed from Felix Struck, and drive the wagon across Bay Street to Lakeside Fuel Oil (in dry season) or down to where the barge tied up in the spring. Luckily, Rudolf Muza, the one-armed former fisherman whose job it was to load the wagon, had long had his eye on Anica for reasons of the heart. He never told his boss that a girl of twenty was hoisting the heavy glass containers out of a honeycomb of wooden crates on the bed of the wagon, depositing them carefully on dozens of doorsteps, picking up empties and marking off names on the list. It was only after the accident, when he himself came under suspicion, that Rudolf Muza "remembered" it was Anica who made the deliveries that Saturday, Anica who carefully set the glass container on the doorstep of August and Marta Wolf near the end of her route.

She was lifting another container of kerosene out of the wagon, hurrying to finish before dusk turned to darkness, when the accident occurred. She heard the loud *whoomp* behind her and spun around, dropping the glass container and dousing her feet and skirt with kerosene. A pillar of flame filled the doorway of the Wolfs' house, and the air was filled with screaming. Seconds later, the flaming pillar collapsed. The screaming ceased as suddenly. Everyone within earshot was already running toward the house. They stopped when they saw Marta Wolf's stepmother, Valentina, emerge from the doorway into the yard, cutting a path through the crowd. Behind her, two men strained to carry a rolled up carpet from the house. A horrified murmur rose from the crowd as word spread—it was Marta they carried, still wrapped in the rug they'd used to extinguish her burning clothes. "Keep her father away from here," Valentina Kubiak commanded, leading the men across the dirt street to her own house. But it was too late. Everyone saw "Governor" Kubiak coming red-faced and full-speed up the sidewalk from his tavern.

As he approached, only three sounds could be heard: the Governor's boots clomping on the wooden planks, the waves washing against the breakwater, and the moans from inside the rug.

It took a few hours, in the confusion, to determine that Anica, not the old man, had made the delivery. Some people hinted at once that she had done it on purpose, had waited until dusk to give the Wolfs a jug filled not with kerosene but with gasoline, knowing that when either Marta or August poured it into a lamp, all hell was going to break loose. Everyone knew, after all, that August Wolf's marriage to Marta Kubiak two years earlier had broken Anica's heart. Others looked askance at one-armed Muza, thinking he had made a grave but typically stupid mistake in loading the wagon. Still others blamed Lakeside Fuel Oil, one of several lakeside companies that stood to gain substantial real estate when the Kaszubes were driven off Jones Island once and for all. Eliminating Muza left only Anica and the company to choose from, and when, on the morning after the accident, she could not be found, her guilt seemed established beyond a doubt. By noon, people would have crossed the street to avoid her.

AT THE END of the sixth long day since Anica had turned her back on him, Joe Iljasic was walking home from the gandy dancers' shack in the railroad yard. His arms, like his heart, felt heavy, and his fingers tingled and curled toward his palms, remembering the handle of the hammer. He stopped at the corner of Hilbert and East Bay Street to look back down at the lake. It was Saturday and he had no second shift to fill. Later he would say that he heard a boom and that he thought of thunder, a weirdly local lake storm brewing at the edge of an otherwise lovely evening. He would say that he saw a thin column of smoke rising across the water and that it filled his heart with dread. But there was no smoke, no boom, nothing to be seen or heard from the corner of Hilbert and Bay Street. Then how did he know that something terrible had happened to her? Why did he walk back down toward the lake, moving faster as his sense of foreboding grew, until he was running past houses, through the railroad yard, past the gandy dancers' shack that he had left only moments before, feeling a chill rise in his bones? His feet were pounding on sand when he became aware of boys running toward him, toward the mainland. Joe shouted to them. Two ran past without stopping, but the third slowed down enough to say that they were going for a doctor. A woman had been burned, Joe thought he said. "Who? Her name?" Joe cried in English, but the boy had run on.

On Governor Kubiak's street, Joe hovered at the fringes of the somber crowd outside the house, keeping an eye out for Anica, afraid to call attention to himself. When he heard someone say, "It was gasoline in the bottle!" he pushed his way to the front. The crowd surrounded the front porch. Two men sat on the wooden steps. One of them Joe recognized as Felix Struck, the owner of the red-brick tavern. Struck gazed straight out into the crowd, very still, like a man holding his breath until the worst was over. The other man—a meaty fellow with huge gray sideburns and a sea captain's beard—sat leaning against a porch pillar and staring at his hands, which he held, clasped together, between his boots. This was Anton Kubiak, Marta's father. He looked, Joe thought, like a cloth doll that had lost most of its stuffing, causing it to sag to one side.

From what he overheard, Joe put together a picture of what had happened that was not too far from the truth. He backed out of the crowd and found his way through crooked streets to the house where Anica lived, which he identified by the curtains in the front window, the same as the ones she had made for Mrs. Tomasic's parlor. No one answered the door, though he pounded on it until his knuckles bled. He even tried knocking on the doors of neighboring houses, but everyone must have been at Governor Kubiak's place. The street was deserted.

Joe knew no one to ask about her—that one-armed fellow,

perhaps, but Joe hadn't seen him in the crowd—and nowhere to look for her. It was possible, he thought, that she had gone back to the boardinghouse, but as he reached the beginning of Bay Street, the thought of finding her there, telling whatever terrible news she had to Mrs. Tomasic, the two of them shutting him out, seemed too much to endure. At the corner of East Bay and Aldrich Streets, he turned left.

His little house was dark and empty. It was furnished with built-in gas lamps—no need for kerosene here—but Joe had put all of his money into the purchase price, and it would be a while before he had saved enough to have the gas supply connected. Erich Schultz told him to forget the gas and have the place wired for electric lights, but Joe thought gas would be good enough. His wife Agnes had never seen such a thing as a gaslight. He put the key in the lock and turned it, trying to imagine Agnes in the house, waiting for him, in the kitchen. He had tried to imagine her here before, tried to believe that she was the mother—and he the father!—of a child who could walk and talk and climb into his lap. But, in his heart, he didn't believe any of it. In his heart, he knew that she was dead—if not in childbirth, then in the war. He had felt the chill every night. He felt it now. Pushing open the door of his empty, empty house on Aldrich Street, he knew he was truly alone.

"Joe?" someone whispered.

He dropped the key. It bounced once on the wooden floor, then landed on something softer. Deep in shadow in the corner of the porch, Anica was curled up into the smallest possible space. She was hugging her knees, rocking back and forth in the darkness. She was crying. Was she crying?

"Joe?" she was saying. "Joe."

Her hair smelled like kerosene.

⁂

"WHAT HAPPENED NEXT?"

It was my grandson Robbie who asked. Mary Helen's boy. He arrived at the hospital shortly after Aggie did, having paid ninety-six dollars to take a cab from Madison to Milwaukee. "You've gotta be twenty-five to rent a car," he explained. His blue hair and leather jacket were frosted with wet snow when he came in, his lip ring and ear studs glittering. "Hey, Grandpa," he said. He was a cold tower leaning over me. "Gramps? Howzitgoing? Can you hear me?" He straightened up. "Mom? Can he hear me? Can he see?"

The doctors didn't think so. In fact, now that Robbie was here, my daughters said, they were going to move me to a private room and take me off the ventilator. What would happen then? Robbie wanted to know. It was impossible to say, my daughters told him. (They were only repeating what the doctor said.) "Maybe the shock will bring him out of the coma," Robbie suggested. It was impossible to say. My daughters had gone together to make arrangements for the private room (I swear they used the word *arrangements*), leaving Robbie and Kata with me in the ICU.

"I'll tell you what happened next," Kata said to Robbie. "They burned my mother's house down, is what happened. Can you imagine what that would be like? How it would feel to know that somebody—all kinds of people, people you thought you belonged to—they hate you so much they would burn your house down?"

Robbie looked a little sorry that he'd asked.

"It was hatred that killed my mother in the end," Kata said bitterly. "It got concentrated in her body. People talked about her birthmark and the cancer, but I think it was their hatred that ate her up. They blamed her for everything—not just what happened to Marta, but the fire, and Kubiak closing his place, he was never the same after Marta—and even the people moving away after that, one by one, and the city moving in, the sewage plant, everything was her fault. The wages of sin."

IF IT'S TRUE that old people remember things, it's also true that they forget. Until yesterday, Kata had completely forgotten her own contribution to the list of things her mother took the blame for. When she plucked that roll of yellowing paper from the nest of broken glass and wood and plaster at the mall, Kata didn't know at first what it was. She stuffed it into her sleeve for safekeeping, together with the torn scroll of the Stations of the Cross, whose brightly colored borders showed how much the sufferings of Jesus had faded over the years through the glass. At the hospital, in a waiting room, she pulled the roll of paper from her sleeve. Two pieces it turned out to be, one inside the other. Slowly she unfurled the pieces and saw angels kneeling at the top of the inner sheet. The *Illegitima* hurt her again, it was true, almost as much as it had hurt her sixty-odd years before, but this time—ah, this time—she found Joe's name right where it belonged, underneath her mother's. She recognized his cryptic handwriting. She knew it so well. The angular "J" and the "f" and the undotted "i." She had found a magazine once with Joe's name written on the back, over and over, as if he were practicing. Sometimes J-o-s-i-p, sometimes J-o-s-e-f. Such funny writing. She liked to trace the letters herself.

In the waiting room at the hospital, Kata held the little roll of paper open for a long time. The instant her fingers let go, it curled back up like a window shade snapping, and she remembered something that made her own heart pound. She had worked very hard a long time ago to forget that Good Friday when Staramajka found her weeping in the bedroom, a little before the sacred hour of noon. In her lap, wrinkled by tears, lay the tattered magazine where she still practiced writing Joe's name from time to time. The baptismal certificate she had crushed in her fist.

"Where is his name?" she cried, raising her fist to the door. "My mother said his name was here!"

Staramajka pulled the door shut and sat down, the featherbed billowing up on either side of her like snowy slopes.

"He went to the priest, Kata, just the way your mother told you. But the priest said, only if Josef married your mother would they let him write down his name on the paper. How could Josef marry your mother? He still didn't know yet if his wife Agnes was alive or dead. When the priest heard that, he sent him away. Do you see? What your mother said was true. He wanted his name written there, only that priest got in the way." It was another indictment of the Catholic Church in America.

"So Joe really is my father?"

This is where Staramajka should have looked Kata straight in her blue eyes and said, "Yes!" But instead she looked down and picked a loose black thread from her apron. When Staramajka raised her eyes again, it was too late.

"Anyone could be my father," Kata said in a strange voice that chilled Staramajka's heart. Kata gazed down at the villains leering from the covers of the pulps in her suitcase. "It could be Putsz!" she cried with horror. "It could even be that priest!" She covered her nose with both hands.

"Kata! You are talking like a crazy person. Your mother told you—"

"My mother lied to me!"

Staramajka crossed herself. "Even now, from heaven, she—"

"My mother is burning in hell!"

"Jesus, Maria."

Thanks to her lessons with Father Wojcek, Kata knew exactly which commandments her mother had broken. Thou shalt not bear false witness. Thou shalt not commit adultery. It was one grave sin after another. With a look on her face that Staramajka could hardly bear to see, Kata leaned over the suitcase and whispered, "Do you know who he is?"

"I can't—"

Kata put her hand up to ward off the answer. "No no no—don't tell me, don't. I'll be really sorry if you tell me, won't I? You have to tell me though."

"Oh, Kata." Staramajka looked sorrowful.

"It must be very bad, isn't it?"

"I promised her, Kata. I gave her my word."

"Was it Putsz?" Kata held her breath.

Staramajka said at last, "No."

Kata's relief—for how could she live with the knowledge that Putsz was her father—lasted only as long as the rush of breath she exhaled. How could it be worse than Putsz?

"Who, then?" she said, narrowing her eyes at Staramajka. "Was it one of the other boarders?" This did not seem possible to her, but it had to be someone.

Staramajka kept a stone face.

Who was left? Who was left in the stories her mother had told her? There was the man—Wolf?—whose wife died in the accident. He had been sweet on Anica, someone said. With a sharp intake of breath, Kata asked herself if the accident had been an accident, or if—she could not complete such a thought.

And this is where Staramajka, mistaking the reason for Kata's gasp, thinking that she had hit upon what Staramajka knew as the truth, burst out, "That old man was not her father! He took her in when she was your age—her and her cousin, the boy who drowned. He should have sent her back to Kenosha after that. They shouldn't have allowed it—that she should stay with him on Jones Island. But her mother was dead, Kata. All those people—the ones who knew?—they looked the other way."

Kata had grown so pale, listening, that Staramajka took her by the shoulders to shake the blood back into her face. "There was no one to save your mother, Kata, like she saved you!"

Kata cried for a long time in Staramajka's arms. When she finished crying, she felt as if she had been turned inside out.

Staramajka went to the kitchen to get her a glass of coffee with milk, Good Friday or not. Alone now in the bedroom, Kata sat up straight. She had made her decision and she had to work fast. She smoothed out the baptismal certificate on a stack of pulp magazines placed on the bed like a desk, and found in the wicker suitcase the pen she had stolen from Father Wojcek's office. After tracing the name of Josef Iljasic one more time for practice, Kata knelt beside the bed and wrote his name where her mother told her it belonged. Then she sat back on her heels to consider her work—the sharp turn of the "J," the cramped and angular "f" and undotted "i"—and she was taken by surprise.

How much easier it was to believe what was written.

Staramajka was still in the kitchen, cutting a thick slice of bread to go with the coffee, when she heard Kata's feet pounding down the front stairs and out the door.

She ran down the alley and through the swampgrass to the railroad yard. No sledgehammers were ringing against the rails at noon on Good Friday. A small curl of smoke threaded up from the stovepipe that stuck through the roof of the gandy dancers' shack. Kata knew that Joe might be inside. He might be reading the latest *Terror Tales* before he put it in the stack of magazines beside the door. He might be alone, the Italians in church at noon on Good Friday. Even if he wasn't alone, she could have gone inside and asked him, calmly now, if what her mother said was true. He would know exactly what she meant. She wouldn't have to come right out and ask him if he really was her father. But if she went inside and spoke to him, then he would also know that she had doubted her mother's word. She would have shown herself to be like all the rest of them. A traitor to her mother's memory.

It was a shame, in a way, that Kata didn't go inside. Joe would have told her exactly what she wanted to hear.

⚜

IT WAS A miracle, people said the day after the accident, if it was an accident, that Marta Wolf's house hadn't caught fire. In that hot, dry weather, the fire might have spread, reducing the whole village to the smoking ruin certain Milwaukee businessmen would have liked to see it become.

Perhaps this very danger is what gave someone the idea of setting fire that night to the house where Anica lived.

She and Joe saw the light the flames made against the night sky from the back window, upstairs, on Aldrich Street. Joe had no furniture, but Mrs. Tomasic had given him a featherbed to get his household underway, and he'd rolled up his trousers to make a pillow for Anica. They couldn't tell what was burning, although she said, suddenly, "The house is empty. He's gone." All night long they heard alarm bells and boys running down the street, calling for help, and in the morning, when Joe walked out to Jones Island to see, a smoky haze hung over the street like a gauze curtain. Nothing remained of the old man's house but blackened stilts.

Joe knew what the old man had done to Anica after the accident. By the light the moon spilled through the curtainless windows of the house on Aldrich Street, he had seen her eye swollen shut, her lip puffed and split, her nose crusted with blood. He knew there were more things that he couldn't see, not even after he carefully lit the lantern. Anica told him how she had left the wagon full of empty bottles in the street and run home by a back route and found the old man there, drunk as usual and full of rage, for one-armed Muza had gotten there before her. Muza had told the old man what happened to Marta Wolf and who would take the blame for it, then fled the bucket flung at him for his trouble.

Holding each other that night, Joe and Anica had felt no desire, they had no thought of it. Joe wanted only to take away whatever evil she had suffered. To do this, he touched her—the back of one hand brushing her forehead, his fingers skimming coolly down her cheek, floating over the scrape on her cheekbone, brushing her swollen lip. The palm of his other hand lightly smoothed her fallen hair and cupped her chin, touched her shoulders. She held her breath at first, and then she sighed, and then she was breathing softly and evenly and it was working. His hands were erasing the other man's touch, healing the bruises he couldn't see in the uncertain light. She didn't know how and neither did he, but it was working. After his hands had given back every aching part of her, his lips returned to the places most damaged—that scrape, the teethmarks, scratches on her breast—until it seemed as though all boundaries between them had melted, as though she had dissolved to take him in, such softness and fullness, like water round and trembling above the rim.

Afterward, in his arms, she had this thought: *if there is a child, now it will have a father.*

Years later, when she was dying, Anica could not think how

to explain to Staramajka what she and Joe had done on the night when her child was conceived. They had performed a miracle. They had transformed an act of violence into one of healing tenderness. It was like turning not just water, but poison, into wine. In the end, Anica said to Staramajka only this, needing a new breath for each word, shaping them one by one: "Your son Joe was very kind to me. Always very kind."

❦

"WELL," KATA SAID, "I hope he could hear me."

We were still in the ICU, waiting for whatever was going to happen next. Robbie sat in one of the chairs, watching my chest rise and fall. Kata stood at the foot of the bed. She started to tug the blanket over my toes, then changed her mind, pulled off the hospital sock, and pressed my bare foot between her palms. I thought I'd lost contact with most of me, but I could feel the warmth of Kata's hand on the sole of my foot. It felt very, very good. She sighed and said, "Joe Iljasic gave my mother that house on Aldrich Street, you know, free and clear. He paid the taxes on it, too, until she died. He killed himself working two jobs his whole life. No offense to his wife Agnes, but he would have married my mother, if he could. I believe that. My mother said I was too small, but I remember them painting that house together. I used to think they moved it there from Jones Island."

"Jones Island," Robbie said, sounding suddenly more alert.

"I'm sorry," Kata said. "I just wanted your grandpa to know how it really was with his pa and the Kaszube girl's mother."

"The Kaszube girl?" said Robbie. "Is that a real person?"

"I guess so!" Kata looked at him. "She's me."

"You're kidding," said Robbie. "I thought he made her up."

"No," said Kata.

"Wow. When I was a little kid, Grandpa told me all kinds of stories about him and the Kaszube girl. On Jones Island. That was you?"

"Yes," said Kata.

There was a pause while Robbie tugged at his lip ring, no doubt calling some of the stories to mind. "So it all really happened," he said. "Wow."

"That depends on what your grandpa told you," said Kata.

"About the birthmark and you coming back from the dead?"

"It sounds like maybe he exaggerated a little."

"But you really had a birthmark like that?" He caught himself up. "If I'm not being too personal."

"I had a birthmark."

"And they had to cut it out of you?" Robbie of the multiple piercings sounded impressed. "With no anesthetic? To save your life?"

"My mother saved my life," Kata said firmly, as if she thought he might argue the point. "Can I ask you a question now?"

"Sure," said Robbie.

"Are you any good with tools—like a screwdriver or a drill?"

My grandson told her proudly (and it was probably true), "Hey. Shop was my best subject in high school."

⚜

WHAT ROBBIE KNEW of my adventures with the Kaszube girl was highly selective. I'd told him about the time we used our trusty swords to turn back a host of evil tax collectors bent on wresting Jones Island from the Kaszubes cowering at our heels. I told him how we ousted the Polish vampire from his warehouse headquarters and then burned the warehouse to the ground with flaming arrows. I didn't tell him how my grandmother made me wait outside on the back steps while she and Kata went into the house to finish the job that Frankie had bungled at Struck's.

On our slow walk home from Jones Island, Kata claimed she never even flinched as he cut where she'd told him to, a slice like a paper cut, as close to the birthmark as he could get. An alarming quantity of blood had welled up immediately, darkening the purple dress and robbing Frankie of his desire. (He said later that he wasn't about to murder somebody, no matter what she promised he could do afterwards.) He dropped the knife and ran. Bleeding, Kata tried to change his mind. She shouted that it was too late, too late—he had touched her, he was already cursed with the curse that had befallen her and her mother before her.

"And he believed you?" I said.

"I told him if he didn't believe me, he should go and ask the priest with no nose."

"I don't get it," I said.

Kata sighed at my ignorance. "I said to ask him how he got that way."

"Oh!" I said, although I still didn't get it.

Staramajka said, "Tch."

Now she and Kata were in the house and I was exiled on the back steps that stretched a whole story from the kitchen upstairs to the backyard below. I was too busy brooding to notice the scuffling in the darkness under the stairs until I shifted my feet and the scuffling stopped. *"Who is it?"* I whispered. Frankie Tomasic stepped out from under the stairway, looking wild in the eyes and clinging to the railing with his no doubt blood-stained fingers. "What do *you* want?" I said.

Frankie looked over his shoulder, then back at me. "Listen," he said, wiping his nose with the back of his hand. "George. Do you think it's true, what she said, if anybody, you know, touched her, I mean, do you think—?" He stopped on a sharp breath and looked up the stairs over my head. I turned to see what he saw.

At the top of the stairs my grandmother stood like an apparition, her loose white hair and long nightgown lit from behind and floating around her in the night. "Tell him, Georgie," she said. Her words were addressed to me, but her deep-set eyes bored into Frankie, pinning him where he stood.

"What?" I asked her in English, for Frankie's benefit. "What should I tell him?"

"Tell him—" she hesitated, searching. Although he couldn't understand what she said, poor Frankie was all eyes and ears. "Tell him," Staramajka intoned, "the Wages of Sin is Death."

My job, I knew, was not so much to translate the Croatian as to remember the English version. The first word eluded me.

"What did she say?" Frankie pleaded.

I couldn't think of *wages*.

"Tell him!" my grandmother commanded.

"What did she *say*?"

I improvised. "You get what you pay for, Frankie!"

That's when I should have belted him, right then, before he turned and ran. I could have saved myself a lot of grief.

Kata recovered quickly from her kitchen surgery. Contrary to my mother's dire predictions, there was no infection, no blood poisoning—only the raw beginning of a wedge-shaped scar five or six inches below her collarbone. (She offered to show it to me.) In less than a week, she was ready to make the trip to Kenosha with Lenz, the Kaszube tavern keeper, in his beautiful maroon Chrysler. I stood on the curb with my grandmother to wave good-bye and keep the smaller Serbs from hitching a ride on the bumper. Kata looked pleased in the front seat with her arm around the Stations of the Cross, Christ crucified leaning back against the velvet upholstery beside her.

"Her mother saved her," Staramajka said to me as the car pulled away. "My hand only held the knife."

IN THE PRIVATE room my daughters finally got arranged, Kata was getting ready to say the rosary for me. She held up the carved ivory beads and the crucifix, gruesomely detailed. "What do you think, Georgie?" she said. Now that I was off the ventilator, she expected me to pipe up any minute. "Do you want Sorrowful or Glorious?" She couldn't do the Joyful Mysteries, she said, because she had forgotten one of them. "I can't remember Number Four. Does anybody know what it is?"

My daughters were talking to the respiration therapist over

by the window. They pretended to be admiring the stained glass masterpiece temporarily installed by my grandson Robbie, who had cleverly hung the wooden frame from brackets intended for the window blind, but they were really talking about my blood gases, which were very bad and getting worse all the time, and my responsiveness to the neurologist's last visit, which was pretty much nil. A lot of people—nurses and staff and other patients' visitors—had come in to see the stained glass earlier. They should have waited until now, when the sun streaming through it colored everything in the room. Even the IV tree was twinkling.

"Is it Christmas?" said Mary Helen. "Is Christmas a Joyful Mystery?"

"Nativity, you mean," said Kata. "That's Number Three, I think." The beads clicked together in her hands—an old familiar sound. "There's Annunciation, Visitation, Nativity, something else, and Circumcision."

"Circumcision?" Robbie said. "That's a joyful mystery?"

"They call it something else," Kata said. "With the Joyful, there isn't too much to pick from. Not like Sorrowful. For Sorrowful, we got more than we need—Agony in the Garden, Crowning with Thorns, Stripping of Garments, Scourging at the Pillar, Nailing, Falling—"

"That's where I'd put the Circumcision," Robbie said. "With the Scourging and the Nailing."

"It's just one sorrowful thing after another," Kata said.

She sighed. She had been in my so-called private room ever since they brought me down from Intensive Care after breakfast. (With her encouragement, Robbie ate my toast and applesauce rather than let it go to waste. They bring you breakfast here until your toe is tagged.) All morning my daughters had been giving people little tours of my stained glass masterpiece. Even Frankie came. (If he had any objections to Kata sticking around here, he kept his mouth shut. I give him credit for that.) All morning I expected Kata to correct my daughters when they pointed out the grapes and the giant spider's web, but she never did. I think I've figured out why. I think she's waiting for me to do it. She's waiting for me to open my mouth and say, "They're lilacs, for God's sake! It's a drying wheel!" Even if I could, I wouldn't waste my breath. No matter what you say, somebody always gets the wrong story. But she's got me thinking. If I *could* say something, what would it be? Here she is, leaning over me. I'd say, *lepa moja. Lepa moja, Kata.* She takes my hand. My fingers thrill.

EPILOGUE

AT THE TRAIN station in Pécs, Mary Helen said to Marie Sinyakovich, "Everyone here looks like somebody I know."

Three different women had bustled by during the time it took Marie to telephone her nephew ("Did you smash up that car yet or can you pick us up?"), and any one of those women could have fooled Mary Helen into thinking that her aunt Madeline's final journey had ended not in the family plot at St. Adalbert's cemetery, but back here, back home, in the place she'd left so long ago. Here came another one, a barrel-shaped woman in a striped dress, her gray hair swept up under a babushka and a huge black purse on her arm, a woman with bright blue eyes and a sharp, narrow nose, maybe a tooth or two missing near the front. She was Aunt Madeline all over again, except for the babushka.

Marie Sinyakovich (a barrel-shaped woman in a plaid dress who carried a fairly large purse herself) said, "Don't go overboard, Mary Helen. Of course they look like you know them. Same blood."

In the village, Mary Helen kept seeing her father's face, his eyebrows and cheekbones and of course his mustache. And she knew at once which old fellow was the son of the Turk and

Nadya. He was the one who looked like Omar Sharif, the one who lived in the house that had belonged to her great-grandmother Jelena—so everyone told her, indicating the house with a subtle jerk of the head or eyebrows raised significantly in its direction. Mary Helen had spent at least an hour in almost every house in Novo Selo, first eating and then sitting on a chair or a bed—there were beds, she noticed, in every room—while people looked her over and said what a shame it was that she couldn't speak good Croatian like her father. She had taken pictures of the Drava River and the four-hundred-year-old church, of thick-walled houses, storks nesting on their chimneys, ancient wells in their back yards (some in the shadow of a satellite dish on the roof), and of many blue-eyed people, each of whom was related to her in a way that Marie Sinyakovich could explain precisely, rattling off names from the family tree in her brain. But at the end of two weeks in the village, Mary Helen still had not set foot in the house of the Turk's son, whose name was Tasz (Hungarian spelling), like his father.

Marie said, "You go if you want. Your father went when he was here. Watch out for the wife, though. She's a crazy one."

On the summer evening before they left for Pécs, Mary Helen was packing her bags snugly into the trunk of the Ford Escort, hoping the ceramics she bought in Kaposvar would survive tomorrow's ride to the train station with Marie's nephew, a young man who always wore tight-fitting tank tops and who passed cars on two-lane roads with the urgency of someone scratching a sudden and unbearable itch. She heard a man's voice calling to her.

"Jelena. Helen? Mary Helen."

She turned around. The Turk's son was standing before his open gate in the pink glow of sunset, two cows snacking on the grass behind him. Not *exactly* Omar Sharif all over again, but close, in spite of polyester slacks and a flannel shirt.

"*Tuka*, Jelena," he called. "Helen, cahm here!"

Inside the house, he motioned her to sit and called to his wife, who brought to the table two small cups of coffee.

"*Hvala*," Mary Helen said nervously. "*Hvala lepo.*" But the wife—Saba was her name—only grunted and went back through a dark doorway into another part of the house. The Turk's son dropped four lumps of sugar into his tiny cup. He stirred and stirred it, his eyes on Mary Helen, who was trying to figure out how to say, "I can't stay long. They're waiting supper for me." *Čekaj*. Check-eye. Wait.

"Check-eye," she said and nodded her head toward the window and the street.

"*Da*," he said. "*Čekaj.*"

He stirred a little longer, still watching her, the spoon ringing against the cup. Then, abruptly, he pulled out the spoon, picked up the cup, and drained it. He set it down as if he had made a decision and must act with resolve. In the center of the table was a well-worn child-size shoe box. Keds. He pushed it toward her.

"*Gledaj*," he said.

Look. "Look?" said Mary Helen, pointing to the box. "I should look?"

"*Da, da.*"

She took the lid off the box. It was full of photographs,

black-and-white and color, old ones mixed in with new ones. The one on top was a graduation picture, a young man who looked pretty handsome in a black jacket and bow tie.

"*Moj unuk*," said the Turk's son.

Unuk, unuk? "Your grandson," said Mary Helen.

He nodded, smiling a little.

Pleased with herself, she set the picture aside and reached for another. Her hand stopped in midair.

The next picture was a black-and-white, three inches square and framed by the scalloped border of a Brownie snapshot. A skinny little girl with long brown braids and thick bangs stood with her hands on the hips of a plaid school dress circa 1958 or '60. She had her chin tucked down toward her chest and looked up coyly at the person taking the picture. Behind her, resting his hands on her shoulders, for she barely came up to his waist, a policeman in a double-breasted coat and visored hat filled the whole frame from top to bottom. He was grinning at the camera.

The Turk's son was watching her. "*Ko je to?*" he said.

"Who is it?" She looked at him. "It's my father and me."

"*Ti?*" he said, pointing to the little girl. "*To je ti?*"

"Yes, it's me."

"*Y otac?*"

"And my father, yes. I have a picture just like this. Where did you get it?"

He sat back in his chair.

"Who gave it to you?" she asked again. "*Ko—uh—ko—*" She couldn't remember *give*, the past tense of *give*, who gave it to you. She gave up.

She shuffled through the box and found her First Communion picture. She found her sister Aggie as a newborn, birth announcement attached. And here they were, the two of them in a plastic swimming pool on the grass behind the house on 4th Street, Mary Helen frowning over the head of the smiling baby in her lap, her scowl so like the ones she'd seen on many faces here. They were all photographs that she had seen before, including the army-issue portrait of her father and a hazy studio shot of him (again in uniform) and his new bride, cheek to cheek. A very handsome couple.

The Turk's son had pulled the little girl and the big policeman out of the pile again.

"Tamo," he said, pointing to the policeman. *"To je tvoj otac?"* He said this slowly, separating the words for her, letting her hear them one at a time.

"Tvoy oh—? Yes, yes, it's my father. I already said."

"To je moj brat."

Wait. Check-eye. Brat? "Brother? He is your brother? Who told you he's your brother?" Who says? *"Ko kaže?"*

"Moj otac."

"Your father. Your father said this is your brother?"

The Turk's son frowned. He tapped the photo, his dirt-rimmed fingernail in the middle of George's double-breasted uniform. *"To je moj brat u Americi."*

This is my brother in America?

Maybe he meant "brother" in the more general sense, Mary Helen thought, as in brethren, family, a member of the clan. That was probably it. He didn't mean that her father was his *brother*, exactly, that they shared the same parents. Or even one parent. Maybe *brat* had another meaning. Maybe he was using some other word altogether. She was trying to string words into a question in her head when Marie's nephew showed up, looking for her. After supper, they made a final round of good-bye visits, so it was not until they were settled for the night in the nephew's living room, side by side on the big straw mattress (which was surprisingly comfortable, layered with feather-beds), that Mary Helen told Marie she had visited the Turk's son after all.

"Congratulations," said Marie as she pulled the covers up to her chin.

"Something weird happened over there."

"I told you his wife was crazy."

"It wasn't his wife. It was pictures. He had these pictures of my family—my sister and me when we were kids, and Mom and Dad."

After a tiny pause, Marie said, "Other people here got pictures, too. Your grandma Agnes sent pictures to her family here, her friends. She wanted them to see her grandchildren. That's all."

For a long time after that, Mary Helen tried not to make the straw crinkle or snap underneath her. She might have slept a lit-tle, on and off, but she spent most of the night watching a blue beam of moonlight from the window over her head fall on the wall opposite, inching its way down over the mirror and dresser and chair as the moon rose, turning the room into a box of sil-ver things. When the moon was so high that the beam reached the floor, she sat up and pushed the featherbed down to her feet, careful not to uncover Marie. She whispered the puzzle she'd been mulling over all night: *"To je moj brat u Americi."*

Marie's voice rose in the milky darkness. "That's the best Croatian I heard you say the whole time we've been here."

"But what does it mean?"

"You know what it means. Don't you?"

Mary Helen said it to herself one more time.

"But why would he say that Dad was his brother?"

There was the rustle of straw shifting as Marie rolled over toward the wall. "Oh, Mary Helen," she said, yawning. "I can't believe your father never told you the story of his mother and the Turk."

Acknowledgments

FOR MAINTAINING HIGH standards while offering all kinds of encouragement, I thank my husband, John Stefaniak; my editor, Alane Salierno Mason; and her assistant, Alessandra Bastagli. For all her efforts but mostly for her faith in me, I thank my agent, Valerie Borchardt. For their helpful comments on many versions of the manuscript, I thank Eileen Bartos, Mo Jones, Kate Kasten, Jane Olson, Tonja Robinswood, Mary Vermillion, Kris Vervaecke, Ann Zerkel, and Elizabeth Stuckey-French. I am grateful to Michael Koch for his advice and for publishing earlier versions of "The Kaszube Girl" and *The Turk and My Mother* (a novella) in *Epoch* magazine. Special thanks go to Vladimir Goss for translation and promotion of my work to the Croatian community in the United States and in Croatia. Thanks, also, to Vida Zei, for friendly language instruction.

For their support during the writing of the book, I thank my colleagues—especially Brent Spencer and Susan Aizenberg—

at Creighton University, my friends at Prairie Lights Bookstore in Iowa City, and the generous founders of the Lillian Smith Center for the Arts in Clayton, Georgia.

I am grateful to Lauren, Liz, and Jeff Stefaniak for frequently referring to me as their mother the author.

I owe my acquaintance with many useful documents—some of them hard to find and long out of print—to my research assistant, Steven Lovett. Additional information and help came from Bruce Brown, Rob Corson, Roy G. Benedict, Alan Moore, Tobias Wittmann, Jamie Merchant, the Milwaukee Public Library, the *Milwaukee Journal* (now the *Milwaukee Journal Sentinel*), and the Milwaukee County Historical Society. Any errors or liberties taken with history, geography, or medical science are my own.

Certain people were so integral to the creation of this book—long before I began to write it—that they have fictional counterparts in the work. I thank them most of all: my father, George Elleseg, for answering questions, drawing maps, and giving me a tour of the old East Bay neighborhood not long before he died in 1983; my aunt Madeline Esperes for letting me tape-record her stories ("What we say this thing catches?") in 1987; my cousin Marie Sinyakovich for taking the real Mary Helen to Europe not once but twice, and for providing many details, including the name of the rooster; and my grandmother's nephew Paul Bunyevacz for history, hospitality, and that lovely bike ride along the Drava.

Of the many works I consulted, I owe the most to these two: *Through Blood and Ice* (1930), by Imre Ferenc, and *Seven Years in Russia and Siberia, 1914–1921* (tr. 1971) by Roman Dyboski. In addition to newspapers of the day, two graduate theses offered indispensable details about Milwaukee: "The German-American Community in Milwaukee During World War I: The Question of Loyalty" by Gerhard Becker (University of Wisconsin-Milwaukee, 1988) and "Americanization Work in Milwaukee" by Isabelle Laura Hill (University of Wisconsin, 1920). Sample English lessons came from Gerd Korman, *Industrialization, Immigrants, and Americanizers: The View from Milwaukee, 1866–1921* (1967).

Other especially helpful books were: Angus M. Fraser, *The Gypsies* (1992); Elsa Brandstrom, *Among Prisoners of War in Russia & Siberia* (1929); Andre Kertész, *Hungarian Memories* (1982); James Forsyth, *A History of the Peoples of Siberia: Russia's North Asian Colony, 1581–1990* (1992); Victor L. Mote, *Siberia: World Apart* (1998); George Stewart, *The White Armies of Russia: A Chronicle of Counter-Revolution and Allied Intervention* (1933); John M. Thompson, *Revolutionary Russia, 1917* (1997); Donald W. Treadgold, *The Great Siberian Migration: Government and Peasant in Resettlement from Emancipation to the First World War* (1957); Harmon Tupper, *To the Great Ocean: Siberia and the Trans-Siberian Railway* (1965).

The Siberian charms on pages 115–18 are reprinted/adapted from *Russian Traditional Culture. Religion, Gender, and Customary Law*, ed. Marjorie Mandelstam Balzer (Armonk, N.Y.: M. E. Sharpe, 1992), pp. 73–74, 75, 79. Translation ©1992 M. E. Sharpe, Inc. Used with permission.

The excerpt from "Gift" used as epigraph and specified line

(*"He whose life was short can easily be forgiven"*) on page 186 of the novel are from pages 277, 278, and 279 of *New and Collected Poems: 1931–2001* by Czeslaw Milosz. Copyright ©1988, 1991, 1995, 2001 by Czeslaw Milosz Royalties, Inc. Reprinted by permission of HarperCollins Publishers Inc.

THE TURK AND
MY MOTHER

Mary Helen Stefaniak

The Turk and My Mother has been called "hilarious, heartbreaking, and deeply touching." Is that the book you set out to write? Which adjectives would you use to describe the book?

I like those three adjectives. I also like "innovative," which is what Sandra Scofield called it, and "brilliantly constructed," which is not, strictly speaking, an adjective, I know. Jim Hazard said in a review that the book is "comic, touching, erotic, sad, violent, innocent, harsh, and crafty, just like the world it describes." So there's a whole list of adjectives, all of which apply. It's also a compassionate book, I think, a book that encourages forgiveness. Hence the epigraph, from a poem called "Gift" by Czeslaw Milosz: "Whatever evil I had suffered, I forgot."

The Turk and My Mother covers great distances in time and space, and yet the stories keep intersecting, like strands in a braid. How did you come up with this braided structure for the book?

I modeled it after the way family stories are told, at least in my experience: piecemeal, with new facts and details emerging over time, different versions from different tellers with different agendas. Like Staramajka in the novel, my aunt Madeline—the real Aunt Madeline— did not trouble herself to explain who was who when she was telling you a story. With her voice and the voice of my (real) father in my head, the novel braided itself as I wrote it. In fact, I had to work at untangling it. I'd make one of the characters say, "Wait a minute, wait a minute!" and ask a question to accommodate the listener (and the reader).

The Turk and My Mother is a novel, and yet the acknowledgments go on for four pages, listing books and people that supplied you with facts. If this is fiction—and if you've got your license to make the facts fit the story—then why worry about all those facts?

You need facts to write good fiction. For one thing, facts feed the imagination. Think of how much would be lost from the book if I hadn't come across that orchestra in Khabarovsk that was mentioned in two different memoirs, one by a Hungarian officer and one by a Polish professor, both of whom were prisoners of war in Siberia. The fact is, I don't know where in Siberia the real Uncle Marko spent the war. I might have had Marko making boots in Irkutsk or Achinsk, with no orchestra in sight. Without the orchestra, there would have been no reason for me to create Heinrich the violinist, and without Heinrich, Marko would have had no reason to tell Nadya about his musical past, which means I would have had no reason to invent the blind Gypsy, and where would that leave Istvan and Staramajka? Fiction writers use facts—whether from their own experience or from research—to furnish a novel with setting details and historical background, even with characters and events. Research gave me the Jones Island fishing village, pre–World War I Milwaukee, the geography and the political position of far eastern Siberia during the Bolshevik era and White reprisals that followed. It gave me the very young and very cruel Major General Kalmykov, the armored trains attacking villages, the peasants with their bellies ripped open, and, of course, the orchestra and its fate. I found these events and circumstances in history books, memoirs, and, in the case of Milwaukee, the newspapers of the time. Many smaller details that help make the fictional world in the book feel solid and authentic also emerged as I did my research: from the tunnels through the mountains around Lake Baikal to the smell of the Russian soldiers' uniforms to the carp sales in Milwaukee's second ward and the architecture of Milwaukee's city hall.

Alice McDermott says that once a historical or geographical or biographical fact enters a fictional narrative, the "fact" is transformed into something else, into fiction; it belongs now to a fictional world and leaves its historical/geographical/biographical existence behind. I like that idea. I believe it's true. In a wonderful, hilarious story called "The Dolt" by Donald Barthelme, the narrator's wife asks him if the story he has written is historically true—if it really happened. He responds, "It does not contradict what is known."

You don't want your fictional world to "contradict what is known." So you research carefully, you check the facts. But the facts are not the point. The facts are malleable. As a fiction writer, the reason you're creating your fictional world (apart from the pleasure of creation) and the reason for readers to enter it (apart from the pleasure of doing so) is, in *fact*, to use the power of what can only be imagined in order to better understand "what is known."

If this book is based on your family history, then isn't it really "creative nonfiction"? Why call it a novel?

The short answer is: because it is a novel. *The Turk and My Mother* is not my family history. It's a fictional family history. Some characters have real-life counterparts, it's true. I think of them as actors playing themselves in a fictional story.

And the long answer?

It's true that my grandmother Agnes did spend the years surrounding the First World War in Europe while her husband was in Milwaukee. It's true that my aunt Madeline conceived her first child before she married; and, according to Aunt Madeline, it's true that my grandmother punished her in the cruel way the story describes. It's also true that my father used to catch snapping turtles in the river as a child in Milwaukee and that he liked to swim in the filthy water of the canal with his friends and that he himself became a policeman in part because of his admiration for the neighborhood policeman who becomes Pete the Cop in the story. It's true that my grandfather's brother Marko served as a courier in the First World War, that he was wounded and taken prisoner, and that, as a prisoner of war, he worked for a shoemaker somewhere in Siberia. (Aunt Madeline claims that the shoemaker *wanted* Uncle Marko to marry his daughter, but the real Uncle Marko was a good boy and came home to the village instead.) Pretty much everything else in the story is fictional, including some of the main characters: the Kaszube girl, for example, and her mother Anica (with the "c" like the "zz" in *pizza*), also Nadya, Pitkin, Heinrich, the blind Gypsy Istvan, even Staramajka and the Turk himself. All made up.

This is what fiction writers always do, though, isn't it? We always begin with something "from life"—a comment overheard, a gesture observed, a story someone told us about a terrible or puzzling or odd thing that happened the other day, or when they were young, and so forth. This novel grew out of that story Aunt Madeline told me about my grandmother punishing her for being pregnant. It was a story that suddenly gave me a different picture of my grandmother from the one I had carried around in my head since she died, when I was seven. The story was disturbing enough to me to make me need to imagine my grandmother Agnes in a new way. It required me to invent a whole life and romance for her in the village before she came to America so that I could explain to myself what she did to Aunt Madeline. I know almost nothing about the real Agnes's life before she came to America. I had to invent a past for her that would make it possible for me to understand and ultimately forgive her.

So that's what I did. It worked, too.

That's a pretty labor-intensive way to forgive somebody—writing a whole novel. Do you always write novels when you need to forgive someone?

For me, writing fiction is a way of figuring things out. I've discovered that one of the reasons I write stories is to be able to understand how characters behave, to understand whatever weakness or pettiness or even downright evil is part of them. Once you've gotten inside a character's experience, you're more likely to empathize, even if that character is very different from you or does things you don't understand or approve of. Czeslaw Milosz calls compassion "that ache of imagination." I think that's exactly right: you have to *imagine* the other person's experience in order to feel for or with them. That's what literature is for, I think, or at least it's one of the great services literature can do for us: it enlarges our capacity for compassion.

Of course, I didn't realize what I was doing—creating Agnes in order to forgive her—until after I had written the first part of the book. The writer is often the last to know.

Then what did make you write this particular novel—consciously, I mean?

From the beginning, I've thought of *The Turk and My Mother* as a novel about storytelling. I'm interested in how stories create who we are and how we see the world, how stories hold off death, how a story can change the listener, how a story can unharden a heart. This is why I was so pleased by Lan Samantha Chang's comment that the novel "reinvents the family saga and the art of storytelling as we know it."

In a way, the whole novel grows out of my Aunt Madeline's storytelling voice. She was always talking about people she knew, all in her wonderful nonstandard English, with Croatian and Hungarian words thrown in here and there. You knew what and whom she was talking about oh, maybe half the time. Listening to her, you really did wish you had an index. I wanted very much for the reader to experience that kind of storytelling. It was a great pleasure to listen to Aunt Madeline. If you could let go of your need for absolute certainty and clarity, then you could immerse yourself in her voice and the details. All kinds of vivid scenes would rise up in your head. Who, exactly, they were happening to didn't seem important.

One reader told me that, reading *The Turk and My Mother*, she felt the same way she did at her husband's family reunions, trying to keep everybody straight. I could tell that she wished I had made it easier for her to do that—in fact, I created the "cast of characters" to help her out—but the truth is that I was delighted to hear her say it. If I had written the book in a more linear way—if, unlike Aunt Madeline, I'd made clarity my goal—then reading it would not introduce you to the way in which these characters experience their own lives. You would be looking in at them from the outside. I wanted to immerse myself and the reader in their way of being in the world, their way of understanding, all of which is "embodied" in their storytelling voices. A friend of mine said, "I wasn't always sure who *I* was while I was reading." I think that is a very interesting place for a reader to be.

Reading *The Turk and My Mother* is like overhearing someone telling a story at a bus stop or in a café; you don't know everything about the characters, but you get caught up in the story. You feel as if you're eavesdropping.

You *are* eavesdropping most of the time. Every story in the book is being told by one character to another character for a particular reason, and you're listening in. Then, when the storyteller fades away to let the scene unfold directly, the reader is often in the same position as the intended listener. In Part I, for example, Staramajka is really telling the story of Agnes and the Turk to *Agnes*, in order to make her remember what it was like to be young and in love, in order to "open a door in her heart"; so when we drop into the story that Staramajka is telling, we usually find ourselves experiencing the scene from Agnes's point of view. It's as though we are remembering the story with her. In Part II,

Staramajka is the most important listener for the tale told by the priest's letters. She's the one Marko wants to reach. She needs to imagine what Marko experienced, to see and feel from his point of view, in order to understand why he didn't return to her. In Part III, when Kata is telling the story of Josef and Anica, George has become the listener, the one who needs to unharden his heart, or at least to accept the truth about his father. To do this, George has to imagine what it's like to be Josef living in that boardinghouse in Milwaukee. So Kata tells most of the story from Josef's point of view, the point of view in which George has the greatest stake and interest. (She can do this, by the way, because storytellers—as opposed to mere fictional narrators—are omniscient. Pay attention to the next story you overhear at the café or, for that matter, the family reunion, and you'll see what I mean.) We can always pull back, as the narrative does at times, to the thoughts and words of the teller of the tale—whether it's George or Kata or Staramajka—but most of the time, we find our eavesdropping selves exactly where the storyteller wants the listener—whether it's Agnes or George or Staramajka or Mary Helen—to be, busily filling in the scene that someone wants us to remember or to imagine unfolding before us.

The narrative also has a layered effect, as you keep finding out things that change the picture. You have to pay attention!

The book does make the reader work a little to put things together. Those are the kinds of books I like the best, where the story is told in layers and circles. I'm thinking of books like Margaret Atwood's *The Blind Assassin* or Alice McDermott's *Charming Billy*. *The Stone Diaries* by Carol Shields. As a reader, I enjoy having to figure it out, having to wait. I love backtracking in a narrative, having something show up on page 100 that really happened between pages 9 and 10, seeing how events shift meaning when some new scene, formerly hidden, comes to light.

That certainly describes *The Turk and My Mother*. The last line of the epilogue is the most dramatic example. That line asks you to reconsider everything—the whole story.

Many readers have told me that they got to the end of the book and felt a strong desire to go back to the beginning and start reading it again.

Now of course most people don't actually do that—they might go back and skim a little here and there—but I spoke to one book club where every one of them had read the book twice! Not only was I flattered, but my secret, impossible wish was fulfilled.

Your secret wish?

To write a book whose ending would make the reader feel *compelled* to go back and reread the book, at least up to a certain point. I don't mean that I wanted to write a book that forced readers to go back because they felt they didn't understand. I wanted readers to be pleased by the first reading—not frustrated or confused beyond endurance—but I also wanted them to feel, having read the last line, that they now understood the book in a different way, they could see a different picture. When I finished the book and was preparing the manuscript to send it to my agent, my secret wish was so strong that I was tempted to copy and paste the first part of the book—up to a certain point, a certain scene—into the manuscript again, *after* the epilogue. I don't think my agent would have seen that as a very good idea.

Another way to look at it is that the last line of the book makes you see George and his storytelling in a different light. In fact, the epilogue repeats many elements—details, actions, words—that occur in an earlier scene, way back in Part I. That earlier scene answers the question raised by the last line of the book.

I don't suppose you would tell us which "earlier scene" you're talking about.

No, but I'll give you a clue. Look for a loom "like a harp with silver strings." Or maybe a "room like a box of silver things." You could say that the epilogue rhymes with the earlier scene.

So there's a mystery in *The Turk and My Mother*?

Maybe "puzzle" is a better word, or maybe "mystery" and "puzzle" are both ways of talking about the "braided structure" you mentioned at the start—where a detail or a character suddenly reemerges and events you thought you understood take on a new significance. Little pieces of information are always coming to light as the novel proceeds that make your whole picture of the family click into a new picture. Isn't that the way we get to know people in "real life"—especially people in our families? You think you know somebody—I thought my aunt Madeline was a little old woman who sat in the corner of her darkened living room praying the rosary—but then you find out some previously unknown "fact"—she ran away with Gypsies when she was fifteen (not true, at least of Aunt Madeline) or she conceived a child out of wedlock, as they used to say—and suddenly the little old woman is not who you thought she was. Those moments—when a bit of information changes the whole picture—happen again and again in *The Turk and My Mother*. They happen for the characters and they happen for the reader. And they certainly happened for the writer. I can't tell you how surprised I was when the blind Gypsy turned up at the door!

Publishers Weekly praised your "easy familiarity with the vernacular idioms of the old country and the new," your "zestful, respectful ear for different voices." Where do these voices, different from your own, come from? How do you cultivate them, get them to the page?

I've already mentioned listening to my Aunt Madeline's particular variety of English when she was alive and to the two precious tape recordings she let me make. (When my children were small, they liked to listen to the "Aunt Madeline tapes" like bedtime stories, even though they had no idea what she was talking about. They liked the sound and rhythms of her voice, the funny way she pronounced words, her favorite expressions, like "niceway," for "nicely," and "overdue particular," which meant "too fussy.") I also made a point of studying Croatian and, to a lesser extent, Hungarian before I went to visit the village of Novo Selo. (I live in Iowa City and Omaha and make the four-hour trip between them two or three times a month. I like to listen to language tapes while I'm driving.) Then, too, Croatian was my father's first language, and since I spent my early years in my grandmother's house, I heard Croatian and nonstandard English spoken around me. The rhythms and syntax and diction I picked up in all those ways show up in the dialogue and the narrative style of *The Turk and My Mother*. I wanted it to read, at least some of the time, like a translation.

What was your biggest challenge in writing *The Turk and My Mother*?

The biggest challenge in writing this book was trying to make sure the reader knew exactly where she or he was on any given page. You might start a sentence in Milwaukee in 1934 and by the time you get to the end of the sentence you're in Siberia in 1917. Lots of shifts in time require very careful attention to providing cues for the reader as to where we are and when. I don't mean the date or the name of the place—you don't always need to know that. I mean the reader must feel the world rise around the characters (the straw in the stable in Lemberg, Poland, or the ice on the breakwater in Lake Michigan, or a bowl filling with water in the moonlight) without ever thinking that the characters are somewhere they're not.

The big challenges were the management of time, the creation of place, and moving from time to time or place to place without unduly disorienting my readers. Not that a reader can't be in uncertainty—but I think you have to feel as if you're in good hands, that the author knows where you are even if you don't for a moment or two. You have to feel as if all that's needed will be revealed to you in good time. I hope I succeeded in making the reader feel that way.

What do you think is the greatest challenge for the reader of *The Turk and My Mother*?

Aside from the cast of dozens of multilingual characters and the zooming around from time to time and place to place? Aside from that, I think the book introduces some readers to a way of thinking they are not accustomed to. There is a deeply felt sense of the hidden meaning in everyday things in eastern European cultures. "Now there is a miracle and no matter what," Aunt Madeline was always saying. Everything happens for a reason. There are no coincidences. Everything is taken very seriously, with the result that everything is often hilariously absurd at the same time. These are people, as one reviewer said, who believe in the evil eye and the wages of sin. I guess you could call it magical thinking. It's anti-ironic. Milosz talked about writing poems in "a bucolic, childish language that transforms the sublime into the cordial." I don't know if he was talking about Polish or Lithuanian, but he could be talking about the language of Staramajka as well, and in the language is her worldview, her way of being in the world. It's a way of being that allows her to insist, against all evidence, that her missing son, Marko, is on his way home. When someone reminds her of how many years he has been gone, she says, "It's a long way to walk." And she means it. And in the end, it turns out that she was right.

DISCUSSION QUESTIONS

1. In Part I, George tells his daughter a story that his grandmother, Staramajka, told him and his sister Madeline. The story is mostly about George's mother, Agnes. Why does Staramajka tell the story to George and his sister? Why does George tell it to his daughter?

2. How would you describe the relationship between Agnes and the Turk?

3. What about the relationship between Agnes and Staramajka? What role does Staramajka play in the story of Agnes and the Turk?

4. What is the significance of Agnes's final words to Pete the Cop in Part I?

5. In Part II, why doesn't Marko write to his mother? Do you believe that Staramajka could forgive Marko for not writing to her? Why does "the steam go out of her heart" after Istvan's visit?

6. The other main story in Part II—the story of Staramajka (Jelena) and the blind Gypsy (Istvan)—is told to us as if we are within Staramajka's memory after she has died. How does the story's point of view (from beyond the grave) affect its meaning and impact on you? What do you think of a novelist presuming to show us what the afterlife is like?

7. What connections exist between Marko's story and the story of Jelena and Istvan? What is the significance of all these connections? In what ways is Marko very much his mother's son?

8. Does Part II help you better understand Part I?

9. Part III opens with the dying George wishing he could tell his daughter a story about his childhood with Kata. What does this story reveal about him?

10. How does George's adult relationship with Kata compare to his childhood relationship with her? What does Kata mean to George?

11. Why is Kata so eager to talk to George before he dies?

12. When Anica thinks about the night that she spent with Josef, she thinks, "They had performed a miracle. They had transformed an act of violence into one of healing tenderness. It was like turning not just water, but poison, into wine" (p. 296). How might this passage and its biblical metaphor relate to other parts of the novel?

13. What is the significance of Marie's final words in the Epilogue? What parts of the novel do they force you to reconsider?

14. In what ways do the events of Part I and Part II affect the meaning of Part III—and vice versa?

15. How much do you think George knows as he sets out to tell his story to Mary Helen?

16. The novel opens with an epigraph: "Whatever evil I had suffered, I forgot." How do these words by poet Czeslaw Milosz shed light on the novel's meanings?

17. Can people really forgive one another they way they do in *The Turk and My Mother*?

18. Are Agnes and Staramajka immigrants or exiles? What is the difference between an immigrant and an exile?

19. Do you think of Staramajka as a victim of circumstance? a heroine? something else?

20. How do stories get told in your family? What purposes do they serve?

21. Do any of these characters remind you of people in your own family?

22. Readers who have immigrant grandmothers tend to identify strongly with *The Turk and My Mother*. One such reader said, "That's just the way I would write it, if I could write." Did you find the characters and tone of the book mostly familiar or mostly strange? If you were to write about these characters, how would you go about it? What would you do differently? What kind of advice or suggestions would you give the author?

AUTHOR'S NOTE

I've been fascinated by my father's family history at least since fifth grade, when I wrote a story about my grandmother and her five-year-old daughter traveling from their village in Hungary to Ellis Island on their way to join my grandfather in Milwaukee. I had them take a train from Paris to London—not possible in those days and not the route they traveled in any case—but my fifth-grade teacher let me get away with that, unwittingly issuing my very first fiction-writer's license to make the "facts" serve the truth of the story.

Many years later, my father took me on a tour of the old Milwaukee neighborhood on East Bay Street, where he grew up, and where I, too, lived, at least as a very small child, in my grandmother's upper flat. (This is the same upper flat where I picture Staramajka answering the door with a scowl on her face, the same house where I imagine Agnes pressing her ear to the ductwork in the basement.) My father died later that year, at the age of fifty-nine. In my book, though, he gets a chance to live past eighty, and he tells his daughter Mary Helen more stories than my father ever told me. This was a great source of pleasure for me in writing the book—sitting down with my father and imagining his voice, as I remembered it, telling me all of these stories.

Some years after my father died, I went with my elderly cousin Marie Sinyakovich (who is not from St. Louis, nor is she the daughter of the "real" Uncle Marko) to visit the village of my ancestors in Hungary, which is Marie's hometown. Novo Selo—or, in Hungarian, Totujfalu—is not much larger today than it was in 1921, when my grandmother saw it for the last time. It's a few minutes' walk to the Drava River, a short swim from there to the Croatian border on the other side. In the village, cousin Marie made fun of me for aiming my camera at everything. I took pictures of houses with foot-thick walls and red tile roofs (including the one where Marie was born), pictures of pigs and red brick barns, of cows coming home down the village street, each one turning off into her yard and ambling back to the barn behind the house—like so many cars pulling into their driveways. I took many more pictures than I needed of the storks that nest on chimney tops and telephone poles. I took pictures of the 400-year-old church and of the empty lot where my father's mother, the real Agnes, used to live. The house had burned down years ago.

This novel has its roots in that village and a few other real places, and in three or four events that really happened to four or five people who really existed. You could say that I planted those events and places and people in my imagination, like cuttings from a grapevine (maybe a grapevine brought to Milwaukee in the lining of a suitcase), and there they sprouted more characters and details and scenes, until they grew into a novel. My real father's real sister Madeline, who liked to tell stories even more than my father did, was an important source of those details. She was kind enough to let me tape-record her twice. All the "ethnic" voices in the book—but particularly Staramajka's—are echoes of my real Aunt Madeline's voice. I realized after I wrote the first part of the book that it was about forgiveness, that I'd written it in part to forgive my real grandmother (Agnes in the story) for something she did to her daughter, something my real aunt Madeline had told me about a long time ago. In order to forgive Agnes, to understand why she did what she did, I found I needed to imagine my way into her existence. The rest of the book developed from that beginning.

The Turk and My Mother opens with a reference to *Dr. Zhivago*, and like a Russian novel, it has a large cast of characters with unfamiliar-looking names. Before George launches into the story of his mother and the Turk—a story his grandmother, Staramajka, told him when he was a boy—he warns Mary Helen that Staramajka had a style of story-telling "that did not accommodate her listeners in any way." Although most of the stories she told took place in her tiny village, they "had casts of thousands," George says. "You needed an index to keep track." Well, it doesn't take long for the reader to figure out where George learned *his* style of storytelling.

The Turk and My Mother not only introduces a large crowd of characters, it also takes readers into unfamiliar territory: a Kaszube fishing village in the Milwaukee harbor, a tiny Croatian village in the Austro-Hungarian empire, the city of Khabarovsk in far eastern Siberia, and several places in between. We meet Croatians, Hungarians, Slovenians, Gypsies, Russians, Germans, Cossacks, Siberians, Kaszubes, and more. The characters are often negotiating two or three languages at once—a feat that I witnessed myself when I went to visit the village—and there's a lot of translation going on, all of which is delivered to the reader in English, of course, with the occasional Hungarian or German word here or there and a more generous sprinkling of Croatian. Words like "Staramajka" and "Lukovisce" may look forbidding, but they are, in fact, completely pronounceable. (See the pronunciation key below.)

With thanks to Professor Mary Vermillion and David Medaris.

CAST OF CHARACTERS

Introduced in Part I
Georgie (the narrator who starts the story)
Mary Helen (his daughter)
Madeline (Georgie's sister)
Agnes (Georgie's mother)
Staramajka (Georgie's grandmother, Agnes's mother-in-law). Stara-majka means "grandmother." Her given name is Jelena.
Rosa (Agnes's sister)
Tomas Novakovich (Rosa's young man)
Josef Iljasic (Agnes's husband, Staramajka's son)
(Uncle) Marko Iljasic (Josef's brother, Staramajka's son)
Tas Akbulut ("the Turk" of the title)
Mrs. Ludmilla Tomasic (Agnes's friend, who runs a boardinghouse in Milwaukee)
Frankie Tomasic (Mrs. Tomasic's son, Georgie's friend/rival)
Other Milwaukee characters: Chuey Garcia (Georgie's boyhood friend), Mr. and Mrs. Beymor (Madeline's employers), Mr. and Mrs. Solapek (tavern owners), Madeline's young man
Villagers in Novo Selo: Widow Begovacs and her son Andras, Mrs. Dragovich the wax lady, Mayor Bunyevach, Vincent Zarac (a cousin of Agnes)

KEY TO PRONUNCIATION OF
CROATIAN WORDS

(Generally, J sounds like Y in Croatian; C with a mark above it sounds like CH; S with a mark above it sounds like SH.)

Staramajka = star-a-MY-kah (stara-micah)

Iljasic = ill-yah-sheech (or, in English, ill-jay-sick)

Wojcek = woy-check (or any way you like to pronounce it)

Kaszube = kah-SHOOB

Gospođa = go-spoh-jah (Mrs.)

Begovacs = beg-oh-vatz OR beg-oh-vach

"Lepa moja" = lay-pah moy-ah (my pretty one)

"moj stari čovek" = moy starry cho-vek (my old man)

"dobro jutro" = do-bro-YOU-tro (good morning)

hvala = fala (thank you)

Jabotevrag = Yah-boh-tay-vrahg (name of the rooster!)

Places: Pécs = Paych; Barcs = Barch; Lukovisce = Luke-oh-veesh-cha